STOLEN FUTURES

PRESENT

DANGER

M. Drewery

edited by

NATE RAGOLIA

SPACEBOY BOOKS

Denver, Colorado

Published in the United States by:
Spaceboy Books LLC
1627 Vine Street
Denver, CO 80206
www.readspaceboy.com

First printed March 2020

ISBN: 978-1-951393-01-4

For Richard, a good friend.

My thanks to my family and friends for their support.

Shout out to Scott, Stolen Futures' biggest fan.

THE NEW FUTURE

The girl was not actually a girl. Not any girl I had ever met before anyway. I think she was in her early twenties. She had dark hair flecked with strands of copper, her eyes were large and bright and also gold in colour. I had to marvel at them they were so unusual. I then noticed that she was doing the same to me, except she was looking at my scar with curiosity, as if she recognised it.

Then together we both turned back to Antumbra and asked at exactly the same time:

"What is going on?"

We shared an annoying glare, each thinking the other a mimic.

"Antumbra, please explain," we said, again in sync.

Antumbra was not looking at us, it was looking off into the distance as if trying to reconcile some memories or information.

I looked at the other aliens. They were doing the same, cocking their heads and looking confused, as if trying to file/collate something new, except for Pebbles, who was as inactive as a brick.

"This is odd, I have two sets of memories in my head, or maybe one set is my memory and the other is a dream of the same, with slightly different events. The question is which one is the dream and which one is the truth?"

"What does that have to do...?" I began and the girl began in sync. "With..." I said slowly and so did she. "...what's going on?" I said quicker than normal and she did the same.

"Stop that," I said, as did she.

"I said stop it," we both said.

"I think I know what's happened," Antumbra said at last.

"Explain," we said, waving our hands in frustration.

"I think we successfully created a new timeline in the multiverse, however, I think that it was so similar to the original one combined with the new one."

"Combined?" me and the girl asked.

"Yes. I have memories of both of you doing the exact same thing to achieve our escape from the thieves. You both were in a pod opposite me in the museum, you broke open our cells, were chased, freed the others, stole the ships we stole. Essentially both universes became in-sync enough that the multiverse brought them together."

"How is that possible?" the alien with the large mouth said.

"Yeah, for one thing we're not the same person," me and the girl said.

"Well I didn't say completely in-sync, just enough for both universes to combine. Creating a new timeline is like creating a new universe, where did all the matter and energy come from? How does the universe create it? How does it organise it? Maybe it can't handle it and so it combines universes together to prevent total entropy. Or, maybe, the great creator just prefers things tidy..." Antumbra said. "But that means..."

It drifted off, and I wondered what conclusion it had reached, but then I remembered that I had a copycat.

"So we're saying the same things because we have had the same experiences?" we both asked.

Antumbra was staring into space.

"Antumbra?"

...

The alien wasn't moving instead it was staring into space with a blank expression on its face.

"Antumbra?"

"Yes. At the moment, there are not enough differences in your experiences to make your word choices different."

"How – do – we – stop?" we said using broken speech, which failed to break our bond.

Antumbra stepped forward and grabbed my arm. Its energy-like form sizzled my arm, after a second it let go.

I screamed in pain and held my arm up. My enhanced body started the healing process, but the pain was still terrible. I bent over cradling the arm.

"Why did you do that?" the girl asked Antumbra.

"Yeah why did you do that to me?" I said, then I realised I was free.

"I gave him a different experience, Ada," Antumbra said.

"Why did you have to hurt me?" I cried out.

"It seems like the simplest way," Antumbra said. "Plus from where I am from it's rude to attack a member of the opposite sex."

"Are you a male?" I asked, realising that I didn't know how Antumbra should be addressed.

"No I'm female," Antumbra said.

"You think I'm a girl," I said.

"Antumbra I'm a female human," the girl said.

Antumbra looked at us both and made a funny noise, which sounded like disbelief.

I inspected my arm, the scarring had already faded, and I huffed in annoyance then turned to the girl.

"Who are you?" I asked.

"My name is Ada," she replied and she looked at me up and down. "I don't know you, either, but you seem familiar even though your universe was just folded into mine."

"I think your universe was folded into mine, actually," I said.

"He's right," Antumbra said. "Two and Me..." and she motioned to herself and Ada "didn't send anything back in time."

"Which means you're from the universe we created when we sent the message back in time," I said. "Wait you're also called 'Two'?"

"My real name is Ada, however I was called Two for a lot longer than I was called by my real name. I prefer Ada now."

"Did you ever know a guy called One?" I asked.

Ada rocked back on her feet like she had been struck.

"If you know One then you must be an Arkonaut," Ada/Two said.

"I was. In fact, I'm the last. My name is Callum," I replied.

Ada/Two stepped forward and reached out with her hand. She traced a line from my forehead down to the bottom of my cheek, right where my scar was.

"You are Callum, you're older."

"Decades older," Antumbra said.

"How are you? How do you feel?" she asked.

"I'm... fine," I said.

Ada/Two backed off, but stared into my eyes. She shook her head, as if I lacked something she was expecting to find.

Ada/Two then looked off into space as if calculating something. "So you did send the message after all. Everybody was wondering."

"Who are you? You weren't on the Ark when I was?

"I was there... in storage," Ada said. "I was awakened after the General and Minister were defeated. Your message saved the lives of everyone on board. The Arkonauts had good lives after you sent the message."

I stood a little taller, prouder, and smiled, I had saved the human race. Well, technically Antumbra did, but I had made it happen.

"Tell me about it, I want to know what happened to them... what happened to me."

"I only know what happened to the Arkonauts up to the point I was put into the pod."

"The pod that ended up in the museum?" I asked.

"Exactly," Antumbra said, "Somehow your pod, in your universe, ended up in that museum. The events in your timeline then fell into sync with ours, which somehow led to both merging and... here we are."

I nodded, despite not quite understanding all of that. "Tell me what happened," I asked Ada/Two again.

She started to tell her story.

SYSTEM ONLINE

CHECKING RESOURCE DEPLETION

WITHIN DESIGNATED PARAMETERS
SOLAR SYSTEM SCAN REPORT

1. SHIP ON COURSE
2. APPROACHING OORT CLOUD, ONE WEEK BEHIND SCHEDULE
3. PASSED THE VOYAGER SPACE PROBE
4. REACHING THE EDGE OF THE SUN'S GRAVITY WELL 0.8 LIGHT YEARS

PHASE THREE IN EFFECT

ROUTINE SCHEDULE OF TASKS ESTABLISHED

1
THE FIRST RECRUIT

I had a plan. I had carefully worked everything out. Step one was getting two accomplices, one who would be kept in the dark because he might blab, the other was One, who could be trusted to keep quiet. The first of my accomplices was always first in the cafeteria. He was the earliest riser on the Ark. He would be alone in the cafeteria and I could ask him for a favour without anyone over hearing.

I couldn't set an alarm. My watch was long gone, my phone had no more power. The only way I could get myself up before him was to drink lots of water the night beforehand. So one morning I woke up bursting for a pee. I relieved myself, dressed quickly, and put my ear to my door. I listened through my door, and when I heard the click of his door opening I too emerged from my room.

Ogwambi was pulling his door shut when I exited my room.

I smiled at him. "Good morning Ogwambi," I said.

The Ugandan boy jumped a little at my surprise warm greeting and joyful entrance.

"Oh hello, Callum. You're up early?" he asked.

"Yeah, for some reason I woke up an hour early this morning, couldn't get back to sleep. When I heard you leave your room, I thought I might as well join you for breakfast."

Ogwambi shrugged. "Okay. It's Wednesday, so I think the robots will be serving us sugared cereal today as a treat."

I nodded and we both fell into a slow walk down the residence corridor toward the cafeteria.

I smiled at the thought of a sugar rich cereal. Every day of the week had a regimented food menu. The little treats the robots would throw in were always welcome. Wednesday always gave us a sugar rush. Thursday was dessert day. Saturday always had chips. It gave us something to look forward to.

We never saw the robots at work, however we knew they were there, one level above us preparing our meals. Every single one of them had come from somewhere else. Schools, office buildings, hospitals... All repurposed to serve us on the Ark.

"How do they wash their hands?" I asked Ogwambi. This was part of my plan, engage him in conversation and lay the ground-work for the favour I needed.

"What?" he said and yawned.

Maybe he wasn't fully awake yet? Was the morning a bad time? What if he was grumpy? I decided to plough on.

"Well they prepare us food, but they are robots, they can't wash their hands or the water would break them, right?"

"I saw robots out in the rain all the time. I think all the designs are waterproof," Ogwambi answered.

"Good point," I replied.

We made it to the cafeteria and strolled up to the dispensers. A segmented tray suddenly appeared on a small dumbwaiter. There was a bowl with the cereal, a cup of milk, dehydrated, unfortunately. There was also some fruit and some fruit juice.

Once we had out trays we sat down. The room was completely empty. We were alone. I wasn't sure how long it would be until the others arrived, so I decided to go for it and ask my favour now.

"Ogwambi, you're in the Control Centre aren't you?"

"I am for the next few months, why?"

"Erm could I, erm do a swap with you for a day shift?"

"Why?" He asked.

I knew this question was coming, so I had an excuse ready to go.

"Gerlinde is in the Control Centre too and she told me that the ship is passing the Oort cloud tomorrow and that she can't wait to see it. We won't see it out of the observational room, but if you are in the control centre you can. I want to be there when we pass it by."

"You want to do a shift in the control room just to see a cloud?"

What I told him was partially true, we were passing the Oort cloud, however I didn't care about it. Gerlinde had also told me some details about it. "It is the limit of the solar system, after we pass through it that's it we're out of the sun's reach. I want to see it this one time."

Ogwambi spooned some cereal into his mouth and considered it.

"Where are you now?" he asked.

"Engine room," I replied.

He mulled that over, "I've haven't worked in the engine room yet. And I do like the idea of seeing it and working there before the rest of my group."

"So it's a deal? One shift."

"Hang on. If this Oort cloud is as special as you say then I might want to see it."

I panicked. "It's not really a cloud," I said, "I mean you won't see a sort of cumulus nimbus in space. The cloud surrounds the solar system we'll be passing through it."

"Sounds dull," he said.

Yes, I thought.

"Wait why do you want to see it if it's not a thing in one place? Won't it be scattered around and barely visible?"

Oh, no, I thought.

"Does it matter? I'm specifically intrigued about astral landmarks, even if they aren't super cool to look at." I said, and metaphorically brushed aside his comments with a wave of my hand.

Ogwambi looked at me chewing his most recent mouthful slowly. "No," he said. "I guess not."

"Good," I replied. "Then I get to look at the cloud and you'll take my engine room shift."

9

"You don't care about the Oort cloud do you?" he asked.

"Yes! Yes, I do," I replied a little too quickly.

"Really?" he said. "I don't believe you. What's the real reason," he asked, and now he was smiling.

Was I blushing? It felt like I was blushing at that point. My plan was crumbling from the beginning. I had to go to my contingency.

"If you don't want to swap that's fine," I said, shrugging as if my requesting was the most unimportant thing in the world.

"Who is it?" he said.

"Who is what?" I asked.

"Is it Ernesta?"

I said nothing, not because I thought silence was the best option, but because my mind was not providing me with a response that would be a convincing answer.

"Pilar?"

I didn't reply.

"What other girls are in my group?" he mused to himself aloud.

"Alba, Gerlinde, Maiara..." he listed off.

I stared into space when he began his list. Did my eyes dilate or my cheeks flush when he hit the right name? Hopefully not.

"Come on, Callum. Tell me," he said.

I shook my head.

"Ah, so this *is* about a girl," he said, and he pointed at me like he was a cop breaking a criminal in an interrogation.

I squirmed.

"Are you going to give me the exchange or not?" I asked, staring down at my food.

He sat back in his chair.

"Her name and it's yours."

I glared.

I wasn't entirely sure why I was keeping it a secret. I guess maybe giving voice to what I wanted might, rob me of it, or maybe I wanted it to be special and by sharing the secret with someone else might mean making it less so. That was an odd reason. The human race was down to 250-odd teenagers. Every relationship was special and I had already witnessed others forming.

"Name," he repeated.

"No," I said.

He turned away, and considered his situation.

"Doesn't matter, I'll swap with someone else," I said.

He frowned losing his chance to get some juicy gossip first.

"Give me two shifts and it's yours," he said.

I smiled. "Okay, you do two shifts in the engine room and I'll do two in the control centre."

"No I mean you'll do my two shifts in the control centre and I'll take two days off."

"Wait. What?" I said.

"You'll have to do your engine room shift, and then go to the control centre." Ogwambi said.

"That's crazy! That's two full days of work," I countered.

"Give me the name and we'll go back to your original proposal," he offered. He sat back in his chair like a gambler who had played a straight flush in the certain knowledge that his opponent was bluffing.

I weighed my options, and I didn't like either of them.

"One shift. I'll cover one shift," I said.

"Two."

"One and a half?" I offered.

He looked off into space. "Very well," he said, and offered his hand.

I quickly grabbed and shook.

"Thank you," I said, sitting forward in my chair, munching on an apple.

The next stage of my plan was falling into place.

"Whoever it is, it better not be Moana," Ogwambi warned.

"Don't worry it's not... Wait, you and Moana?"

He smiled and raised his eyebrows.

"Wow," I said.

2

THE SECOND RECRUIT

After breakfast I went to find One in the control centre preparing it for the morning shift.

He was there alone, another lucky break.

"Hello Callum, how can I help you?" he said.

With One I could be more direct and honest, because he wouldn't tell. "Hi One, I need a favour."

"If it's reasonable, then I will grant it," he replied as he stared down at a computer screen, tapping away at the controls.

I took a moment to marvel at how easily he was controlling a ship the size of large city.

"I'm switching shifts with Ogwambi in the control centre, I'm going to need the training a little early."

He stopped typing. "I hope you're not planning to switch groups. I would prefer it if you stayed where you are. If you change then others might want to do the same, and it will cause disagreements."

"Don't worry. It's just for a shift and a half."

"Why?" he asked.

"Ok, you can't tell anyone this. Alright?"

He smiled and he took up a relaxed stance. "I see. Some sort of secret. Yes. I can keep secrets," he assured.

"There is a member of the current control centre's group I want to spend time with."

"Can't you just talk to them in-between shifts?"

"I could however to get her on her own might alert others to the fact I want to speak with her on her own, and right now I don't want people to know that."

"Her?" One said, his smile broadening.

"Yes 'her.' If I talked to her in the control centre I wouldn't have to pull her from a group, and it would be less embarrassing."

"There seems to be a flaw in your plan," One said.

"A flaw?" I stammered back.

"You're going to be working here, so you won't have free time to talk to her, whoever she is."

I hadn't thought about that.

"There must be moments where people talk?" I asked.

One smiled again and turned back to his control panel.

"Perhaps. Meet me in the medical bay just after lunch and I'll give you the control centre training, so you can switch the shifts."

"Thank you One," I said.

"I don't suppose you'll tell me who this person is?" he asked.

I paused. I knew he wouldn't tell if I did, but saying her name felt like it would curse my chances.

"I'm not going to. No," I said.

"Very well," he said with the hint of disappointment.

I backed out of the control centre and headed off to start a normal day. I couldn't help but smile. Everything was falling into place.

3
ASKING OUT

Ogwambi was in the engine room and I was heading for the control centre. I was itching the crook of my arm, still sore from yesterday's injection of nanites One had given me to work in the control centre.

I was walking very slowly to the control room.

I had reached a crunch point. I was committed.

I had a sudden stab of fear. What if she wasn't interested? That was actually an easy question to answer. I simply had to back off and let the thing go, however it was now creating other questions, other avenues of anxiety and terror.

For one thing I would be stuck doing extra shifts that served no purpose. What if me being there made her uncomfortable? What if I couldn't talk to her, what if—?

I stopped in the middle of the corridor, thinking about backing out entirely. But I still had go and serve in the control centre. I kept walking. I had no choice.

She'll probably say no, a part of my brain said.

Shut up, I told it.

The control centre was only a few metres away. I couldn't stop now.

I took a deep breath and wandered in.

The control centre was notable for a domed ceiling that was actually a giant computer screen. The floor was another screen. It had two doors on either side of the room and was ringed with consoles, some alien, and some human. The alien consoles were extremely hi-tech, sleek, and shone with green light. The human computers were touch screens, with some levers.

One was there and when he heard me walk in he glanced up, quickly smiled, then went back to his work.

Everyone else looked up and frowned when they saw me. I felt my face go red and I panicked. I hadn't realised that everyone else would question my appearance here. Now, I just had to roll with it.

"Callum, what are you doing here?" Waris, the boy from India asked.

"I'm filling in for Ogwambi," I said.

"Where is he?" Moana asked.

Don't you know, you're dating aren't you? I thought. "I owed him a favour," I said.

"One can we do that, cover for others?" Waris asked One.

One shot me a flash of annoyance that my favour had generated this question and a possible change in routine, then smiled at Waris.

"Only in very rare occasions," he answered.

Thankfully, everyone lapsed into silence, wondering if they too could trade favours in other part of the ship. They were preoccupied enough that they ignored me, and that meant I was in.

"Callum, you're at that work station over there," One said pointing at a vacant chair. "Your work assignment for the day is already on the screen."

I nodded and went and sat down, finding myself a spot right next to the girl I wanted to talk to.

I looked at One who was ignoring me now. *Did he know? Had he planned this?* It didn't matter right now. This was a gift and I was going to take it.

I turned to the girl next to me and nodded, playing it nice and cool.

She smiled and then looked away. I couldn't tell if she was pleased to see me or not.

I couldn't jump right in with a conversation. I needed to look like I was really covering for Ogwambi.

The new nanites that had prepared me for working in here gave me everything I needed to know about how to operate the computers. My assignment for the day was to check the ship's projected flight path for the next forty-eight hours, and scan for any obstacles or potential problems.

I brought up the ship's course on a small section of the larger dome screen in front of me. It showed a green trail heading through otherwise empty, boring space. I initiated a scan of the whole area along the projected path. First, I ran a close scan within a few miles of the ship. When the computer was done, I initiated a wider scan going up to a thousand miles.

The computer would be busy for a few minutes so I took this opportunity to start talking.

"Hey Maiara, this is my first time working in here. It this a fun assignment?" I asked.

She looked at me, then glanced over her shoulder at One. "Not really, but when One goes we can muck about a little," she whispered.

"He can hear you," I whispered back.

"Yes, but he's not listening," she said.

"I think he is," I warned her. I suspected he was paying particular attention to us right now, given what he knew.

"Don't worry. When he leaves I'll show you what I mean," Maiara said.

"When does he leave?" I asked.

"When he needs to check on the other systems."

As if on cue, One picked up a small tablet and then left the control centre.

"Watch this," Maiara said, projecting CCTV footage of the cafeteria on the screen.

"We can watch anyone from up here," Maiara said, "and you see some funny stuff." She laughed.

"You're a little stalker aren't you?" I said to her as playfully as I could. I didn't actually think she was, and I didn't want her to think that I thought that either. *Oh dear! Was I overthinking this whole thing?*

She brushed her hair back and laughed. "We're actually supposed to be looking. We flag problems as soon as possible. Check this out." She grabbed the arm of my chair to pull me over. "Watch Illarion and Gerlinde."

I saw them on the screen.

"I thought Gerlinde would be in here today," I said.

"Like everywhere else, we split the shifts," Maiara said.

I looked at the pair on the screen. They were holding hands.

"Wait. Gerlinde and Illarion?" I said.

"Indeed."

"How have I missed these couplings?" I asked.

"What do you think they're saying?" she asked, ignoring my question.

I realised that I had a chance to impress Maiara, and make her laugh, so I cleared my throat and waited for Illarion to speak. Although we couldn't hear the words it was like I was dubbing him. "I love your hair," I said in my best Russian accent.

Maiara cackled.

She spoke for Gerlinde in her best German accent. "Thank you I did it myself."

We both laughed.

"Is this what you do all day? Watch us? What have you seen me do?" I asked.

"Nothing yet," she said.

"But you have been watching me," I said trying to sound offended.

She didn't reply, just looked away.

"These screens can do other things too. Sometimes while the computer is performing my commands I look at space stuff," she said.

"Nice dodge," I said, "What space stuff?"

She brought up the picture of a planet on the screen, "This is the Goblin, a very small planet in our solar system."

"Wait, I thought Pluto was the last planet."

"Nope we're still within the boundary of the solar system. There is yet another called Sedna."

"Do you ever get to steer the ship?" I asked.

She rotated a little on her chair to talk to me. "Unfortunately not, the course has already been set by One. Plus, we don't really have the fuel for exciting course corrections. This isn't the Enterprise."

"The Enterprise?" I said. "I didn't figure you for a Star Trek fan."

"I'm not a real fan, I just saw some of the movies, and they were good."

I wanted to shout in joy.

"Speaking of *Star Trek* films, did you see the last one?"

She nodded as she turned back to her computer to continue doing work.

"I liked it, I'm glad they started doing films based around those other TV series like *Next Gen* or *DS9*." She said.

"*Next Gen*? *DS9*? You are a real fan," I teased her. "Only a real fan knows about those things."

"My dad loved them and he showed them all to me," she said. "I couldn't tell you what the characters were called or their backstories. I just enjoyed watching them."

"Fair enough," I said.

This was my moment to ask what I had been waiting to ask.

"Do you like movies?" I asked as innocently as I could.

"Of course I do," she replied. "Who doesn't?"

"Do you want to watch one, maybe tomorrow evening?" I said as quick and as nonchalant as I could.

There was a painful silence.

"Yes. I would," Maiara replied.

Yes, I said internally.

"Who else is coming?" she asked.

"What?" I stuttered, "Oh I meant just...I mean who do you think would like to join us?"

Maiara then barked a laughed and covered her mouth stifling her giggles.

"I was just joking," she said, looking across at me and smiling.

"What?"

"Callum, I'm not dense! You're asking me out on a date, and I'm glad."

"That's good," I managed to say.

"Saved me having to ask you," she uttered quickly.

"What?" I asked, "You were going to ask me out?"

"Uh huh," she said.

Now, I was a little annoyed. I still had to cover for Ogwambi and I had to put up with an early nanite injection when I could have waited.

"You did all this just to ask me. Why not ask me in a corridor?" she asked.

"I haven't had the chance to talk to you one-to-one, and I wasn't sure you liked me."

"Well I do, so thank you for allowing me to avoid the hassle of doing the same things just to talk to you."

I huffed in good humour.

"I'll pick you up at your room tomorrow evening, is that alright?" I asked.

She nodded. "8pm?"

"That's fine."

"Fine."

"Excellent."

"Amazing."

"Looking forward to it."

4

NERVOUS AS HELL

So she had said 'yes.'

For the rest of that session I felt the things you're supposed to feel. There were butterflies. My heart beat faster. That sort of thing. I also felt huge amounts of anticipation and anxiety. Because now I had to make sure the date would go smoothly.

I already had a fairly good idea of what we could do, and I had already laid the groundwork.

Thankfully my shift ended before hers, so I had a little time to get away and prepare. Then I had another shift, my real shift, in the engine room. After that I went to sleep thinking about the big date.

I awoke early still feeling the anticipation. I would not see her until the evening, but my mind would focus on nothing else.

I wanted to talk to her alone, so I planned to take her somewhere where no one else went, or had a reason to go. We also needed food. Thankfully I was prepared. I had saved some food over the last week and made an ad hoc picnic.

I also needed a spectacular end to the night—something that would amaze her, and make it memorable. There was only one place on the ship for that.

I went to the engine room that morning and worked, clock-watching the whole time.

I wondered if anyone else knew Maiara and I were going to meet up later. No one shot me cheeky grins or knowing glances, which was great, because then I didn't have to put up with any irritating suggestions or meddling.

The shift ended and I scuttled out of the engine room leaving everyone else in the dust. Evan may have called out after me, but if he did I didn't hear it properly as I raced back up the stairs to my room.

I didn't see Maiara anywhere, which was good. I somewhat felt that seeing her beforehand might ruin it or make it more awkward.

In my room I had to pick out my best clothes. I chose jeans, a shirt, and my best shoes. I don't know how these nice smart clothes had made it into my case. My mom clearly thought I needed to be well-dressed during this trip. As I laid them out on the bed, I thought about my mum and then the rest of my family.

It was the first time in a few weeks I had thought about them. I had been into the flow of life on the Ark, in sync with this new place. Not thinking about before.

If I had been living on earth, getting ready for a date, my parents would know and be supporting me. My mum would be questioning my clothing choices and my dad would be showing me how to iron my shirt so that the seams could cut someone.

I teared up.

They weren't here to help me. They weren't here to listen afterwards when I told them how it had gone. There weren't here to see how happy or sad I might be, or the possibilities afterwards.

Then I suddenly thought of Jack. He never had, and never will have, the experience of dating anyone. He'll never have a relationship with someone. He never felt that way about anyone as far as I knew. Here I was having a life, while he didn't.

Awful feelings of guilt and shame washed over me. I was safe, and having a relatively normal experience everyone my age goes through.

I was living, while my family was dead.

I sat down on the edge of the bed to process my thoughts.

I resisted the urge to cancel the date. My family would want me to live. They would want me to be happy. Wouldn't they?

I quickly dressed, then washed my face sending a few droplets of water on top the shirt, which made me look like I was incapable of washing myself properly. I flirted with the idea of changing shirts but opted against it. Surely she would forgive it. We were both in the same situation, with limited clothing and less than ideal washing facilities.

That was the only thing Dr. Ghost had never thought about—a decent laundry. We had to build a makeshift one, and dry our clothes in the engine room.

I slicked back my hair and applied the last of my deodorant.

There was no mirror, so I had to assume that I looked great.

This was it. I was ready. No turning back. This could be the beginnings of a long-lasting relationship, hopefully without a bitter breakup. I could think of nothing worse than being trapped inside a spaceship with her if it didn't go well... if it soured.

I set off, closing my door and heading down the corridor toward her room.

I reached her room. At least, I believed it was her room. She had said her door was green with the number 34 painted on it. And so I stood before that very door. I checked my breath, and reached out to knock.

Deep breath.

I panicked suddenly, worried I was underdressed or maybe overdressed. I lost confidence for a second and the knock came out weak and timid.

Would she hear me? Would my soft knock sound pathetic?

I overcorrected, knocking as loudly as I could on her door a second time. I wondered if that was a mistake, too. Did I sound a bit too forceful?

"You idiot." I said to myself.

Finally the door opened.

Something I had not smelled in ages wafted over me. The smell of plant life, of flowers.

Then a flash of memories erupted in my mind. I felt crazy. My brain was throwing up all sorts of things that didn't make sense, and I couldn't turn it off.

LIVESTREAM

Back on earth I had a habit of exploring the military base where my family and I had been sequestered.

I was kind of irritating to the soldiers and base personnel because I didn't care for the rules. I didn't really need to. I mean, I knew that I was going to be teleported away onto an alien spaceship. It made no sense for me to follow the ridiculous rules like "don't touch that", "don't go there" and "do as you are told". The base commander, an air force colonel, once dressed me down in front of my parents. Skirting "the rules" was one of only two things that could take my mind off what was going to happen to me. So I ignored him.

The second was the invasions.

Near the end the British populace were starting to riot against the government, and military bases became the favourite target for protests. Sometimes people tried to infiltrate them believing that they were safe zones from the calamities caused by the Destroyer.

The base I stayed on, although highly secured, still had to deal with the violence. To this day I don't understand how the soldiers were able to stay focused and on duty. They must have known why they were there. The base had housed several children from different countries. The military personal must have known that they were guarding the ones who would survive the destruction of Earth.

What had Dr. Ghost told them? How had he convinced them?

I found out when I met one of the many people who had tried to infiltrate the base.

I was outside on the surface, sneaking my way out through exits known only to cleaners and janitors. Every base had to have them and the senior personnel didn't check because they weren't part of their remit. All the locks were coded, but I had seen the codes entered, so I knew the way around.

I went to the surface that day hoping to see my dog come back to me for a little bit. We had brought her to the base as a family, however people were starting to think about eating her, or at least putting her down, because of the water she consumed.

I had snuck her to the surface and released her. I doubted she would come back to me because I had to shout at her and throw rocks to get her to leave. I just wanted her to live for a while longer. I hate that I had to do it.

I wandered around surprised to see wildflowers and grass still growing in places around the base. Most of the plant life was dying. The Destroyer had leeched so many resources, and the destruction clouded the sun. I bent down to smell every flower. Since I came to the base, I had realised that these moments were precious, and I always took the time to notice the little things.

When I got tired waiting for my dog I decided to head back inside the base.

That's when I caught the guy trying to get in.

He had a backpack—two stitched together, actually—overloaded with equipment and bottles. He had long shaggy hair and a massive beard. He was blocking the door back into the base.

I approached him carefully, not exactly afraid after what I'd been through, but still cautious. I just wanted to get back inside.

He had his back to me and was jabbering to himself as he tried to break in.

"Hello?" I said.

He spun around toward me, and the sound of junk clanking together in his bags rang out in the cool night air.

His hair was wild, but he had no eyebrows. He couldn't have been older than twenty-five.

For a moment he appraised me and I was surprised to see he was not confused. The base was crawling with soldiers; I thought he might be surprised to find a child on the base.

"I knew it. I knew it," he said.

Then he went back to jimmying the lock, like I was a non-event.

"What are you doing?" I asked.

"I knew it," the man repeated.

"You knew what?" I asked.

He turned to me again. "You're one of the special ones right, the new crew of the Ark!"

I was taken aback then. How he could know that?.

In retrospect, I shouldn't have been surprised. Millions of people were ultimately involved in the Ark project. Its existence would have had to have leaked at some point.

"I don't what you're talking about," I said, heeding my parents and Dr. Ghost's constant warnings about sharing my situation with outsiders.

The man appeared to believe me. He started pacing and speaking.

"So they're keeping the truth even from the ones they intended to send. Of course! Can't have them running away! But you should have figured it out. Why else would they bring children to a base," he added pointing at me accusingly.

"Why are you here?" I asked.

"To let the world know the truth, so the Plan can be changed."

"The Plan?" I asked him.

The man sighed in frustration.

"The Plan! The Plan to send a couple of hundred children out into space to save them. It's nonsense! They should be sending people like me; scientists, rational men and women. But I'm going to tell the world! I'll get past their evil ways of keeping us compliant..."

He trailed off and his eyes went wide.

"But now, I'm late for my treatment," he said.

He pulled out a square gun from his bag then pointed it at his head.

I stepped back, terrified that I was going to watch a man blow his brains out.

He pulled the trigger and the device fizzled a bit. He seemed unharmed.

"What was that?" I asked.

"It keeps them quiet!" the man said.

"Who?"

"Doesn't matter. I have to get in find the proof. Let the people know the truth, so a better plan can be made. Yes. A better plan."

The man loomed over me.

"They're taking ignorant teenagers and planning to send them up there in a ship to save them." He pointed into the sky at a bright light, the Ark, floating over our heads. "That's why you're here. You're one of those children! They're saving you!"

He knelt. Now we were eye-to-eye. "You. A mere child. I understand their reason. Save the lowliest amongst us, the poor children. But, humanity needs people like me as well. I'm smart! I'm scientific! I'm rational. And I can make a difference. I can help with the new humanity!

"I need to stop them. I need them to know others like me are willing to go and can serve. They will have no choice once I broadcast the truth to the world. The people will demand a change. Don't worry, you'll still be going. But I'll be going too. I deserve to go! I have a right to go!"

I was shaking. He was harried, mad, in a way I'd never seen.

Then, the man went back to the door and continued trying to break the lock.

Clearly he had snapped. He had figured out that the Ark was our salvation, but not in the way the people of earth had been told. Everyone had been told the Ark would be dropped on the Destroyer. The governments of the world were still telling people that lie, through social media and the news. The truth had made him desperate. Not wrongly so, but dangerously so for me, in this moment.

The door latch finally broke, and he sighed in relief.

He then pulled out a smartphone and activated the camera. He activated a live stream.

"I'm here, followers," he said.

I looked at the screen and saw he had about four hundred followers total.

"I'm about to go inside the military base where I will find the proof. Proof that the government has lied! Proof that they are in our heads. Proof that they have a plan to save humanity! Proof that it's a dark plan that is a mystery to even those who are a part of it! Proof that they are making a tragic mistake in overlooking us who can resist them!"

He then pointed the camera to face the door.

"In we go," he said.

The door flew open and soldiers burst out, wrestling him to the ground.

The phone was stomped on and destroyed.

I backed away as they forced the man to the ground.

He screamed. He wouldn't stop. Even as they pinned him.

A captain surveyed the scene, then turned toward me.

"Get back inside," he ordered.

"What about him?" I asked.

"What about him?" the captain said, staring coldly.

I returned his gaze, wishing they would show some compassion, then turned and went inside. I went straight for my room.

My mind raced with questions. Why had he used that device on his head? How had he discovered the Plan? Why was it a dark plan?

I needed to find answers to these questions, but could I trust answers from Dr. Ghost?

No. Probably not.

But, there was someone I could trust.

5
THE DATE

...So I made memories fade away and I stored them back where they had come from.

Or maybe I just stopped daydreaming, because what I had just seen didn't feel real. There was no connection to those thoughts. They didn't seem to be mine. Where were they from? The mind of another? Was one of the Nanite memories I had been given malfunctioning?

Every Arkonaut had been given 17 Memories to help us prepare for this mission. Clusters of nanites. Small robots had been put in our brains to give us new knowledge and purpose. Maybe something was wrong with one of them.

I shook it off because the truth is I didn't care. I was about to go out with someone I had been trying to get close to for weeks. I wasn't going to pass this up. I composed myself as the door swung fully open.

It was Gerlinde who stepped out.

I frowned a little, "Oh, Gerlinde. Sorry! I think I have the wrong room."

She smiled at me in pity, "No Callum. You're in the right place."

She then closed the door a little then I heard her whisper, "You'll be all right. He's as nervous as you."

Gerlinde sidled past me saying, "Excuse me," awkwardly and briskly walked down the corridor.

She had pushed the door wide open behind her, and that revealed Maiara, and her room. It was the same size as mine although decorated very differently, with things I assume she brought with her from Earth. The most striking difference was that she had actual plant life in her room, which explained the smell from before. She had flowers in bloom and creepers growing up the wall, and even a cactus.

The American girl was standing in the middle of her room standing straight. Her black hair was tied back except for some stands that were braided.

She was wearing a light blue dress paired with shiny black shoes. It fit her perfectly. It looked tailored.

"You look nice," I said. And she did. In fact she looked amazing.

"Thank you, this is actually a prom dress I never got to use," she said.

"Oh. I'm sorry," I said automatically.

"Don't worry. I get to use it now," she said.

She stepped through her doorway, and turned her light off, then closed the door behind her.

She looked at me expectantly.

For a second I was flummoxed, taken aback by how good she looked, and how I was looking forward to talking more with her. I then realised that I was the one who had asked her out, so it was my responsibility to kick-start the evening.

My confidence started to rise. Some of the nanite memories were telling me to get on with it.

I started walking, "So erm..." I licked my lips, which had gone very dry all of a sudden. "I'm so glad we're doing this. I've wanted to ask you out for a while."

"I'm glad you did. I was hoping you would," she replied.

"It would have been easier for me if you had done something to let me know. Come on, Maiara, it's the 2030's. Boys shouldn't be expected to ask the girl out."

She smiled, then chuckled. I felt immense joy that I had said the right thing and made her laugh.

"I was brought up by old school parents, so I was taught to wait for the boy to ask," she said.

"Well, I think that tonight will not disappoint. I may have taken my time, but I spent it thinking about what we could do."

"So what are we going to do?"

"I want to get away from the rest of the crew for a bit, spend some time alone," I said.

"That's hard on a ship like this."

"Thankfully I know a place."

I took her away from the residential area and the main ship systems to a stairwell that went down past the cargo bay, the engine room and up to another floor above where most of our daily lives happened.

"What's up here?" she asked in curiosity.

I opened a set of doors for her, revealing all the robots that serviced the ship.

The room was huge, two stories high at least, and continuing for probably half a mile. It was human, so it was built of recognisable architecture. The entire floor area was occupied by robots. When the Ark had been converted for our use Dr. Ghost had clearly thought ahead and placed them here to operate and maintain some of the systems that we couldn't take care of.

Some of the robots looked the same, however there was a hodgepodge of various makes and models; some old and some new, a mixture cobbled together for whatever purpose the Ark project could possibly need them for.

"So all these robots do various things for us," I said. "That's a medical droid," I pointed at a familiar robot that had been of use to us during what was known as the Invasion.

"I've seen a few during the day," she said. "One even cleaned my room for me while I was in it."

"Well I had to come up here during the Invasion and in weeks following I returned to check them out. My family never had a robot. I always hoped we would get one. As a kid I wanted one as a best friend."

"My family had one," Maiara said. "An Azimo, he was a cute thing and very useful to have around."

"I thought that most of them would only be useful, but I discovered some that could be fun."

"Fun?" she asked. "Robots were never fun."

I led her to a robot I had come across in my explorations. It moved around on a set of caterpillar tracks.

"This was for the next round of Mars missions. For us it routinely scans all the seams where human built structures were added to the alien Arkitecture."

"Funny," she said, noticing the pun.

I stepped up onto a platform behind the robots' body. Then offered my hand.

She took it and gracefully stepped up onto the platform to join me.

The robot had a trunk that rose telescopically from the middle of the caterpillar tracks. It also had multiple arms.

"Hold on," I said.

She gripped an arm tightly.

I pressed a few buttons on the control panel on its chest.

At first the robot jerked forward and Maiara screamed a little. The scream became a laugh as the robot settled into a slow but steady forward momentum.

It zoomed through the rows of robots, heading to a pre-programmed destination.

Maiara smiled in joy, she even sort of wrapped her legs around the machine and then raised her hands like she was on a fairground ride.

She motioned me to join her, but I shook my head.

"Too scared?" she asked.

I nodded. Then decided to let go with one arm and raise that hand up.

We both neared another part of the bay and the robot slowed down.

I climbed down, offered Maiara another hand, and she stepped down to join me.

We were now next to a very large robot almost the size of a house.

It was shaped like the marriage between a crane and a dumptruck.

"This one was designed for construction purposes. I think it's here to help us unload the cargo bay stuff when we arrive on our new planet," I explained.

"Okay. But, why did we stop here?"

"Because this one has a 3D projector," I said. "Probably to display the plans for building it was supposed to build."

I tapped at its control panel and turned on the projector.

The display showed a title card for one of my favourite classic films. It's something my dad had shown me years ago. I had loved *Independence Day.*

Maiara walked around the image. "How did you—?"

"I got One to download this from the ship's stores and help me put this on the robot. I figured it'd be fun to watch a movie, alone, together.

She looked around. "We need something to sit on."

I waved my hand to beg her indulgence, and picked up a remote I had left on the big construction robot.

I pressed a button. From behind Maiara a curious crate suddenly came to life. It broke into thousands of pieces, all of which were actually scuttling robots that looked like beetles.

The crate reshaped itself from these smaller robots into a chunky, angular sofa.

I went over to it and sat down, then patted the empty space next to me.

She peered at me, and this robot couch, then walked over and reached out to touch the sofa.

"It's a collection of small robots designed to clear the blockages and clogs in the pumping station, as a mob they move through eating away at blockages. The thing is, they can form a myriad of shapes that don't eat things or people. This is the closest I could get to something resembling a seat.

She turned around and sat down, bringing her leg up underneath her to get comfortable.

"You really did plan this all out, didn't you?"

"Yeah," I said, "I wanted it to be different than any other date, but also just like any other back home." Then I started the film. "I hope you like this. It's one of the best.".

6
STARDUST

We barely watched the film.

We talked instead.

In hindsight I'm glad that we didn't get too much into it because the film is about a giant alien spaceship wreaking the earth, a poor choice.

Instead we asked each other lots of questions, getting to know one another more.

I talked about how I felt I was just an ordinary boy, basic grades at school, normal lower middle class family, living in one of the lesser-known English counties. The most exciting things to ever happen to me only happened when the Ark and Destroyer landed. I told her about my parents and family. My dad was the owner of a small building company, my mother an actuary. They had met when he needed someone to do the books for his company and she was the one he hired.

When I mentioned my baby brother I clammed up a little bit, and she didn't push it. It was still hard to talk about. In some way I had left him to die, and in other ways I had no choice. I wanted him here with me, surviving.

She asked about my scar. I think to distract me from my brother. No one else on board had broached the subject.

I told her about the kidnapping and she was enthralled by the story especially about my heroism when I earned my scar and escaped the kidnappers.

She then asked about my efforts during the invasion, when I was the one who helped One to retake the ship. I told her about the nanite injection I had given myself in my butt, which she found hilarious. She pressed for details about that injection. It had contained military strategies and combat techniques, meant for One. I told her I could do several forms of martial arts now.

She wanted a demonstration, but I declined. Those memories were things I kept repressed. I didn't like the kind of person they made me.

And I asked her about her life.

Her parents had met in an odd way. Maiara's mother was Native American and her father was a Texan.

Her mother had actually been protesting a development on an important indigenous site, and her father had been one of the lawyers for the development company. They had met at a protest and her father fell in love with her mother to such an extent that he quit his job and started working for the charity protecting the land. He helped get the development project overturned. The rest was history.

Maiara grew up in Texas, and her parents taught her to embrace both cultures. She was the mix of her boisterous father and her contemplative mother.

Her father taught her how to fire guns, and taught her mother spirituality. Her father was big and bold like most Americans and so was she. Her mother was thoughtful and wise and Maiara claimed to be that also.

I playfully teased her about it referring to when she shouted down the Colonel when he invaded. That was big and bold, and not wise and thoughtful.

We sat far apart at the beginning of the film, and then gradually she inched closer, then I moved closer until our legs were somewhat together and bodies touching.

The best moment in the film came and went, and I hardly noticed. Maiara jumped up from the couch when the good guys launched their final attack on the Mothership. When she plopped back down onto the sofa, she was even closer to me, and staring right into my eyes.

I stared back into hers.

With the film over, I thought now was the perfect time to show her *the* big surprise. We shut everything down and returned the robots to where they were supposed to go. Then I led her down to the engine room, and we kept going down.

The engine was like a skyscraper hanging from the ceiling. At the top were gangplanks and walkways to monitor and adjust the engine's settings. There was also a lift to the base of the room.

Maiara and I took the lift all the way to the bottom.

At the base, the giant engine hung suspended about a hundred feet above the floor. Wires extended down into the floor around a hatch, which led to the bottom section of the Ark, where all the water once vacuumed into the ship was stored.

I lay down and looked up at the engine, as she lay beside me.

"This is one of the best views on the ship."

"It's just the engine, Callum."

"Yeah. But watch."

The engine routinely flushed a build-up of some fuel elements. When it happened, clouds of tiny, shimmering particles floated down to be reabsorbed into the engine to be used again. Each burst of these elements created a shower of multi-coloured snow.

Maiara had not yet worked in the engine room, so she had no idea that this happened, and had no idea it looked so spectacular.

She gasped at the spectacle. In multiple bursts, clouds of green, yellow, pink, red, gold, purple, blue, silver, orange all drifted down like fireworks. Each ejection from the engine mixed the colours anew. And as they reached the lower section of the engine, lightning like you'd see in a plasma ball lamp, reached out and pulled the particles back to the absorption medium, keeping us perfectly safe.

It was the most spectacular display of colour. We both oohed and aahed aloud.

But an errant particle here or there, and the finger of lightning reaching out to grab it was still enough to make us both jump.

That was when we both grabbed each other's hand.

And both looked down at our fingers, entwined together.

At first I felt embarrassed and and loosened my grip. But hers tightened.

We looked into each other's eyes, just staring. We were content to be in this moment.

I wondered if now was the time to kiss her.

Then another lightning bolt crackled through the air, and we jumped again, laughing nervously.

"I think we should maybe leave this area," I said. "Just to be safe."

She agreed.

It was late and we made a long walk to her room, hand in hand. No one else was up to see us or give us a hard time.

Everything had gone perfectly.

"That was a great first date, Callum," she said, standing at her door.

"I hope I haven't used up the best ideas I have," I said. "I don't know if I can top this evening."

"I'm sure you'll think of something," she said.

"What are you doing tomorrow night?"

"My shift in the control centre is in the evening, but how about lunch together in the cafeteria?"

"I can do that," I replied.

"Great."

"Great," I repeated.

Suddenly another moment of awkward quiet descended. Was she expecting a kiss? I knew I shouldn't presume so.

I decided to at least test the possibility, so I leaned closer.

Her eyes went wide and she leaned in too.

Then our lips met.

It was brief, but soft and pleasant. The first time in a long time that I had kissed a girl. And after a night as great as this one it was really special.

Her hand went to my cheek as she kissed me again, and then backed off.

She smiled and looked into my eyes one more time.

"Now that's how you end an evening like this," she said.

She then opened the door and stepped into her room.

"See you tomorrow, Callum," she said, closing the door.

"Goodnight, Maiara," I answered.

As I started off down the corridor, I looked back wanting her to leap back out and kiss me again. She didn't come out again. She was doing the wise thing, letting the evening end on a really high note.

I practically skipped back to by room. I felt as light as a feather and my heart was beating fast.

I reached my room and fell into bed, ready to sleep so I could wake and meet Maiara for lunch. My head hit the pillow and I drifted off.

That's when my memories of the military base resurfaced again.

FINDING NEW FRIENDS

I was back inside the base travelling, but instead of heading to my family's quarters, I headed to a different side of the base.

There was a different squad of soldiers on this side, and they didn't give me a second glance as they went about their chores.

I passed another residential area. I knew this was where another future member of the Ark crew was living. He had a huge family and they had set up a kind of miniature village centred on their bunk rooms. The crew of people ranged from young to very old. And a flag hung forlornly in the middle of the corridor; a Ugandan Flag.

I hadn't met the Ugandan representative before. I hadn't really met any of my future crewmates. I had wanted to keep away from them as much as possible because they represented the new life I'd have, and made me sad for the one I didn't want to leave.

Now I needed to talk to this guy and any of the others on the base. What I had just seen outside concerned all of them.

Sitting outside the first room I came to was an old grey-haired guy sitting on a wooden seat, smoking. I imagined that if he was still in his home town in his own country, he would be doing exactly the same thing.

The old guy didn't seem to care that I was approaching.

"Hello. I'm looking for someone who's about my age," I asked the old guy. I didn't want to get into specifics. I had no idea if this Ugandan representative's family even knew what they were here for.

The old guy turned to me. His eye had cataracts, so he probably didn't even know what I looked like. He shrugged his shoulders, and then took a draw from his cigarette.

I walked past him and peered into any of the open rooms.

In one, a family sat on the floor eating their meagre rations. They paused, food halfway to their mouths, when I appeared in the doorway.

I quickly scanned the faces in the room. None of them seemed the right age.

I waved awkwardly and said "Hi." Then I moved on.

In the next room was a family of five. A big lanky father and equally tall mother sat with a boy who looked my age and two younger siblings.

This looked right, I thought.

The Ugandan representative could have been male or female, but I took a chance that there wasn't a girl my age elsewhere in one of the other rooms.

"Hi. Sorry to interrupt. I'm Callum. I looking for the—" and I lowered my voice to a hushed whisper, "Ugandan representative of the Ark."

The boy looked up at his parents.

They were looking at me, evaluating me. I felt their eyes fix on my scar for a moment.

The family then starting speaking amongst themselves, but I didn't understand the language.

The boy appeared passionate as he argued with his parents, pushing until they relented. It was then that he greeted me. He offered a hand and we shook.

"My name is Ogwambi," he said.

"Callum," I said. "Can I have a word?"

"I've only a minute," he said.

I ushered him into the corridor and leaned in to whisper. "Look, I don't know you, but we're both future crewmates."

"Uh huh."

"I ran into someone the other day, and he said something strange."

"Strange? I hate strange. Strange means bad to me. Ever since a giant, alien spaceship crashed down things have only gotten stranger."

"I get that. This guy came to this base and he tried to sneak in. He said he was going to find out the truth behind the conspiracy."

"Conspiracy? You mean the gigantic lie that Dr. Ghost and company are telling the world? The one where they tell everyone that everything is going to be ok so people don't totally freak out?"

"I don't think he was talking about that. He seemed to already know it was a lie. It seemed like he was talking about something else."

Ogwambi looked uncomfortable to hear this. His posture changed and he crossed his arms and gazed past me.

"What?" I asked.

"I suppose I should say you're crazy or that you've lost it due to stress, but you're the second future crewmate who expressed these concerns to me."

"The second? Who was the first?"

"A guy called Koyla, the representative from Australia."

"Oh that guy? He's nuts though," I said.

"You sound nuts, as you put it," Ogwambi countered.

"We need to talk to him."

"Follow me. I know where he is," Ogawambi said.

He led me through the base to Koyla's quarters.

Kolya was only living with his grandfather. Their room was sparsely decorated. He had brought barely any of his personnel belongings from the looks of it.

Ogwambi knocked on the door and Koyla answered.

"We need to talk to you," I said.

"Tell him what you told me," Ogwambi said.

Koyla yawned and then said, "I didn't hear this from an official source. It's just something that Koamulu and Gerlinde were talking about."

I rolled my eyes at Ogwambi, and he shrugged.

A few minutes later Koyla had led us to a community room where we connected with Koamalu and Gerlinde. After a few moments of pleasantries, Koyla engaged the other two.

"Tell them what you told me," Koyla said.

"I've told you lots of things," Gerlinde said.

"About the secrets Dr. Ghost is keeping from us," Koyla clarified.

Gerlinde looked uncomfortable. She brought her arms up to hug herself and she backed away.

42

Koamalu motioned for her to tell us.

Gerlinde's eyes darted all over, then she spoke.

"It was something I noticed about the government officials who brought me here," she began. "I saw them getting injections of nanites, too. One on the plane trip over."

"So maybe they needed new information? And that would have been the quickest way to get it?" I said.

"Yeah, but they sort of got the injections reluctantly. The people who administered them were guards, soldiers. The ones working directly for Dr. Ghost. Afterwards the officials on the plane seemed more compliant. They didn't have as many complaints as they seemed to before. Less vocal about the decisions being made and how they were the wrong ones.

"I didn't like getting the injections, either. Did you?" I said.

"There is other stuff too. When the plane landed and the group was greeted by Dr. Ghost and his team, they mentioned something about the 18th."

"It could be anything. Just a meeting," I said.

"But they said it while talking about me."

"Are you the 18th something?" Koyla asked.

"Germany is the 18th best," Koamalu said.

"Nonsense! We're always in the top ten," Gerlinde said.

"So what can 18th mean? Didn't you ask?" Ogwambi asked.

"I was too scared," Gerlinde said.

Ogwambi then motioned for me to share what I'd just seen.

"So I met this guy the other day who was breaking into the base. He seemed a little weird, but he said that Dr. Ghost was keeping something from the general population, and that he had 'manipulated' things."

"What things?" Koamalu said.

"I don't know," I replied.

"He probably means the lie he told the world. The one about the Ark being dropped on the Destroyer. We know that's not going to happen." Koamalu said.

"The guy said that we didn't know the truth. Us! Why are we being lied to? Especially when we'll be the last members of the human race. Is there anything we shouldn't know?"

"I think we have to find out," Ogwambi said.

"Do we ask Dr. Ghost?" Koyla said.

"Would he even tell us the truth?" Gerlinde said.

"Hang on guys. Maybe we should talk about this somewhere that doesn't have a camera," Koamalu said.

I started turning to look.

"Don't move. If they know we're looking they'll definitely want to know what we're talking about," Koamalu said.

"Ok. Let's meet during the next dinner period. We haven't eaten together before, but it makes sense that we would want to meet, and we can talk more there," I suggested.

We all agreed, and then headed our separate ways.

The conspiracy talk made me uneasy. The world was already coming to an end and now something hidden might be plotting against us.

Nothing felt safe.

7

CONFUSION

I felt a chill run through me as those old memories filed themselves away again. Nothing about them seemed real. Were they a fantasy? They didn't feel like my memories. It was like they belonged to someone else, like the nanite-implanted memories did.

I began to wonder if they were nanite memories. Did I have memories from someone else in my brain? Had someone else experienced this, and left their past in my mind? But that didn't make sense. It was me, Callum, in those scenes emblazoned in my brain. How could they be someone else's memories? I was the narrator. The events were from my perspective.

Could nanite memories be programmed to make the recipient believe they belonged to them? Why would anyone do such a thing if it were possible?

I needed to know more, and there were only a few people that I knew could help me.

8

REPORT

First thing in the morning, I got up to greet Ogwambi across the hall from my room.

I waited for him in my doorway, and when he finally stepped out, he jumped a little seeing me standing there.

"Callum," he said, "Are you waiting for me?"

"Yes, I am," I replied.

I looked down the corridor left and right to make sure it was clear.

"I have a question for you. Do you remember us meeting up in the base in the Lake District before arriving on the Ark?"

He looked confused by the question. It might be weird for me to ask? It felt like a lifetime ago to me.

"No. We didn't talk at all before coming here."

"So, last night some memories flashed up in my brain, memories of..."

"Oh! Yeah! Last night! How did that go?" he asked, smiling and winking.

I suddenly remembered my date with Maiara. A wave of elation came over me. And anticipation that I'd see her again at lunch.

"It was great! It went really, really well."

"Maiara and you, ay?" Ogwambi winked again.

"Wait... I didn't tell you who I was seeing."

"Gerlinde knew and word got round," he said.

I blushed and sighed. "She needs to learn to respect people's privacy."

"What did you do for your first date?"

"We watched a film, talked, and I showed her that lightshow that happens when the engine purges itself."

"Nicely done. That lightning is spectacular," he said.

I nodded and then made a serious face.

"Listen, I really need to know. Do you remember me and you, Koyla, Gerlinde and Koamalu all meeting up in the base to talk about something we thought Dr. Ghost was up to? Even a little bit?"

His eyes darted upwards. "Nothing rings a bell, Callum. Why do you ask? It would have been months ago. And if we did why wouldn't I remember? Those memories couldn't change."

"I don't know, Ogwambi. I remember it really clearly and it's not a dream. I don't even think it's a nanite memory."

"Then ask the others, I guess? I don't remember it at all. It's probably nothing. We've been through a lot since we left Earth, Callum. It wouldn't be crazy if we were a little scrambled by it."

I hoped he was right. It probably was nothing. But I couldn't dodge the feeling that it was important.

9

THE METEOR STORM

I was lying on the right side of her bed, she was on the left. This was, I think, our twenty sixth date. Yes I was counting. All of them had been amazing so far. The last month had been brilliant and I had forgotten all about those pesky memories I didn't understand.

We were both on our sides just staring into each other's eyes.

Somehow all the staring had become a competition.

The corners of my mouth twitched toward a smile, hers followed.

I tried to get a grip and keep my eyes locked on hers, but they started to water.

Then I had an idea.

I crossed my eyes, which I managed to do without blinking.

Her smile broadened.

I started raising my eyebrows in a flirty manner.

She broke. She laughed in my face, blinking the moisture back on her eyes as she did.

I relaxed, and blinked as well. I watched her laugh, so full and warm, and thought, *She is the best.*

She was fun.

This relationship was fun.

I loved it.

She stopped laughing and looked at me again. This wasn't an invitation to another stare down. I leaned closer.

She pursed her lips and leaned toward me.

Our lips met and we kissed, just like that. The best kiss I had ever had at that age. It was tender, simple, equal, and fun. I could have kissed her like that for hours.

Suddenly, the ship's intercom blared and we separated to hear it.

"Arkonauts, this is a ship wide announcement. We are approaching an asteroid-heavy area of space. They are relatively small and will do no damage to the ship. However we will get hit and will experience some turbulence. Everyone in the engine room is to evacuate. I don't want you on those walkways. If you can get to the larger rooms, the antigravity room will be the safest place. The impacts won't last long, as the Ark is going very fast. Brace yourselves. We will enter the field in a few minutes."

"What shall we do?" I asked.

"Let's just stay here," Maiara replied. She wrapped her arms around me, and hugged to my chest. "I have a shift in the control centre soon, and for the moment I just want to relax."

She started to curl into me, but then pulled back and looked me in the eye again.

"I just remembered... I wanted to ask you something," she said.

"Ask away."

"Could we play a game? One that could help us get to know one another better?"

"I hate icebreaker games," I replied.

"No. This is a challenge. Listen it works like this: whenever we meet up, the first one of us to ask the other about an embarrassing story from our past has to get an answer, and the other person can't ask one back for the rest of that period of time we spend together. If you have a good memory you can be the one to get all the juicy stories," she explained.

"Aged ten, tell me a story," I said quickly.

She sat back a little from me, "No. You're supposed to say 'yes' to the game. Then I ask a question. You ruined it. I was supposed to be first."

"I'm a little cleverer than you think," I said.

49

She scowled at me, and then smirked.

"Aged ten, tell me a story," I repeated.

"Fine," she replied in faux anger. "My parents had church groups around our house sometimes. Once I came downstairs in just my underwear, looking for a set of clothes that I thought my mother had washed."

"Oh no," I said, guessing the end.

"So I burst into the living room to ask my mom where my clothes were and there was the pastor and the rest of the group in the middle of a bible study."

I stifled a laugh.

"I ran back to my room and refused to go to church for two weeks."

"That is a funny story," I said.

Maiara shook her head, but still she smiled.

Suddenly, the bed, the cabinet, and everything not bolted down in the room slid toward the far wall.

A vibration passed through the entire ship. A shockwave.

We both sat up with a start.

"That must have been an asteroid impact," I said.

Everything shook again. The bed drifted from the wall and then flung back into it, harder than last time.

"The Ark used to get hit by missiles all the time. But that's got to be different than being hit by a solid rock travelling millions of miles an hour, right?" I said.

"Are you worried that this might get worse?" Maiara asked.

"Maybe," I replied.

Then the ship groaned.

"What was that?" She asked.

And it groaned again, louder.

"That didn't sound good," Maiara said. "Sounds like the bridge..."

"What do you mean?" I asked.

"Back home, one of the Destroyer's pipes wormed its way up a river near to my house. It eventually met a bridge and instead of going under, it smashed through it. I remember watching the bridge collapse. It made the same sound."

"That's not good," I said.

"Callum," Maiara said, pointing at a cactus on her bedside table.

It slid on the tabletop, and just as it reached the edge, Maiara leapt over me, jabbing me with her knee.

"Ow!"

She plucked the plant from the table's edge, before it could fall. "Sorry. This is my favourite."

"We need to get out of here," she said.

"Why?"

Then the whole room tilted dramatically. All the furniture slammed to one side. We barely avoided smashing face-first into the wall.

"Come on, Callum," Maiara said.

She hopped off the bed, and took my hand, pulling me from the bed.

The room was still at an angle. We had to balance on an uneven floor to get to the door. Maiara tried the door with one hand cradling her plant with the other.

"It won't open," she said.

I looked at the frame. It was bent and buckled. I grabbed the handle with both hands and pulled as hard as I could. The door inched open so I yanked again, and it finally came open.

The room suddenly shifted again, tipping further.

In the hallway, other Arkonauts were running down the corridor, yelling.

Moana lived opposite Maiara. She was huddled in her doorframe.

"What's going on?" she asked. "I thought the asteroids wouldn't hurt the ship."

I looked down the slanting corridor. The hallway was dipping a few metres from where we were. It was as if a sinkhole was opening under the corridor and everything was falling into the empty space.

"We have to go," I yelled.

I pushed Maiara up the corridor and waved for Moana to follow.

The two girls ran uphill towards the section of corridor that was still level.

This entire area was sinking downwards. Just as we reached the level corridor, the floor collapsed a little more.

Maiara and Moana stood steady on the flat bit.

I hadn't made it there yet.

I yelped and then fell to the floor. There was nothing to grab onto, so I started to slide backwards.

Moana and Maiara knelt and reached to grab my arms.

Then the floor disappeared from under my feet entirely.

Everything in the corridor and the surrounding rooms fell away. I was dangling over the edge of the hole that had opened. My heart raced. I wanted to scream, but I couldn't catch my breath.

I looked over my shoulder, past my flailing legs and saw the section of corridor that had just collapsed fall and crash into the floor below; the cargo bay.

Maiara's and Moana's rooms tumbled down and broke apart as they smashed on the shelving units below. Furniture splintered on the floor, crates filled with supplies from Earth burst open. Sparks from torn conduits nipped at me as I dangled between floors over the chasm. Broken pipes flooded the cargo bay.

"Pull me up!"

"You think?" Maiara said. She strained with one hand on my right arm and the other still holding her plant.

"Put the plant down. It's safe," I screamed.

Maiara quickly set it down and gripped my arm with both her hands.

She and Moana then counted down and heaved me up over the ledge and onto the level corridor. Maiara then grabbed me by the belt and dragged me further away from the hole.

We gazed at the damage. A section of corridor forty feet across, including Moana's and Maiara's rooms, had fallen away. We were staring down into the cargo bay, filling with water.

"We need to shut that water off," I said.

Suddenly, the ceiling above us bowed, and another hole appeared. A robot from the level above fell into the cargo bay, crashing into a pile of furniture, foodstuffs and some of Maiara's and Moana's clothing and furniture.

"What is going on?" Moana asked.

"The asteroid impacts must have weakened the ship's structure where they built our rooms."

The internal speaker system crackled.

"Arkonauts in the residence area, what is happening down there?" One asked.

"Maiara's and Moana's rooms collapsed into a sinkhole. I would like to report shoddy workmanship." I replied.

10

SEEING THE DOCTOR

The floor of the entire section of the crew quarters had to be rebuilt. The cargo bay needed to remain airtight to preserve certain foods, materials, and the seed vault.

One told us that was no way to rebuild Moana's and Maiara's rooms, but there were a couple of unused, unfurnished rooms available. They wouldn't be fancy, but at least they provided private places for the girls to stay.

After that, One demanded we all go to the medical bay for a check-up.

As we sat around the beds being scanned by a robot doctor One tried to explain the situation.

"What about my bed?" Maiara asked.

"The frame was destroyed when it fell into the cargo bay, but the mattress survived, so you'll have something to sleep on," One said.

"Did my keyboard survive?" Moana asked.

"You played?" I asked as the robot grabbed my chin and shone a light into my eyes.

"No concussion," the robot, in a cheerful voice in an attempt to have a good bedside manner.

Moana nodded.

"I am sorry Moana. The keyboard's casing shattered when it hit the floor of the Cargo bay," One said.

"Maybe it will still work," she mused.

"If you want to try and fix your furniture, we have the tools in the cargo bay, and I will help you as I am available."

The robot addressed One: "Physically and mentally they are fine. Although a bit of extra rest would do them good."

"Take your next shifts off," One said to us all.

"Yes," Maiara said, pumping the air.

I smiled, but my mind drifted. How had they assessed our mental state? Could that mean it was also capable of understanding why the strange memories of the base were re-surfacing?

"Callum, will you help me retrieve my stuff?" Maiara said.

"I'm going to find Ogwambi," Moana added.

"Maybe we can let the men do all the work? They're supposed to be big and strong," Maiara quipped.

Moana looked at me and shrugged. "Erh... strong may be the wrong word."

I didn't respond to the ribbing and banter. I was still thinking about the robot.

"I'll be with you in a minute," I said. "I have a pain in my foot and I want to the doc to take a look at it."

"I will go open the cargo bay," One said. "The other robots have started repairs on the floor."

"See you soon," Maiara said, not questioning my fib. Then she, Moana, and One all left the room.

I slid off my bed and approached the robot.

"Hello Arkonaut, how may I help you?" it asked.

"I have this problem. I'm remembering things that don't seem like my memories. They seem foreign."

"Please take a seat," the robot said.

I seated myself again on one of the medical benches, like I used to do with my old GP, and wondered briefly if I would get a sweet at the end of this consultation.

"Have you had any significant brain trauma recently?" the robot said.

"No. I don't think so," I answered.

Even during the recent invasions, I hadn't hit my head.

"Have you taken any psychotropic drugs?" the robot asked.

I laughed, and the robot cocked its head curiously.

"No," I replied.

"Are you sure?" the doctor droid asked.

"Yes," I said, firmly.

"Here is a pamphlet just in case," the robot said.

A slot on the front of the machine opened, and a small pamphlet popped out. *The dangers of psychotropic drugs.*

"What else could it be?" I asked the droid.

"Have you received nanite implants?" it asked.

"I have," I answered.

"Please lie back on the bench," the robot said.

I did what I was told.

The robot used a device attached to one of its many arms to scan my head. I felt nothing and it took only seconds.

"It seems as if some of the nanites in your brain are not performing optimally. They are trying to render the memories you prefer not to remember inert, however they are struggling to do so. This could possibly be due to the presence of so many nanites in your brain. I suggest a simple reboot to remedy the issue."

"Sorry did you say 'inert'?" I asked. "Are there Nanites in my head trying to make me forget things?"

"Yes, some of these nanites are designed to render some memory cells inert, however they are currently inactive," the robot explained.

"Are you saying they are purposefully keeping parts of my memory hidden from me?" I asked.

"That is correct. Shall I restart them? Or would you like a moment to prepare and talk to love ones?"

"Why would nanites hide my memories from me?" I asked.

"These nanites expedite recovery from traumatic experiences by effectively preventing the brain's capacity to remember them," the robot explained.

What trauma were the nanites trying to hide from me? Was this Dr Ghost's way of making sure I could become an Arkonaut to move on from the trauma of losing my family and my home?

That didn't make sense to me. I had never been told about this before. As far as I knew all the nanite injections were meant to infuse helpful new memories, not erase old ones.

"Is it possible for you to make all those trauma blocking nanites inert?" I asked the doctor.

"I can," the doctor said.

"I want to remember everything."

The robot raised its arm, revealing a needle attachment, and pointed it at me.

"This won't hurt a bit," the robot lied.

OLD MEALS

I met the others in the cafeteria as we had arranged.

We all arrived far too early for a meal, confusing the chef, who made it very clear that food wasn't going to be served for half an hour at least. He emphasized that this was why a sign stating the cafeteria hours was posted outside the room.

We all played dumb and begged him to let us wait, and he reluctantly waved his hands toward the many empty tables

We choose a table on the far side of the room, out of the view of the cameras. Koamalu, Koyla, Ogwambi and Gerlinde, plus Waris, the boy representative from India, sat with me.

"How did you find out about this?" I asked Waris.

"Koyla told me," he answered.

"Koyla, don't you know the meaning of the words secret meeting," *Ogwambi said.*

"I thought we were all in this together?" Koyla pointed out.

"Good point, I suppose. Welcome, Waris," I said.

"So, you think something's being kept from us?" he asked.

"Yes."

"That makes no sense. We're going to be the last human beings left alive. Why would they care what we know?" he asked.

"I don't think that's how it works," Gerlinde said. "During this entire process no one has told me about the truth behind the JFK assassination, or who released those files on former president Crumb that got him imprisoned for treason, or if UFO's landed at Roswell. That last one is moot now, I guess. Point is no one is sharing all the secrets with us."

"Look guys, we need to figure out a way into Dr. Ghost's office so we can log into his computer and find out the truth. How we do that?" I said.

"Accessing his office should be easy enough. I can pick locks," Waris said.

Koyla beamed, proud that he had recruited someone useful.

"How do you know how to pick locks?" I asked.

"After the Destroyer attacked, my family had to walk from India into Eastern Europe. We broke into abandoned houses along the way to survive," he explained.

"Hmm, well that'll get us inside. Now, how do we avoid being seen?" I said.

"We don't have to worry about that either," Ogwambi said. "Once you entered Dr. Ghost's wing of the office building there are no more cameras. Seems like he does like keeping secrets."

"But someone watching the cameras might spot us go into the corridor, so if we take too long, they might get suspicious," I said.

"And you expect me or Koamalu to distract the guards or something?" Gerlinde asked.

"You watch too many movies," Ogwambi said. "Besides, couldn't the boys distract the guards too? "

Before Gerlinde could reply, I interjected.

"We're not doing any of that. We'll just have to take the risk. If someone comes to investigate, we'll just pretend we were expecting Dr. Ghost to be there, and that the door was open," I explained.

"Believable," Ogwambi agreed. "Hopefully."

"It's not like they can do anything to us. We're the last humans and they need us," Waris said.

"If they're still hiding secrets right before the inevitable end of the world, I don't think we can trust them to be rational," Ogwambi said.

"It's still a military base, and they're not going to like us hacking his computer, either way. We need as much time in Dr. Ghost's office as possible," Koamalu said.

"Which bring us to the third problem: hacking his computer," I said.

"So, how do we hack his computers? We need passwords."

"Unless he keeps hard copy records," Gerlinde added.

Soldiers, and other civilians started trickling into the cafeteria. It was nearing mealtime.

Everyone went silent for a moment. No one seemed to know how to gain access to Dr. Ghost's computers. His passwords could be anything.

"Look at you all. This is perfect," someone said behind us.

We all jumped with surprise and looked toward the voice.

It was Dr. Ghost.

"Why do you say that, Dr. Ghost?" Ogwambi said,

He laughed

"It's good to see you all getting together on your own, making friends. This is great progress."

The old man, who resembled a thinner Santa Claus, sat down at the table beside us.

"What were you talking about?" he asked.

We all looked at each other.

Someone needed to say something, before we started contradicting each other.

"We were just trying... to... to get to know one another better," I said.

Dr. Ghost smiled.

"That's great. Really good," he said.

"You know," Gerlinde said, "We don't know anything about you, Doctor."

I looked at Gerlinde.

She winked.

I wondered what she had in mind.

Dr. Ghost leaned back and took a deep breath, " Oh, I don't think I should waste your time talking about myself. The sad truth is I'll soon be dead. Hmm. Yes. It's something to hear it out loud. What matters now is your relationships."

"But we all want to know more about the man who... who saved us," Gerlinde said.

Dr. Ghost studied her carefully.

"A fair query I suppose. I'm only the man with the idea. Countless others have worked very hard to get you here."

"Come on, Dr. Ghost. We want to know more. Do you have a family?" Ogwambi asked.

The old man looked off into the middle distance for a moment.

"I have a son," he said.

"What's his name?" Gerlinde asked.

"Joshua," he replied. "His name is Joshua."

"And where are you from?" Gerlinde asked.

"Canada,"

"Canada? Really? Do you like hockey?" Koyla asked.

My new friends definitely got him talking...

Dr. Ghost smiled.

"The Calgary Flames. It's a shame they played their last game just two weeks ago, their Ice rink was cut up for the water. Even at the end of the world it's hard to imagine traditions ending, despite being for a good cause."

"Did you study to become a doctor in Calgary?"

"No, no. I went to the University of Toronto."

Suddenly, the PA system crackled on and the voice paged Dr. Ghost.

He frowned.

"A shame," he said. "It was nice speaking with you. Keep getting to know each other. You're going to be connected for a long time."

He stood and exited the cafeteria.

Once he was out of earshot, I asked, "What was with all the questions?"

"Passwords," Ogwambi said.

"We know a little more about him, and people often make passwords about close personal things," Koamalu said.

"Genius," I said, "We should probably learn even more."

"Let's go to the library. There's still internet in there," Gerlinde said.

"Good idea," I said.

Our chairs screeched along the floor as we all stood up, leaving a bemused chef behind.

THE INFILTRATION

Our room on the base was actually three rooms, plus a communal kitchen and dining area, and two bedrooms, with one containing a sink and toilet. Showers were taken in a communal block down the hall.

My little brother and I slept in one room, while my dad and mum slept in another.

We kids had been sent to bed an hour ago, but my parents were still up.

When they finally went to bed I waited another hour to be absolutely sure they were asleep. I spent that time worried about what I would learn from Dr. Ghost's office. I checked my digital watch repeatedly, waiting for the face to read ten to midnight, when we all agreed to meet.

When 11:50 struck, I carefully and quietly unzipped my sleeping bag, then slid out of it and off my bed.

I moved through our little flat as silently as I could, being sure to step carefully. I tiptoed down the hallway to the main room, and approached the front door, turning the knob carefully and precisely and drawing the door open, letting a shard of light in from the flood lamps outside.

Just as I stepped out the door, I felt a tug at my shirt.

"Callum?" someone said behind me.

I jumped, stifling a gasp.

It was Jack. He grasped my shirt with one hand and wiped his sleepy eyes with the other.

"I want—"

I covered his mouth in my hand.

"Whisper," I whispered.

He nodded.

I took back my hand.

"—a drink of water," Jack whispered.

"You don't need me to do it for you," I whispered, gesturing toward the kitchen.

Jack didn't move.

"Where are you going?"

"I'm going to... to meet a girl," I said.

"A girl?"

"Yes!"

"What for?" Jack asked.

"For snogging. Okay?"

Jack's face scrunched up. "Can I come?"

"No, go back to bed," I hissed.

"I'll tell mum and dad!"

"I'll do you a deal, Jack," I said. "You can have my dessert for the next week if you don't tell them. Okay?"

He thought for a moment, and then nodded.

I gave him a pat on the head, and left the flat.

The corridor were still lit and bustling with soldiers, so I was careful to look as though I knew where I was going and had somewhere to be. If they thought I was sleepwalking, they might stop me and take me back.

When I turned the corner, I met up with Ogwambi and we made our way to the meeting spot together.

"What if we find something we don't want to know?" he asked.

"At least we'll know it together so we can decide what to do next," I answered.

That was when we heard Dr. Ghost's voice. We slipped into an open doorway and tried to be as quiet as we could, so he would hopefully walk straight past.

As he passed us, I saw whom he was chatting with. It was the vice president of the United States!

"Why's he here?" Ogwambi asked, with awe in his voice.

"I haven't a clue," I replied, my mouth had dropped open.

The vice president was perhaps the only international celebrity left in the world. Unlike his mediocre president, the vice president was always travelling the world trying to hold things together.

"I've always wanted to meet him," Ogwambi said, and he stepped forward a little and I had to raise an arm to stop him.

"I want to meet him too, but we have something important to do."

Ogwambi sighed.

Once we were sure they were far away, Ogwambi and I stepped back out into the hallway.

"Callum?"

It was Jack. Again. He was holding a glass of water, looking at us.

"That's not a girl," he said.

I sighed.

"Do mum and dad know that you're gay?" he asked.

"If I was gay I would have told mum and dad already, and besides, it's not like that," I said. "Now, please, back to the room."

"But I want to stay with you," he said.

Ogwambi looked at me and shook his head.

"I had to ditch six younger siblings, and you couldn't lose one?"

I knelt down before Jack. "Okay. You can come with me, but you have to be super silent. Quieter than a mouse in socks. Do you understand?" I asked.

Jack raised his glass to his mouth and took a generous gulp. "Yes," he finally said.

"Don't fall behind either." I said.

"Really?" Ogwambi said.

"It'll be fine."

When we reached our meeting point, everyone else was there including another small child. Koamalu's younger brother stood next to his big sister, holding her hand and making funny shapes with his lips.

"You too?" she said, eyeing me, Ogwambi, and Jack.

"He's so cute," Gerlinde said. "Like a little tiny Callum."

"Yes. He's wonderful. Can we please go?" I said.

"We just saw Dr. Ghost, so he's not in his office," Ogwambi said.

64

We made our way to Dr. Ghost's office, watching for other workers from that corridor and doing our best to be deathly quiet. When we got to the doctor's door, we saw that the lights were off, so I tried the door handle.

As we expected, it was locked.

"Waris, you're up," I said.

He smiled and approached the door, pulling a number of bent metal trinkets from his pocket; a bushel of homemade lockpicks. As he started on the lock, we all huddled around watching down both ends of the corridor.

After a few minutes Waris said "Yes!" and opened the door.

We all piled inside.

I picked up Jack, and placed him on a sofa across from the desk.

Koamalu did the same thing with her brother.

The two little children sat there quietly, dozing off and on.

Gerlinde got to the computer first. She touched the mouse and the computer activated, waking from sleep mode, and requested the password.

"What do we try first?" she asked.

Meanwhile, Waris went to one of the filing cabinet and started picking its locks.

"This might be a problem," Ogwambi said, pointing at an object on the desk.

The small metal box had a tiny glass window on top.

"A fingerprint scanner," Gerlinde said.

"Does anyone know how to crack one of those?" I asked.

"I probably could with some jelly beans and a copy of his fingerprint," Ogwambi said.

We looked at him.

"They show you how to do it on YouTube."

"We'll have to settle on what's in those cabinets," I said.

At that moment, Waris stepped back from the cabinet and the top drawer slid open.

"Grab a file," I said. "Ogwambi, watch the door. If someone comes down the corridor we need to know right away."

As Ogwambi slipped out the doorway, I took a file and opened it. Inside I found a dossier on another Arkonaut, but I didn't know them. The name on the file was Leif, the representative from Norway.

"Apparently Leif has a nut allergy," I said.

"Whose Leif?" Koyla asked.

"The guy from Norway," I said.

"Stop screwing around," Gerlinde said. She had already speed read her way through three files, and grabbed for another.

"What are we looking for? It's not like we're going to find a file marked 'top secret,' or 'my plan to conquer the world or something'," Koyla said.

"Just look for anything suspicious," Ogwambi said.

"We don't even know what's suspicious and what isn't," Gerlinde said, slapping another file down on Dr. Ghost's desk.

"You're right. Let's put these files back. We can't leave a mess," I said.

That was when Waris opened the bottom drawer.

"This stuff looks more interesting," he said, leafing through the first folder in the drawer. "Resource allocations," he declared.

We all shifted our attention to the bottom drawer files, grabbing a handful each.

"I've got something in here about orbital trajectories of the Ark," Koamalu said.

"This one's about the storage project on the Ark," Waris said.

"Mine is about the acquisition of the worldwide nanite stores," I said. "Probably just to prepare them for injecting into us."

"There's nothing here," Ogwambi said, dejected.

"If only we could get into that computer," Gerlinde said.

"We still don't even know what we are looking for!" Koyla said.

"Hang on. Yes. Yes we do. The crazy guy that you met, Callum," Gerlinde said. "He was talking to them about being in our heads. And he pointed that gun thing at his head which he said kept the voices out."

"So?" I replied.

"What is in our heads, right now, that would make voices?"

"Nanites." I said.

I looked down at the file I was still holding about the gathering of the world's nanite stores.

"What does it say?" Koyla asked.

"It's just a spreadsheet of how many nanites Dr. Ghost was able to produce."

I turned that page over.

"And this side has some calculations on it... in his handwriting."

"Just how many nanites did he acquire?" Gerlinde said.

"1,780 cartons," I said.

"1,780 cartons?" Gerlinde asked.

"That's what it says," I replied.

"That's seems like a ridiculously huge amount," she said. "There are about two hundred fifty of us. So, 1,780 divided by two hundred fifty... It's more than seven cartons per kid."

"It also says he tried to get all of it, but only managed one quarter of the world's existing nanites at the time."

"Maybe he was trying to get as much as he could?" Ogwambi said.

"How much does one person get per injection?" I asked.

"A hundred millilitres, probably a lot less," Koamalu said.

"So seventeen thousand and eighty cartons is overkill," Gerlinde commented.

"Or he's stored the extras on the Ark? Nanites are really useful," Koyla said.

"I don't know. Some of these acquisitions are dated after the Ark was placed in orbit," I said. "He couldn't use rockets to put them on the Ark or teleport them on board the ship. Imagine trying to teleport trillions of tiny machines onto the ship, the power requirements and computer memory required to send us up there is already stretching the world's capabilities to breaking point."

"Guys, Dr. Ghost is hoarding nanites. Maybe he intended to use them on other people," Ogwambi's said. "Maybe he used them on the people building the Ark to make them complete the work."

"Umm... I have another file here," Waris said. "It lists the memories we've been given with details about the people they came from. Oh, and check this: the compensation they were given."

"Compensation?" I said.

"Yes. They were all paid in water," Waris said. "A lot. Thousands of gallons."

"That isn't surprising, water is hard to come by."

"But why would they take so much? The world's about to die," I said.

"They might not know that," Gerlinde said.

I nodded.

"Guys, that's might not be the most important bit," Waris said. "This list of names... It's wrong. There are eighteen names here," he said. "I only got seventeen nanite shots. And unless one of you got more, there's a mystery memory we don't know about."

"So what? We just have to get another shot," Koyla said.

"No. That's not right. I was told I had all mine," Koamalu said.

The rest of us nodded.

I had had all seventeen shots too. They had told me that was it.

"Why would Ghost give us another memory and not tell us?"

"So we wouldn't know it was affecting us? It must be a secret memory. One that we're not supposed to know about. Maybe it brainwashed us?" Ogwambi said.

LEAVING

"Brainwash? Memory injections can't do that. You've all seen the adverts for the technology. It doesn't influence anyone to do anything. All it does is impart skills that someone needs. It's why university degrees all take less than a year to complete. They just fast track your brain to be more efficient," I said.

"There is no other reason for giving us a secret memory. Why would we need skills that were secret from us?" Ogwambi asked.

"Dr. Ghost did invent the technology," Gerlinde interjected.

"Yeah... along with the vice president of the United States."

"If anyone would know how to use nanites to brainwash, it would be Dr. Ghost," Gerlinde said.

"How would that even work?" I asked.

"Maybe it's a kind of suggestion," Gerlinde said. "People used to think that smoking cigarettes was healthy, but then doctors and scientists told us different and that changed people's perspectives and behaviours."

"So what you're saying is the 18th memory is like an anti-smoking advert?" I said.

"Of course not, Callum! But Dr. Ghost could have given us information that changed our opinions and our actions," Koamalu said.

"Fine," I said. "But I know what I know! I know what memories are new and what memories are old."

"You might know a few of them, but some of the nanites in our heads aren't even active yet. What if this eighteenth memory activates after we get on the Ark?" Koyla said.

"Why are there so many little nanites?" my brother asked.

"Yeah! Why so many tiny robots?" Koamalu's younger brother asked.

"Stay out of this, Jack," I said.

"No!" he screeched. "I'm not stupid you know. I want to know what's happening to you!"

"Yeah! Me too!" Koamalu's brother said.

"Dr. Ghost gave us special knowledge with the nanites... We're part of an... an... experiment," Koamalu said.

This seemed to quiet Jack and her brother.

"I wish we could get into that computer. There have to be answers about the eighteenth memory in there," Gerlinde said.

We all stood there for a moment, unsure what to say. We had asked a lot of questions and imagined some answers, but we were no closer to the truth.

"Guys," Waris said. "I think we're thinking about nanites the wrong way. They do impart information related to skills, but it's not like they're pre-programmed. They first have to learn the skill from a human who performs the action first."

Waris grabbed some paper from Dr. Ghost's desk and started drawing a stack of little rectangles.

"Let's say Dr. Ghost wanted someone to learn bricklaying. He'd inject a bricklayer with blank nanites and have the bricklayer build something. The nanites would see the areas of his brain that light up while he did the work and would copy those patterns and loops. Then Dr. Ghost would extract the nanites and give them to someone else so when they were building that same thing they'd know precisely how to do it.

"I thought they could only copy memories? Memories of someone building a brick wall for example" I asked.

"Nope," Waris said. "Nanites can copy the function of any brain cell activity to make it portable and implantable. So, what if Dr. Ghost sent nanites from when someone, like a soldier, was being compliant, just following orders. The Nanites would see the parts of the brain lighting up, and go towards the grey matter that accepts orders and obeys. Then they would copy that brain activity. When it's extracted from the hosts brain they are implanted in someone else and used to replace someone's natural tendency to disobey... like a bunch of teenagers?" Waris theorised.

"You think we've been injected with nanites to make us follow orders like soldiers?" Ogwambi asked.

"It's not impossible," Waris said.

"Who supplied the 18th memories?" I asked. "That should tell us something."

Waris flipped through the file folder in his hand. He read for a moment. Then looked up at us, confused.

"An historian," he said.

"An historian?" Gerlinde asked.

"Did Dr. Ghost teach us some secret history?" I asked.

"It must do more than that," Waris said. "Historians don't have special training to make them obey."

"Wait, this eighteenth memory aside, if the nanite memories work how Waris described then Dr. Ghost could make anyone obey him, not just us, or at least be very agreeable," Ogwambi said. "If he's still acquiring nanites, what if he's distributing them all over the world to force people to comply with his plans?"

"That's crazy. Isn't it?" I said.

"Haven't you ever wondered why only 250 children were selected when the Ark is so big?" Ogwambi said. "And why would all these people work so hard to help us when they'll end up dead?

"Humanity is not this altruistic. Governments all over the globe working to save just a handful of people from all over? That's not how it works. The first person on the Ark should have been a billionaire or a president or a prime minister, Not us.

"I bet Dr. Ghost is using these nanites to make sure all those people sacrifice themselves for his plan."

"You mean that more people could go?" Gerlinde asked, excitedly.

"We could take our families," Koamalu said.

"Go where?" her brother asked.

"Who's going to be dead?" Jack asked.

Koamalu didn't answer.

It was clear that neither of our younger siblings knew the truth. And it was probably better that way. I made the 'cut it out' signal with a finger across my neck to let the others know that they should drop the death talk.

"No one's going anywhere and no one's dying, Jack," I lied. "Ogwambi's being... dramatic. Besides we don't even know if Dr. Ghost really is brainwashing people."

"Callum, he's lying to us. He gave us secret nanites injections," Gerlinde said.

"Yeah," Koyla said, "If anything he's oppressing people."

I wanted to argue more, but my skin was crawling with the idea that there was some other memory forcing me to be someone else."

"What do we do now?" I asked.

"We need to confront Dr. Ghost," Gerlinde said.

"Are you mad? He'll just put us in a prison until we are ready to teleport! Or worse, he'll take us off the project," Koyla said.

"He can't do that," I said.

"He's brainwashing everyone on earth! He can certainly do that," Ogwambi said.

Ogwambi marched toward us and took the nanite file from Waris. He crumpled it in his hands, angrily, and threw it at the desk.

"He doesn't care about us. In his mind he's just saving humanity!"

"What if he intends to teleport with us," I said.

"What do you mean?" Gerlinde asked.

"As far as I know there is no leader on the Ark who's going to take care of us?" I suggested.

"You think he's going to save himself?" Gerlinde asked.

"It makes sense. He's cooked up this crazy plan to save us. What if he's like that Bond villain who always wants to destroy the world except for those he deems worthy and start again."

"That sounds mental," Koyla said.

"Maybe not, but maybe this is how he survives."

We all went silent and took this in. We had all thought of Dr. Ghost as a hero. He was the genius who was doing all he could to save the human race from extinction. If he was secretly controlling other people all over the world,

72

how did we know he wasn't controlling us? How did we know that we weren't just like robots, programmed to perform tasks at the doctor's bidding?

"We have to confront him. But just him. And we have to have leverage," I said.

"Leverage?"

"We have to get him on his own so we can force him tell us everything. Then we have to stop him," I said.

"Stop him!?" Gerlinde said. "Callum, the fate of humanity is still on the line and the Ark is still our only lifeboat."

"Clearly, more people fit on the Ark. Maybe we can force him to let us take our families too," I said.

Jack and I looked at each other.

I saw that Koamalu was looking at her little brother, too.

I felt energised by a flush of hope.

Maybe I had found a way to save my family.

That was when the office door creaked open, and Dr. Ghost stepped into the room.

"I hoped this would never happen," he said.

CAUGHT OUT

Dr. Ghost eyed us as he walked deeper into his office.

We all couldn't have looked guiltier. The door to his office was open, his cabinet was open, and we had his files in our hands. There was no way to bluff our way out of this.

We all glared at Ogwambi for giving up the watch.

Sorry, he mouthed.

Dr. Ghost sat down at his desk, and sighed.

"You have questions, no doubt," he said.

We all gathered across from him, keeping the desk chairs between the doctor and us, as an extra barrier.

"What is this eighteenth memory?" Gerlinde and I blurted in accidental unison.

The doctor slumped back in his chair.

"It was, as you have no doubt figured out, given to you secretly," he said. "Its purpose is to ensure that once you and the others on the Ark meet you stay together, and you leave any bitterness, resentment, or bias for each other behind."

"How would an historian's memory do that?" Waris asked.

"In layman's terms, it gives you an outlook and curiosity that allows you to move beyond historical conflicts. To see the bigger picture of humanity's millennia long story."

"So you've brainwashed us?" Koamalu said.

"I guess that would be a way to put it," Dr Ghost said. "Though I would prefer to think of it as cutting the bruised pieces of a perfectly fine apple."

"Why would do something like that?" I asked.

"Because you are the new humanity," Dr. Ghost said. "If you are going to restart humanity elsewhere in the universe, why would you do so without a clean slate? I needed to make sure that you would be better than your forebears. I needed you to leave some of the old ways behind to start afresh."

"What about everyone else you brainwashed?" I asked, holding up the file of nanite acquisitions. "What did you get them to do if they're not going on the Ark?"

"The world would never have come together to finish the Ark and make sure you would survive without these treatments. They would have started wars, murdering millions... billions just to get aboard the Ark and survive. Remember how the world's governments picked at the Ark after we stopped it, like vultures at a zebra's carcass.

"I acquired nanites, and re-programmed them to guarantee the plan came to fruition, and humanity would have a second chance."

"You brainwashed the world to complete your master plan," Ogwambi snarled. "You couldn't be sure they'd all kill each other. You didn't even give them a chance."

"History gave them thousands of chances," Dr. Ghost said. "This was the only way."

"There must have been other plans," I said. "What makes yours the right one?"

Dr. Ghost sighed.

"I'm a psychiatrist by trade, and when I first invented nanites to heal the conditions of the human mind I became a celebrity of sorts, so I started a business.

"My technology was revolutionizing the world. Soon I was asked to advise several governments on it's applications. I made many friends.

"The vice president of the USA also worked on the technology and he used his money from it to propel him into politics. When the Ark became ours he got me involved, to help train the astronauts who would fly it. Back then all the nations of the world became partners in rebuilding the ship so we could use it as mankind's first interstellar craft.

"When the Destroyer came, and we knew there was no chance of defeating it, the Ark became the clear choice as a lifeboat. But I saw the rifts among our partners grow deeper. Nations were suddenly eyeing the ship thinking about going to war to obtain it and save themselves.

"So I infected the world leaders with nanites that I knew would make them think like I did. Allow them to see the wisdom of my plan. They, in turn, infected other people for me, getting construction workers on my side, soldiers to guard and rescue you from your countries. Of course I could not control everyone in the world. That was why we lied to the planet, telling people that we would drop the Ark on the Destroyer.

"And that led me to all of you."

He was right.

That is what would have happened. I had watched the news with mum and dad and it was clear that no one was going to get along. But it didn't sit well with me all the same.

"Dr. Ghost, how many people can the Ark support?" Gerlinde asked.

Dr. Ghost coughed and looked at Gerlinde.

"Why would you ask me that?" he asked, flipping through the files on his desk.

"You've lied about pretty much everything else," Gerlinde said. "Maybe you're lying about that too?"

He pursed his lips and furrowed his brow.

"The water and air on board could support about one-thousand five-hundred people over the time it would take to get to the nearest planet we've discovered," he said.

"How many?" I said.

He nodded. "The Ark has the means to support that many passengers," he said.

"That's six times more than the chosen crew," Gerlinde yelled.

"Our families could go with us," I said.

"Perhaps. That number of passengers could make it to the nearest planet on the other side of the wormhole, but we don't know if that planet is a habitable one. If they could not survive there, they'd need to be able to make to a second planet, and if not that one, a third, and so on. Not to mention the needed reserves of oxygen and water to last you during any kind of terraforming process. We had to leave some margin for error. I could have

76

put over a thousand people on the ship, but any mistakes, an unexpected loss of water or air would limit options. With only two hundred fifty odd crewmembers things could go wrong, but they wouldn't seriously hurt the mission. I had to make sacrifices, take the fewest risks.

"But our families," Koamalu said.

"In fairness, I don't need two-hundred and fifty-two of you either, a new colony requires only about half that many settlers. I choose you all because I wanted you to represent all that you are leaving behind.

"My plan is not a megalomaniacal one," Dr. Ghost said. "I'm giving every nation, every people, an equal place from which to start a new world."

"But you've told a massive lie! And we're all complicit in it," I said.

"You will never know you were complicit in anything," Dr. Ghost assured.

Then his office door opened, and a soldier stood there.

"Dr. Ghost?" the soldier asked.

The memory faded.

I heard screams, voices in pain. I felt my arm wrench behind my back, and my face smashed against the desk.

And, almost a whisper, I heard my brother screaming.

11

WHAT ONE KNEW

I hadn't fallen asleep, I was just remembering everything. I closed my eyes and tried to reform my memory of what happened next, but there was nothing. Presumably it was a memory of the soldiers grabbing us, and administering another nanite injection to suppress our memories.

I had probably lost a whole day. But even my parents wouldn't have noticed. It wouldn't have changed me as person.

Just as I was going to ask the robot doctor why I couldn't recall any more, One stepped into the medical bay, and I clammed up.

"Hello Callum," he said. "Are you okay? I saw on the computer that you were still being treated in the medical bay."

"Did you know about the eighteenth memory?" I blurted out.

For a moment, One looked flustered. It was something I had never seen him exhibit before.

"I did," he said. "When I awoke on the Ark, such information was accessible to me. I am aware that Dr. Ghost erased some memories in your mind."

"Why didn't you tell us?"

"What would have been the point," he said.

"Your father took away our freedom!"

"No. In fact, he didn't."

"He did," I screamed at him. "He lied to you and to us. Remember our first night on the Ark when I caught you watching an old recording of Dr. Ghost? In that video, he said we had to make our own mistakes... that we needed to be free to do wrong. And he was lying because he made sure that we'd always stay together by messing with our minds. Instead of freedom, he made sure we would think a certain way and behave a certain way, all so his vision could happen."

"And his vision saved your life," One said. "It is the path that allows humanity to endure. What if the last humans simply fought each other until they shared a single ending? If you were in charge what would you have done?"

I had no answer for him. Well, not a good one.

"Would you have told people the truth? Would you have hoped that they would do the right thing?" One asked.

"I..."

"You know what would have happened," One continued. "Every government would have attempted to seize the Ark. Everyone with power would have fought to get on board. The world would have devolved into violent chaos... a mad scramble that may well have destroyed the Ark in the process, rendering everything moot."

"I know," I said, images of the resource wars flashing to mind. "But maybe that's what should have happened."

One stared at me, silent.

"You would have allowed humanity to die?" he asked.

"No... Well, maybe," I said. "It's just that everything Dr. Ghost did was wrong. How can something built on such dishonesty be right? I have to live with the knowledge that I owe my place on this ship to the brainwashing, murder, and violence done to people who resisted his plans?"

"But you did not do any of it. You are not guilty."

"I feel guilty," I said.

"Do not. You have done nothing wrong. It is wisest to accept this and move on. That is what the eighteenth memory does: it allows all of you to move past mistakes, yours and those of human culture," One said.

"How does this make you feel?" I asked.

"I am not sure that I understand?" he answered.

"Your father made everyone bow to his will. He kept secrets from us; the last remnants of humanity. He killed to make sure such secrets remained hidden until the end of the world, and lied to the people so that they died with false hope," I said. "What do you think of your father now?"

"Everything he did was required," One said.

"But it was wrong."

"Callum, he used bad actions to produce tremendous good. How can that be bad?"

"They just are! People should always be free to make their own choices so the consequences are theirs to own, not palm off on someone else."

"Even if that means humanity dies in horrible violence?"

I knew what One was saying. He was talking about necessary evil. But all that does is taint any goodness that comes from that evil.

"Yes," I said. "If the ends justify the means, then there is no right or wrong at all."

"I see," One said. "Do you now plan to undo time and correct this mistake?"

"I've done it before."

"And was it right to change time?" he asked. "Are there not potentially dark consequences to altering the past?"

"I... I... don't know. That Callum wasn't me."

"And you would go back in time to doom all of your fellow Arkonauts to their deaths? They would all die, Callum," One said. "If I gave you the power to go back and stop my father from ensuring all the people on Earth worked to save a remnant of humanity, over saving their own skin, would you? You know very few people of their own accord would make such sacrifices."

"Don't make me the bad guy, One," I retorted.

"I do not wish to. But consider your decision. You can choose to go back and undo all of this, and you, and all of the young people on this ship will perish. Or, you can choose Dr. Ghost's lie, and all of you remain alive, as the last bastion of humanity."

"You are excusing all of it! Thousands of people could be here with us! My parents... Jack..."

Tears welled in my eyes.

One paused and his expression softened.

"Callum, this guilt is natural. All survivors experience it," One said.

I wanted to hit him, or cry, or both.

"I won't alter time, but maybe I can undo the memory." I said. "I want you to remove my eighteenth memory."

"You all need the eighteenth memory," One said.

"Maybe we should all decide that for ourselves? Let me tell the Arkonauts. Let them decide," I said.

He looked away, considering my request.

I stared at him, knowing that he could probably grab me right now and erase this entire conversation with a fresh injection of nanites, preventing anyone else from ever knowing. I would walk out of here without ever discovering these repressed memories.

What would he do?

12

EIGHTEENTH MEMORY

The theatre was filling up fast. I watched the Arkonauts stream in from the back. They would enter laughing and chatting, but once inside they all seemed to sense a sombre mood.

I stood on the small stage at the front. My cheeks were already burning with embarrassment at being the centre of attention.

One stood beside me. He appeared totally calm, though I could see the muscles in his cheeks tensing. He was probably not too thrilled to have this meeting. He was only going through with it because of a supreme sense of duty he had to the truth. But maybe to him it seemed like failure that it had come to this.

All the kids who had been with me on the army base, all of us who had had our memories erased, sat uncomfortably in the front row. Like me, the robot doctor had given them back their memories.

Maiara was with them. She, too, was fully informed about what I had learned. And she beamed me a smile of encouragement.

Once the theatre was full, One called us all to attention.

"Hello Arkonauts. Thank you for coming to this ad hoc meeting. You are here because it is time to reveal a secret." One paused and took a deep breath. "Since the very day you first met Dr. Ghost, you have all carried this secret with you. While I have reason to believe revealing it may not be the best choice, I am bound by honesty and honour to allow you all to make up your own minds. I will now let Callum explain."

One stepped aside, giving me centre stage.

Hundreds of pairs of eyes stared at me. I looked at the back wall, trying to avoid making direct eye contact, and panic myself in the process. What I was about to share could be devastating, and I didn't want to really see their faces.

"Before the earth was destroyed I, and several others, were sequestered on a military base in the north of England," I said. "Dr. Ghost was staying there for a time. After a ranting and raving man tried to gain entrance to the base, I learned that Dr. Ghost might have been keeping something from us. We were able to sneak into his office, and there we learned that we had been manipulated. In order to ensure the success of this mission, we were all given an eighteenth memory that we were never told about."

"What does it do?" Dion, from Greece, asked.

More kids started asked questions then. I could barely pick them all out from the din.

Some of the couples I knew about were chatting with each other in concern.

And suddenly I had a thought. Would deactivating this memory change how I thought about Maiara. Or how she thought about me? I began to question the whole idea.

I bit my bottom lip, and raised my hand to quiet all their questions. It was too late to back out now.

"The memory's primary purpose is to make us all get along," I said, voice quavering. "It prevents us from getting into arguments and squabbles, and it forces us to be friends essentially."

One then stepped forward.

"I must clarify that the eighteenth does ensure that arguments and squabbles of disunity do not take place, however, it does not force you.

"My father did not want you to be forced to do things that that you would not do. He always believed in humanity's innate freedom, however he desired to provide you the best tools to make strong decisions that would hopefully keep you, and humanity, together.

"It is a memory, not a doctrine. The memory came from an historian. Dr. Ghost chose her because she understood humanity's story. She saw how all the wars, political divides, races, and peoples were knitted together.

"Dr. Ghost believed that only someone who can see the whole story can make the wisest decisions. He hoped that if you had her perspective then you would see the benefits to forgetting the past and moving towards a brighter future.

"Before you ask questions, I have one for each of you. 'If I were to die, who would you look to for leadership?'"

Silence reigned as everyone thought the question through.

"Raise your hand if you would answer: Callum," he said.

I was shocked. Everyone raised their hands.

"Callum is not special like I am," One said.

"Dude. I'm a little special," I said.

One waved my sarcasm away.

"However, after me, Callum has the most experience. A version of him has crossed time for us. He is the logical choice.

"Without the eighteenth memory many of you would likely have answered differently, perhaps due to jealousy or selfishness or boundless dislike. But the eighteenth memory grants you all the ability to weigh all the facts dispassionately, and make the best decision.

"This is what the eighteenth does. It brings those with it to good conclusions, not by force, but by logic and the wisdom of a cumulative knowledge of history."

The theatre fell silent again. The Arkonauts were all in deep thought.

"What do we do about this?" Luciana from Columbia asked.

She wasn't the only one asking.

One looked at me, and stepped back.

"We have the option to disable the eighteenth memory. We will be as free as we have always been, but no longer manipulated by these memories."

"How do we deactivate them?" Sandi from Denmark asked.

"Yeah, how?" another Arkonaut asked.

One presented a device shaped like a bit like a blocky gun.

"This device will target and deactivate an individual set of nanites in the brain. Just point and click, and the memories will deactivate," he explained.

"Should we get rid of these memories? They're not hurting us," Urraca From Panama said.

Mumbles started to fill the room.

I looked around, worried that they all might not agree. I didn't want to be the only one to deactivate,

"We all know there is nothing wrong with the other memories we have been given," I said. "But these memories change our minds and change who we are, without our permission. I don't want to live that way."

"Why?" Nebaioth from Palestine asked.

Jacob from Israel added, "Yeah! Why?"

"We're human," I said. "We need to be free to make our own choices. What kind of new world would we be starting for humanity if we didn't have free will?"

The Arkonauts continued mumbling.

I had to show them not to be afraid, so I turned to One.

"I'll go first."

One dutifully raised the device and placed it to my temple. He didn't argue with me. He didn't even ask if I was sure. He just pressed the button and the machine made a single click.

"Is it done?" I asked, feeling no different.

"Yes. It is done," One said.

I waved to the Arkonauts in their seats.

"See. I'm fine. Still the guy you've gotten to know. Be free with me."

There was a rumble in the crowd, and then a hush as they all queued up to have their nanites deactivated.

SYSTEM UPDATE

EIGHTEENTH NANITE INJECTION DISABLED

DISUNITY PREDICTED...

...TWO ACTIVATION INITIATED

13
CONFLICT

I raised a spoonful of soggy cereal to my mouth, contemplated how gross it looked, and then took the bite.

It was breakfast time in the cafeteria. It was also the day after One had deactivated our eighteenth memories. Dehqan sat across from me. He looked tired, as he munched on a banana.

I hadn't talked to him since I sat down. I was looking forward to seeing Maiara again at lunchtime, and that's the only place my mind was. She still wanted to see me. Still as boyfriend and girlfriend. That's what she'd said. I was relieved that the memory implant One had deactivated hadn't changed the way we felt about each other.

Plus, I didn't feel like a completely different person.

And neither did she.

We talked for hours the night before, imagining what the change would mean. We even chatted about our feelings. It seemed we liked each other because of mutual respect and admiration, plus attraction, but it wasn't because of the nanites.

She said she came to like me when I saved One, and helped take back the Ark. I told her I fell for her when she stood up to the Colonel and his rogue American team. She was so courageous when she looked him in the eye and called him out on his cowardly and hypocritical behaviour. I had never seen someone do that before.

Then we laughed and joked about a few things, and kissed some more.

That's where my mind was, but there was also something in the air making me feel anxious.

The cafeteria was very quiet. Much quieter than usual. The distribution of people was different, too. Kids came in from their shifts, took their meals, and then sat down far away from anyone else. There were a few pairs here and there, but they seemed wary of sitting with anyone else too.

Ogwambi seemed off, as he sat down opposite me and took a bite of his fruit. He gave me a nod, but then looked all around the room like he was watching for someone following him.

Maybe I was just being paranoid.

"Morning," I said.

"Morning," he replied.

"Things seem to be going okay," I said, shrugging.

"It's quieter," he said. "I think deactivating the eighteenth has had an effect."

"I bet it's just the shock of knowing what Dr. Ghost did. We'll process it and move on," I said.

"Yeah. *Move on*," Dehqan muttered.

"That sounded sarcastic," Ogwambi said.

"It's nothing," Dehqan replied.

"Come on, Dehqan. What's wrong?" Ogwambi pushed.

"For some of us, living with these facts is going to be harder."

"Wow! You should be a cop, Ogwambi. You broke him pretty fast," I joked.

Dehqan scowled at me.

"Shut up, Callum. Nothing's funny."

Ogwambi and I went silent. We traded a look, one that said, *"What's his problem?"*

"Sorry Dehqan," I said, finally. "I'm just trying to lighten the mood."

"You don't get it do you? We found out that more people could have come with us." Dehqan's face reddened as he spoke.

"I told everyone that Dr. Ghost felt we needed backup resources just in case the world on the other end of the wormhole isn't safe," I said.

"And we all left people behind too," Ogwambi said.

"Covering for him... No surprise," Dehqan scoffed. "I doubt anyone else from Afghanistan would have made the cut anyway."

"What's that supposed to mean?" I asked

"You know exactly what I mean," he said.

"I don't think we do," Ogwambi said.

"If more people were taken on the Ark, they'd all be Americans or Brits or other rich countries. That's what they were doing right? Hoarding the resources, surviving in comfort, for as long as possible," Dehqan said.

"He's right," said Kaam, from the table next to ours. "All aid stopped to my country for two years, but Western TV still continued parading your celebrities around, and they were as healthy and fit as they had ever been."

"Not everyone experienced the end of the world the same way," Dehqan said.

"I never said they did," I replied. "The Western nations were the ones making our escape possible, we needed more resources for them to make it happen. Without us the whole plan would have failed."

"So you're saying you deserved it because you were the better nations. My nation could have been rich too you know, if it hadn't been stolen from for centuries."

"That's not what I'm sa—"

"Does it even matter now Dehqan? Everyone is dead. Let it go," Ogwambi said.

"They were my parents. They were my friends and family, They all suffered in their final days, just so others like you could have more," the Afghan said.

Then he got up and sat with Kaam.

"What was that about?" I asked Ogwambi.

"I don't know. Although..." he said.

"Although what?" I asked.

"Uganda wasn't a rich country like the U.K., and honestly, I only spent my last days in relative comfort thanks to Uganda still being in the Commonwealth. My nation's leaders had connections that got me to the U.K. But if I had stayed in Africa, I would not have been living in safety and security. We didn't have the means to stop rioting or keep the peace.

"You have to admit, Callum, living where you did gave you the best seat to watch the end of the world."

"The best seat? Are you kidding?" I said. "Maybe Dehqan isn't wrong. The U.K. was better suited to weather the Destroyer. But I suffered too. It wasn't my fault though! What could I do? I was 15 years old!"

I scowled at Dehqan and Kaam, their backs to me, and wished they had never spoken up.

14
MEETING TWO

The next day One called us to a special meeting in the theatre.

I sat next to Maiara, and we were holding hands. It felt really comforting.

"What do you think we're here for?" I asked.

"Maybe One is going to reactivate the eighteenth memory? Have you noticed what's been going on? I've seen two fights already today. And our shift in the command centre was definitely not as smooth as it had been in the past."

"Fighting there too?" I asked.

"No fights, but everyone was irritable. And there was lots of complaining. I don't like it."

"I've noticed similar stuff," I said.

I sat back and my mind drifted. Whatever the eighteenth memory had done to us before, its absence was going to take some getting used to.

"He won't reactivate it," I said. "Maybe this is a pep talk or just about something that happened elsewhere on the Ark."

"We *are* getting close to the wormhole," Maiara said.

"Ooh. Yeah. What that will be like?"

"It's supposed to take us millions of light years across the Galaxy in seconds. I'm hoping it will be a wild ride," she commented.

"Not me. I've had enough chaos," I said, "I don't want to puke."

"Eww," she chided me.

I scrambled to change the subject.

"So... tell me about you at age nine," I said, continuing our game from earlier.

She looked nervous and stared off into space.

Maybe she was embarrassed?

The she smiled slyly.

"When I was nine the most embarrassing thing was the day that I went to school in wearing two different types of shoes."

"That's not even bad," I said.

"Oh, it gets better," she began. "I spent the whole morning worrying about who was going to point it out. During our gym session I decided to swap out my shoes with a friend's."

"You didn't," I said.

"You're right. I didn't," she replied.

"What?" I said, not understanding.

"I didn't swap them with my friend's. I ended up swapping them with another girl's shoes."

"No!"

"She was basically my class's resident bully. Here's the thing, she saw me wearing her shoes just as we left gym class."

"And?"

"She called me out in front of the class, made me give her shoes back. The she threw mine in the toilet."

My mouth dropped wide open. Toilet-shoes sounded like the worst possible thing.

"Didn't your teacher do anything?" I asked.

"I never told," she said. "I'm not a snitch. So, I had to fish them out and put up with being called all sorts of toilet related names for the rest of the week."

I bit my lip and sort of chuckled.

"You can laugh," she said. "I don't mind."

My eyes were watering and I shook my head.

"I'm not laughing. Promise."

Then I heard footsteps behind me.

I looked over my shoulder, and what I saw was a surprise I could never have predicted.

"Maiara, look," I said.

One marched down the aisle towards the small stage at the front. He wasn't remarkable, but the person following him had grabbed our complete attention.

Seeing a new person, when you're one of the last people left alive in the entire Galaxy was a shock, like seeing a mirage.

The girl, who looked to be a few years older than me, had curly copper-flecked dark hair and dark skin. Her eyes sparkled gold. And she wore an outfit that matched One's.

She moved with an easy grace, less stiff and robotic than One, and smiled warmly at all of us as she passed.

Curious chatter was beginning to rise all over the auditorium.

"Who is she?" I asked.

"Another One?" Maiara suggested.

"You think so?"

"Who else could it be, out here in deep space?"

"She must have been stored on board," I whispered.

One raised his hand and we all went quiet.

"You have questions. Do not worry. We will provide you with answers."

The new girl stepped forward past One to put herself front and centre.

"You are all wondering about me, yes?" She said. "I am like One, an altered..." she paused on those last two words as if examining them for accuracy, and then continued, "...human, with much the same skill set as him. However, my mandate is to correct any drop in crew morale. My name is Two."

Maiara gave a little laugh. "Two? How original," she uttered.

I smiled.

"Why haven't we ever heard of you before?" Koyla shouted out.

Two turned to Koyla and smiled a warm smile before crossing the stage to get closer to him.

"It was hoped that I would never be needed," Two said. "Dr. Ghost selected each on the strength your character. He knew you would all be capable of surviving this journey, and that you would have the spirit and the will to unite and uplift the legacy of humanity. You are Arkonauts now and forever more.

"The bonds and friendships you have made prove that Dr. Ghost was right in choosing you. Yet, your minds are clouded with fears and anxieties. As this is a journey the likes of which no human has ever undertaken before, the toll on your minds must be great. I am here to help you in this journey."

I made a skeptical face at Maiara.

She shrugged. "She seems okay. But what can she do?"

I shrugged too.

"You are probably wondering how I can help you," Two said.

On cue, a pair of robots drove into the theatre and down the aisle. They unloaded several crates at the front of the stage.

Two ran her hands over the cases, as if they were her pride and joy, then carefully opened the first one.

I couldn't see what was inside from my angle.

Two reached in and brought out some kind of jacket. It had a zipper at the front, and a hood, quite a big one. It was mostly black, but a design decorated from the bottom right up to the right shoulder. It was a line of white that ended in an image of the Ark, like the vessel was taking off. All across the material were little white dots that looked like stars. And the stars seemed to dim and sparkle.

"This is NanoWear," Two said.

Whispers began all around the auditorium.

"NanoWear is clothing inhabited by a single nanite, living among the strands of material. This nanite resident has a variety of effects."

"Perhaps one of the Arkonauts could come up to the front and demonstrate?" One proposed.

Two and One whispered something to each other.

Then Two replaced the original jacket with another from the crate.

"You will know which NanoWear is yours because each bears a flag on the left sleeve," Two said. "This one belongs to—"

Two rotated the jacket to proudly show a white flag with a red cross on it.

"Callum. From England," she declared.

Maiara exhaled in relief.

I hadn't noticed, but she had been squeezing my hand.

I stood up and walked toward the stage. I heard mumbled words float around me, including one dripping utterance of "Teacher's Pet." It reminded me of the worst days at school, when the bullies would pick me out of the crowd.

Anger surged within me. I wanted to call out whoever said it out, to make an example of them and their cruelty. But I didn't. I was too shocked.

This sort of thing didn't used to happen on the Ark. We had all become friends here. At least I thought we had.

One and Two smiled warmly at me as I got on the stage and took the jacket.

"Why me?" I whispered.

"Because everyone trusts you," One said.

I put the jacket on, but it was a little big. Maybe they expected me to grow into it. The hood had a lining of fur.

"Now Callum will demonstrate the NanoWear features," Two said. "The nanites inside each strand will tailor the jacket to your size. Callum, please press the button on the left sleeve next to the silhouette of a jacket."

There were four buttons on the sleeve. I found the right button and pressed it.

Immediately, the jacket formed to my body. It was now the most comfortable top I had.

"Whoa," I said. "It's like a second skin."

"You can also change the colour," Two said.

I found another button on the sleeve, this one beside a colour wheel. I held the button. The jacket lit up red, then phased to orange, then phased to yellow, and on through the spectrum. When it reached a dark green I let go of the button and the jacket stayed that colour.

"Hmm," I said making a satisfied sound.

"Next, the button with the flashlight symbol activates a light on the end of the sleeve," Two explained.

When I pressed that button, all the stars strewn across the jacket moved to the cuff of the left sleeve. Densely arranged, the stars formed a beam of light.

I looked down at the cuff and was momentarily blinded. It was so bright.

Everyone in the theatre laughed.

"Lastly, you can contact anyone on the ship with communications button. Hold it down, speak the name of the Arkonaut you wish to speak with, and then let it go. Disconnect by pressing the button again."

I pressed the button and said, "Maiara."

Maiara, and the other Arkonauts started to laugh.

"I'm not wearing mine yet, Callum," Maiara called out.

"Just testing," I said.

"Now, you may each come receive your own jackets when I call your names," Two said.

I sat down.

After my demonstration everyone was keen to get up front for their own jackets. And soon the theatre was abuzz with Arkonauts calling each other through their sleeves.

Once Maiara obtained hers, she came and sat next to me. She turned her jacket bright red, and put her hood up. Then she snuggled up beside me.

"This is really nice," she said. "But you'll have to change your colour. Green doesn't match my red."

"Why can't you change yours?" I asked.

She raised an eyebrow at me.

"Yeah. Okay," I said.

Once everyone had their NanoWear, Two spoke up again. "I am glad you all seem happy with these. This is the first of many things I will introduce to keep this crew together.

"Additionally, I am aware that there have been some disagreements of late. If any of you wish to share, please come to me to talk. I am always available.

"I will be hosting an event later this evening. Once you have finished your shift, feel free to join me in the cafeteria if you are interested."

Two and One then smiled and exited the theatre.

"Do you think those too are, like, *together*?" Maiara asked.

"Maybe we should go to this event tonight and see how they are?" I said.

"Yeah," Maiara agreed. "I like her. Especially if she give gifts like this."

15
THE EVENT

I had arranged to meet Maiara at the cafeteria and when I walked through the door she was sitting with Sanna and Gerlinde. They were watching Two inspect the contents of some boxes.

I walked over, waved hello, and then kissed Maiara in greeting.

"Look at you two! Flaunting your relationship," Sanna said.

I turned bright red.

The girls chuckled.

"So... What's Two up to?" I asked sitting on the table next to the girls.

"She won't tell us," Gerlinde said.

Two opened another box and peered inside. She smiled. Then she looked at us.

"I will tell you in a minute when more people are here," she said, grabbing another box to inspect.

One entered the cafeteria next, wheeling a sack barrow loaded with more boxes. He unloaded these next to the others.

"Thank you, One. Could I have another lot?" Two said.

Other Arkonauts filed into the room. Apart from those who were pulling work shifts, it seemed like the whole crew was here.

Two surveyed the group and smiled again, no doubt pleased that so many had accepted her invitation.

"Hello everyone," she said, removing a small cylinder with a red cap—a spray paint can—from one of the boxes before her. Two shook the can, and it clanked as the bearing inside bounced around, mixing the paint.

"I do not know about you, but I do not believe we have put our marks on this ship yet," she began. "While there are some rooms that have been decorated to feel like home, you did not build them. They are not quite your own..."

I nodded as she spoke. She was right. We hadn't changed or added anything to the ship.

"I think it would be good if we all grabbed some paint and started adding our own touches to the Ark," Two continued. "When we land on a new planet, the human race is going to grow again. After we have built new homes and new towns or cities, this ship will become a museum piece. Today is our chance to leave something that future generations will look to for generations to come."

Sanna raised her hand, "But I can't paint."

Her admission helped others admit the same problem. There were murmurs throughout the cafeteria.

Two pulled a syringe from her jacket and held it high.

"This nanite injection contains the memories of a world-class graffiti artist and a graphic designer. With it you can create whatever you want."

"What are we allowed to paint?" Gerlinde asked.

"Anything you want," Two answered. "We have lots of paint, so you can do more, or add on, or paint over something in the future. And I think the best place to start is here in this cafeteria."

Two walked to a blank section of wall between the doors leading back out into the corridor. She proceeded to bash out, with incredible speed, precision and skill, a black and white image of the Ark. She set the diamond-shaped ship amid a white glow and a backdrop of stars.

The cafeteria erupted in excited, impressed chatter.

Two then signed the picture, with the number two set in a circle, and stepped back to admire her work.

"A good start, I think," she said. "In the future, tours will come through this place, and my art will be here front and centre. What will they see of yours?"

That last question sure sounded like a challenge to me.

A rush of Arkonauts clamoured to get their injection and their spray cans.

"Now just a moment," Two bellowed. "This is not free."

There were grunts of confusion. I grunted, confused, too.

"You will have to give me something in exchange."

"Like what?" Koyla asked.

"The flags patches from your new NanoWear jackets." she replied. "They are attached by Velcro. Remove yours and trade it for the injection and paints."

I saw other kids shrugging and ripping at their patches.

I looked down at my left arm, at the St. George cross. It was the flag that had flown at every sports game I had ever attended. It was a rallying symbol for my country. It even told a story of a knight slaying a dragon. I knew that I would never forget the flag, but I knew Two was asking for it for a reason.

I don't know why it was such a difficult decision. The flag of England didn't used to matter that much to me.

Finally, I pulled the patch off the sleeve, savouring the crunchy ripping of the Velcro. I looked at the patch one more time. It's just cloth and dye. It's not like handing it over to Two means giving up my country and culture. Right?

Other kids were thinking about it too, even as Two formed us into lines.

Maiara and I were halfway down the line. She also held her flag patch out in front of her.

"Why are these so difficult to give away?" I asked.

She didn't look up at me, her eyes studied the stars and stripes. "People back home made such a fuss about this. I keep thinking that if I give it away millions of people will be angry with me."

"Yeah. I know what you mean. But England's gone. So is the U.S., and everywhere else for that matter."

"Do you think that's why she's doing this? To test us? To make us forget about the places we used to be from?" Maiara said.

"What other reason could there be?" I said.

We shuffled forward slowly. Other Arkonauts seemed to be labouring over the decision too.

Finally it was my turn. I looked down at the flag, then up at Two.

She was smiling at me as if she knew what I was going to do.

I wanted to give it away because I really wanted to paint. I didn't really care for the flag patch. It wasn't the object that mattered, though, just what it represented. If the flag came to be more important than what it stood for, then what it stood for was lost. England was gone. As the last Englishman, maybe I should be the one to give it up.

I gave the patch to Two.

She nodded and quickly gave me the injection, before letting me choose paints.

After I made my selection, she gave me something else: a new patch for the empty spot on my sleeve.

The patch had my name stencilled on it, with a symbol of the Ark as a backdrop.

"There, Callum. That's who you are," she said.

Maiara gave up her flag next, and when she came over to me, she let out a heavy exhale.

"That was tough," she said. "But when you think about it, the American flag never stayed the same, there were always more states and more stars to be added. Maybe it's up to me, or up to all of us, to make a new one."

"I think you're right," I said.

Arkonauts had already claimed their spaces on the walls. There was going to be a giant mural from the cafeteria bleeding into all the adjoining corridors.

Maiara and I walked a long way to find blank space.

"What are you going to paint?" she asked.

"I don't know. A flag?" I said.

She laughed.

"Something for people to see in the future," Maiara mused.

I thought about the voyage so far. About Mum, Dad, and Jack. About traveling through space-time...

Then it came to me.

I started spraying. I was thrilled at my ability to draw and wield the cans with the skill of a Banksy Junior. The picture was in my head and it sprang to life in front of me. It was clearer and more precise than any art I had made before. When I was finished, I stepped back to take it in.

"I like it," Maiara said.

It was a corridor. Like any of the hundreds on the Ark. In the middle a vortex swirled, and within it was a faint silhouette of a person reaching through, holding a piece of cloth marked in red with Chinese symbols.

"Why did you paint that?" Two asked, over our shoulders.

"Because it still freaks me out," I said. "Someone, somewhere in all of creation, threw a piece of cloth with my blood on it and it saved our lives. It makes my head hurt just thinking about it. Like, who was on the other side, and why did they do that? You said other people in the future will see this. Well, I want to them to ask the same question themselves, and maybe find an answer for me one day."

"It bothers you that this knowledge is out there that you don't know," Two said.

"I guess," I said. "I try not to think about it."

"Maybe this painting can help exorcise it, by giving it form," Two said.

She then walked off, inspecting what the other kids had made.

"What can I do to match that?" Maiara said, taking up her spray cans.

As hers developed, I saw that it expressed how Maiara felt about her place on the Ark.

On the left were a group of people. It looked like it could be her family. They were surrounded by skylines and landscapes that looked like the U.S. There was even a tiny flag. She finished the left side with an image of an elderly Native American woman.

"My grandmother," she said.

In the middle, was a self-portrait, with her arms outstretched. At her feet there was a potted plant. Then she completed the right side. She added lots of faces and images from the Ark. She was reaching out to her past and to her future, but the portrait faced to the right. Toward the Arkonauts, and into what was to come.

"I think I get it," I said.

"Shh," she said. "Keep it to yourself! I want everyone to interpret how they wish."

"I do have a question, then," I said.

"What's that?" Maiara replied.

"Where am I?" I asked. "None of the faces look like me."

She smiled.

"Don't worry. Write your name down there."

She pointed to where our two murals met.

I wrote my name where she'd pointed.

She wrote hers beside mine. Then she drew a heart in red encircling our names.

"Not very open to interpretation," I said.

"It doesn't need to be," she quipped.

"But... what if we... break up?" I asked.

"Then one of us will angrily cover it up," she said.

I laughed.

Maiara leaned in and gave me a kiss.

We admired our work for a moment, eventually holding hands. Without saying a word we both drifted back toward the cafeteria, looking at what the other Arkonauts had painted.

I wondered what people would think of our murals.

And I hoped that the heart stayed around the names forever.

16

THE SECOND LEAK

Two was a welcome presence on the Ark. Unlike One, she was more geared to making our downtime more fun and inclusive.

Over the next month, Two initiated several events and clubs. She ran regular film nights and they always drew a crowd. She started a book club, too, and then a games night twice a week.

She seemed to be everywhere. Like One, perhaps she never slept. And everything she did kept us talking and interacting.

Maiara told me that Two must be here to compensate for the removal of the eighteenth memory. And maybe Dr. Ghost knew a ship full of kids from different backgrounds might not be able to stay together under the stress. Two definitely seemed like a backup plan to keep us together.

Two's origin and purpose were the talk of the Ark. Sometimes we even discussed what would have happened to her if we never needed her at all.

Either way, she was great at her job. She had the air of an outsider, a new face, but we could talk to Two more easily than One, or even each other. She was an impartial observer, and Arkonauts were going to her for advice on relationships, growing up, and more.

And she had found one sure-fire way for every Arkonaut to connect: food.

Each week we took turns cooking, a communal method of making our own meals. One day it was pizza, and everyone liked pizza.

Another we made roasts. Yet another was an ice cream party. Everyone loved food. It was our single universal passion. Two made it a way for everyone to work on a shared project.

She sometimes randomly appeared and started a conversation with us. She always seemed to know how to talk with everyone. Dr. Ghost probably gave her loads of information about each of us, so she knew what to say to bring us together.

Then one day Two's skills at uniting us were tested. I left the cafeteria through the exit where Maiara and I painted our murals, and that's when I saw that ours had been defaced. Someone had drawn a red X through each one.

I barely moved. My one addition to this ship had been ruined. The heart was a mess.

My blood boiled at the random act of vandalism.

Other murals had been defaced, too. I complained to One, and found Maiara, Illarion, Sanna, Julianna, Jacob and Koyla all had as well.

"There is nothing that we can do," One told us. "I am very sorry, and I will investigate this further, but the incident appears at this time to be isolated."

Even so, accusations flew amongst the Arkonauts.

In response, Two ran more and more events that forced us to cooperate and work together, culminating in an Anti-Gravity Olympics that divided us by the season in which we were born so we'd have to unite under a common banner.

For all Two did, she couldn't make our work shifts any more fun.

I was working in the engine room. And it's really just loads of system checks and cleaning. Even with our science and engineering nanite injections instructing us, we didn't know for sure how the Ark's older alien technology worked. That made the job tedious because of all the diagnostics and checks, but it also made it dangerous.

When something went wrong we didn't always know how to fix it. Unlike the other systems—water, recycling, control—the engine's inner workings were mysterious. So, we would all spend every day hoping nothing would happen. We'd check the temperature and particle build-up—one we never really understood—three times during each shift. Every day we'd breathe sighs of relief when everything tested within tolerance.

Otherwise there are these machines that function like vacuums that we use to remove dust and other debris from the engine hull. Keeping it clean was essential, as One had told us, because if we didn't the engine would be less efficient or break down, leaving us drifting in space, unable to make necessary course corrections. So, we'd all be vacuuming, all along the walkways surrounding the skyscraper-like engine, keeping the ship going.

After a few hours of cleaning my section, I returned to the top of the engine to turn in my vacuum and log my work.

Dehqan was there, working at the control station.

I thought back to the last time we talked, and the argument we had had. We hadn't really talked since then. I had caught glimpses of him day to day, and had been avoiding him. I don't know why, but I felt it was my fault that we had ended our previous conversation on a sour note. But avoiding him made me feel trapped, and like I couldn't enjoy myself when we were in the same room.

In retrospect, he had been right about the rich nations hoarding what they could, while other poorer nations starved. But I still didn't know how to tell him that I understood.

When Dr. Ghost had the world's leaders under his thumb with his own modified nanites, he could have made the richer nations share what they had. But he just maintained the system to be as unfair as it had been. Maybe he was unable to rework it, or maybe he realised there was no point if everyone was going to die. And with the world ending, the doctor probably didn't see the point in changing things temporarily.

Was I beginning to think like Dr. Ghost? Becoming a crass and calculating person? I tried to quickly put it out of my mind.

I approached Dehqan, intent on mending fences. Also, he was responsible for logging our work today.

"Hello, Dehqan," I said cheerfully.

"Done already, Callum?" he snapped. "I can't imagine you did a thorough job."

I didn't know what to say, so I just passed the vacuum over to its charging station quietly. A group of other Arkonauts on the cleaning shift arrived to turn their vacuums in too. I waited for Dehqan to pounce on them too, but he didn't.

I waited until the other kids left, and then leaned on the console.

"I need to apologise," I said.

"For?" Dehqan said.

"Our conversation in the cafeteria."

Dehqan sighed loudly.

I could sense hostility in him and I didn't like it, but I bit my tongue.

"You were right before, and I was wrong to argue. Places like the U.K. didn't do anything for other nations at the end. And they didn't because they were selfish."

Dehqan looked at me. His features softened.

"Thanks," he said.

"That's the way things were. And they shouldn't have been that way," I said.

"Yeah," he uttered.

"I wish things could have been different. Every rich country should have been different."

"Yes. Especially yours," he said.

"Ye—"

I didn't like that. Why was he singling out the U.K? The U.S. was even richer. So was China!

"What would you have done differently?" he asked.

I paused to collect myself and sort out the best response.

"I would have pulled every single Arkonaut into one nation with their families," I said. "That would have solved everything because everyone would have shared the same experience at the end."

Dehqan was sceptical.

"But don't you think those from the wealthiest nations would have had the best stuff?" he asked.

"Probably, but you know they would be bringing it with them. It can't be wrong. They would have earned it. Plus, they'd have contributed more to everyone's protection."

"You can't let it go," he said dismissively.

"Let go of what?" I asked.

"That your nation deserved better than mine," he said.

"I wasn't old enough to do anything about that. I was still playing computer games when the U.K. closed its borders. You think I had the ear of the Prime Minister?"

"Playing video games?" he said, "I was helping my family and my neighbours find drinkable water."

"And if you had been me, you'd have played video games too. We're all human. Since we've been up here I've worked as hard as you have."

"Never mind," he said.

He pushed me away from the console and began running another diagnostic.

So, I pushed him back.

"If you want me to get out of the way just tell me. I said I was sorry. What else can I do about it now?"

Dehqan grabbed me by my shoulder and tried to pull me away from the console.

Then I shoved him.

Some Arkonauts gathered around us. Evan, who was working at another engine console started toward us and then stopped as Dehqan waved him away.

Then Dehqan charged at me.

My military nanite memory kicked in. I raised a foot and kicked Dehqan in the stomach.

He flew backwards, struck the console behind him, and fell down, activating all sorts of buttons on the way.

I grabbed him by his jacket and pinned him against the console, activating more controls.

"I'm sorry alright," I said. "I'm sorry about what I said, but you need to understand that none of the things that happened to your country were my fault. It's not my fault."

The engine roared and there was sound like rushing wind beneath us.

Dehqan wrenched my hands free of his jacket and examined the console.

"What did you do?" Evan asked.

"Me?" I said.

"Come on, Callum," Evan said. "We all saw. You pushed Dehqan against the console and broke something."

Evan pushed me away from the console, putting himself between me and Dehqan.

"He's activated a particle dump. We're not supposed to do that," Dehqan said. "It can be done within a planet's atmosphere, but not out in space," he said.

"Can you stop it?" Evan asked.

"The engine's not responding," Dehqan said as he pressed controls.

"I can—" I said, reaching for the controls.

"You've done enough," Dehqan snapped.

Before I could protest Evan interrupted. "The engine's particle network isn't reversing. I think it's jammed open.

Alarms blared all around the engine room.

We also heard a churning sound coming from the base of the engine. We ran to the edge of the gangway and peered down at the base of the engine room.

Some kind of steam billowed from the engine.

Suddenly my science and engineering nanites kicked in.

"We... put too much pressure on the plasma conduits," I explained, words that were not my own spilling from my mouth.

"We?" Dehqan said.

"Me. Okay? We don't have time for that right now," I said.

"If the plasma conduits are broken we have a real problem," Evan added.

The other Arkonauts nodded. They all had the same information in their heads, but no one leapt forward to lead.

"We need to shut them off, and repair the damage," I said.

Then we heard voices, from down below, screaming for help.

Dion from Greece, and Carlton from Scotland, were on the lower walkway. Carlton was limping, and Dion was helping him along.

"Carlton can't walk," Dion yelled.

I froze for a moment. This was my fault. I shouldn't have started things up with Dehqan. I had to do something to make it right.

I rushed to the nearest of four stairways leading down to the engine's base, and darted down to help. When I reached them, the Greek girl and Scottish boy were ascending the stairs.

Carlton's lower leg had been burnt badly. His trousers were ripped and the skin beneath was very red and blistered.

"The venting plasma conduits burned him," Dion explained.

I ducked under Carlton's other arm and we helped him up the stairs, as he winced in pain.

"We've got you, Carlton," I said.

"I would have been fine myself, but I'll take the help," he said.

"Hurry up," Dion said. "That gas is rising, and it'll do to us what it did to your leg."

Below, the white cloud seemed to chase us, seeping through the holes in the walkways, ceaselessly pluming upward.

"We've vented the plasma conduits before," I said. "I don't understand why it's so bad this time."

"We've never let this much plasma out," Dion replied. "The venting pipe is damaged now, and if we don't fix it this cloud is going to fill the rest of the ship."

We hauled Carlton up another flight of steps. My leg muscles were burning.

The plasma cloud kept following.

"How do we fix the pipe if it's beneath us in that cloud?" I asked.

"I don't know," Dion replied. "Maybe One and Two can help."

At the top of the engine room, the others helped with Carlton and rushed him out to the medical bay.

"Everybody else out," I said, panting.

The cloud continued to rise.

"Don't forget to set the engine to low power," Koyla said. "If you don't there won't be time for One or Two to help."

"I will. Now, get going!"

The other Arkonauts ran out of the engine room.

The cloud was only a few metres below me.

My nanites told me what to do next. I activated the controls that lowered the amount of power the ship drew from the engines. In response the engine powered down slightly, not needing to generate it's normal levels of energy. I reset as many of the safety systems as I could to prevent further catastrophe.

Wisps of plasma lapped at my heels.

I looked all over the console for a way to cancel the plasma dump, or a way to vent the engine room, but the cloud was rising around the panel and it was harder and harder to see. My skin itched. The cloud had cooled as it rose, but the chemicals in the air were still irritating.

Dion suddenly came running. She had her t-shirt clamped over her nose and mouth.

"Let's go!"

My throat started to burn. My legs started to tingle like thousands of bugs were biting at once.

The cloud had covered my feet and ankles I couldn't see them any more. It was nearing my knees.

I pulled my shirt up over my mouth and nose.

My eyes started to water.

Through tears, I saw readout display LOW OUTPUT. The engine was no longer a direct danger to the ship.

Dion and I ran for the exit. We ran until we reached the residence level.

The plasma vapour was right behind us. It wouldn't be long before it spilled onto each floor, enveloping the entire upper section of the Ark.

This was a real problem.

And it was my fault.

I wondered if the tears in my eyes were from the plasma cloud, or because I had doomed the entire crew.

17
OUTSIDE

I joined at the back of the group as we climbed to the residence level.

One's voice came over the intercom.

"Arkonauts, lock down your respective areas, then follow the purple lights to an airlock."

The purple light appeared above us and my group followed it. The word *airlock* was passed back and forth throughout the group. We all wondered what it would mean.

The airlocks could be accessed via long tunnels that opened out into a wider area. The tunnels ran through the hull of the ship, making us like rodents in the walls.

I had once helped chuck a nuclear bomb out of the Ark at another airlock when the colonel and minster had invaded the station. But this one was new. The area around the airlock was much larger.

We Arkonauts filled the airlock corridor quickly. And soon everyone knew what had happened in the engine room. Other kids were starting to panic, and glare at me for causing the incident. Though some of them seemed certain that One would save us.

Mostly, though, Arkonauts were banding together.

"Callum," Maiara called to me over the crowd.

Her group was the last to reach the airlock, led by One from the control centre. Two was there, too, inspecting a tablet.

Maiara hugged me, and then took my hand, "What's going on? Someone said that there had been a fight or accident in the engine room!"

She paused when she saw my face, "What did you do?"

"I messed up..." I began.

"Everyone," One said. "There has been a breach in the engine room. Superheated plasma is venting from the lower part of the engine. The gas is cooling before it reaches the upper levels so that is not a problem. In ten minutes it will start to fill this level. The gas is bio-corrosive, so we have to get you all into space suits."

"Space suits?" Koyla asked.

"Yes, they will protect you while Two and I fix the problem."

"Don't you need space suits too?" I asked.

"No. The plasma will not affect us as badly."

One tapped at a key panel on the nearby wall, which opened several hidden wall lockers full of row after row of spacesuits.

"I apologise but they won't be perfect fits," Two said. "You will notice some come fitted with jetpack capabilities. Do not touch the controls on them."

Everyone surged forward to grab a suit. They were clearly made for adults, but some of them fit okay. Many of us looked silly, with arms and legs too long, floppy, and bunching.

I grabbed a blue suit emblazoned with a Chinese logo. It had a jetpack icon on the sleeve, too, and even though the jets were hidden in the back of the suit, it was pretty heavy.

Maiara got an orange suit that was too long in the legs.

"Put on your helmets. I am going to come round and secure them," One ordered.

I helped Maiara with her helmet, and she with mine.

One and Two then went around and double-checked our suits.

One reached me. As he checked the helmet he was not gentle. He gave me a long, hard stare, and then moved on to the next person without a word.

After they finished securing our suits, One and Two made way for the door.

"Just stay here, and do not worry about a thing," Two said. "Do not forget we are all in this together. Please do not leave this area until we have given word."

With One and Two gone, I felt the leering eyes of the other Arkonauts in full force. We may all be in this together, but it was all my fault.

We waited. The other kids talked amongst themselves.

I kept hearing my name.

Maiara and I talked about various things until she remembered our game, and asked me about a time when I was ten years old.

I told her a story of when I was with my family on holiday in York. We could see a field of cows outside our rental house window. My cousin had asked me where all the cows lived, and I said, "in burrows." I really thought they went underground every evening. And no one in the family had let me forget it.

Maiara laughed and slapped me on the back at my story.

Then we heard screams from the other side of the room.

Arkonauts scrambled back toward us. The leaking plasma was washing over the airlock floor. As they all bunched up against us, it dawned on me that we could end up crushing ourselves, so I stood up and pushed through the crowd.

It was all my fault after all. I would wade into the smoke, and show everyone it was fine.

I stood in the billowing gases for a moment, which lapped at my feet, as the other Arkonauts continued to step away.

"Don't worry everyone," I said. "The smoke can't get us in these suits."

The others seemed to relax, as the cloud moved to fill the space. They stood still, letting it wrap around their feet.

After a few moments, the gas cloud was creeping to our knees.

"I hope this gas isn't destroying our possessions," Illarion said.

"By now it's filtering into the rooms. I guess we'll have to wait and see," Gerlinde said

"At least the cargo bay is sealed off, right?" Sanna asked.

Maiara nodded. "It should be fine."

"All our stuff is going to stink," Koyla muttered.

I felt more cold stares again.

"How can this get any worse?" Moana asked.

A crackle from the intercom.

"Arkonauts," One said over the internal system. "We have made effective repairs, however the gas venting will continue for some time, filling all upper levels."

"We have also analysed the gas and discovered that it will corrode some of the seals on your suits. You will be exposed to the gas and prolonged exposure is hazardous to your health," Two said. "As such we are going to direct you to a new safe location outside the Ark."

"Outside?" I said.

I wasn't the only Arkonaut confused by One and Two's plan.

We looked at the airlock door, beyond which lay the cold vacuum of space.

18

SPACEWALK

"The gas will eat through the seals around the oxygen pipes in your suits in the next ten minutes," Two said. "Please proceed through the airlock. And do not worry. You will all be completely safe."

"We'll be outside," I said.

"I know. You need to do this or the gas will infiltrate your suits. The airlock is small, so you'll have to go outside ten at a time. All the suits have magnetic soles so you'll stay attached to the hull."

"Please start moving now."

Evan was nearest the airlock and everyone looked at him to open it. He huffed, and then activated the control panel for the airlock. The screen read: Pressurising. Then with a hiss and an alarm, the hatch opened. It was about the size of small cargo container.

Evan looked back at all of us and then stepped through the open airlock. Nine others followed until the airlock was full of Arkonauts. Illarion was last, and closed the door behind the group.

On the control panel we watched all ten Arkonauts, in ill-fitting suits, step out of the airlock and onto the outer hull of the Ark. Illarion sealed the door again, and the next group repeated the process.

Ten at a time, the entire crew exited the interior of the ship.

I squeezed Maiara's hand when our turn came up.

She smirked at me, sensing my fear through my grip.

We entered the airlock.

Ogwambi closed the door behind us, then Dehqan opened it at the other end, and suddenly we were outside.

In space.

It was amazing, standing in an expanse of stars and infinite darkness, but I knew that the vacuum surrounding us would kill us if our suits failed.

And I was terrified.

Space was vast and deadly and alien. It had never been something I wanted to experience. I took a deep breath, but my lungs were trembling. Everything was.

Maiara practically dragged me out of the airlock.

Once outside, we used our magnetic boots to climb out on the surface of the Ark.

For a moment, I lost myself in the pure vision of the Milky Way in all its glory, glowing against the glass of my helmet.

"Can you believe we're doing this?" Maiara said, staring into the darkness.

The Ark was massive on the inside, and even more so on the outside. What was really strange was that it was flat and virtually featureless. Just a huge smooth diamond of metal, gliding through deep space.

Other Arkonauts were appreciating the view.

Ogwambi and Moana approached me and Maiara. They were bolder than the others, who were huddling near the airlock door.

"What happened in the engine room?" Ogwambi asked.

I shrugged.

"I got into a shoving match with Dehqan," I said. "And I accidentally pushed him onto the control panel."

"That's really stupid, Callum. Why were you fighting?" Ogwambi asked.

"We weren't fi—" I started. "Do you remember that conversation he and I had in the cafeteria? Well, I tried to apologise and he just went on and on about it."

"Are you sure that you didn't say anything to make it worse?" Maiara asked.

"Are you taking his side?" I asked her.

"Kind of. Yes," she said.

I sneered and crossed my arms.

"What? Just because we're boyfriend and girlfriend, I'm supposed to go against what I think is right?" she said. "Everyone else says you shoved him first. You need to own up to this."

"I am owning up to it. You weren't in the engine room. I was trying to apologise to *him*," I pointed at Dehqan. "And we... just started pushing each other. This wasn't my fault, and if you think I meant this to happen then you're all idiots."

"No one thinks you mean this to happen, but I'm not going to be called an idiot," Maiara said.

She stepped away from me and glared.

"It doesn't matter what you mean, Callum. You couldn't just accept that Dehqan feels the way he feels, and because you couldn't, we're all out here."

I fumed.

"Don't look at me like that. You know I'm right," she continued. "I'm not dating you because I worship you. I'm dating you because I think you're the kind of guy who can own his mistakes and learn from them. Isn't that why you got us to get rid of the eighteenth memory? If you're not going to learn from this, then you're not who I thought you were."

I sputtered. She was right and I felt like a fool. But I wanted to fight back.

Then Dehqan walked over, his magnetic boots clanking along the way.

"Why did you just point at me? Are you trying to blame me for this?" he said.

"No. No... I'm not," I said.

"Everyone knows this is your fault, Callum," he said.

My blood boiled.

"Did I stutter?" I said. "I'm not blaming you. I don't blame other people for all my problems."

Maiara scoffed. "It's not like you're owning up."

I looked around exasperated.

Other Arkonauts were looking at me. I was in the depth of space, and was somehow the focus of everyone's attention.

"Fine. I can own up to it," I said looking right at Maiara. "This is my fault. I should never have shoved Dehqan into the panel where he hit the button to vent the plasma."

No one seemed happy with my apology. Instead, there was chatter. Dehqan peered at me. Maiara shook her head.

"What? I said I was sorry," I shouted desperately. "You think I wanted this to happen?"

Maiara jabbed me in the ribs. "You still blamed Dehqan."

I sighed and looked at her.

"I should never have shoved you, Dehqan. I'm sorry for putting us all in this mess."

Dehqan looked around at the Arkonauts. "Fine, you've apologised," he said. "I hope we can all put this behind us."

"Aren't *you* going to apologise?" I asked.

"For what?" Dehqan said.

Even though I knew better. Even though I tried to think of what One or Two would do in this situation, I didn't care. I couldn't believe that Dehqan didn't see that he had started all of this. He was the one who blamed me for something I had no part of. He was the one who wouldn't try to understand me. He was the one blaming a fifteen year old for every bad thing that happened on Earth. It was him who couldn't let it go.

I shook my head and turned my back on Dehqan. And on the others.

Dehqan stomped up behind me.

I waited for him to say something. To apologise.

Instead, he grabbed my shoulder and pulled.

"Turn around and face me, Callum," he said.

I turned.

And I shoved him as hard as I could.

Dehqan's boots came free of the hull and he started floating away from the ship into the cold, emptiness of space.

19

FLOATING AWAY

I saw Dehqan float away, his arms flailing around.

I sniggered for a moment, the absurdity of it mixed with my anger. Then it hit me. He was drifting out into space.

I shouted, and then ran after him, stretching to reach for his flailing limbs. But he was too far away.

"Illarion! Can you grab him?" I called to the tallest Arkonaut.

Illarion reached out, too, but Dehqan was just out of reach.

I stepped back a few paces, giving myself some runway.

"Watch out, everyone," I said. "I'm going to leap for him."

Maiara grabbed me as I started my sprint.

"You can't jump, Callum. You'll float off too. He's not a balloon caught in the wind. He's not going to come down and neither are you."

Dehqan screamed for help. His voice cried in our headsets.

The utter terror he was experiencing made me sick to my stomach. Guilt welled up in me. He had no way back down to the ship. All his momentum was taking him slowly upwards. This was all my fault. Dehqan, the last person from Afghanistan, would die a slow, cold, lonely, cruel death because of me.

"What do we do!?" Koyla exclaimed.

Dehqan kept screaming.

"Help me," he cried out.

"Does anyone have rope or a cable?" Gerlinde interjected.

As we looked for anything on the surface of the Ark that might help, I had a realization. I was wearing a jetpack suit.

I found a pair of buttons on my space suit's right sleeve. The words USE EXTREME CAUTION were printed above them. I pushed both buttons at once, a door opened on the back of the suit, and two flat pieces of metal folded out and then furled into rocket cones. Then two mechanical arms popped out of the sides of the jetpack and extended at my sides. At the end of each was a joystick that I grasped in my hands.

"Callum, what are you doing? You're not supposed to use that!" Maiara said.

"I have to," I said. "This is my fault."

I clicked the thruster buttons on each joystick, and as I did, the jetpack kicked on. My back and legs felt very warm as the engine roared, and I felt the magnets on the soles of my boots release as I jolted upward.

Then Maiara grabbed my foot.

"Are you sure about this? I don't want you to float out into space."

"I have to fix this," I said. "I owe Dehqan. I've been a fool."

She nodded and let me go.

I hit the thrusters again, holding them longer, getting a bigger burst of energy.

Suddenly I was spinning like a top and getting very dizzy. I could see Dehqan, but only in brief pictures as I twirled. I fumbled with the arms and the joysticks, centring my hands to straighten myself out, and then carefully applied the scantest amount of direction and boost. In a moment I had steadied myself. Then I pointed myself at Dehqan and hit the thrusters again.

Dehqan saw me coming, and started waggling whichever arm or leg happened to be close to me, trying to give me something to grab.

"Come on, Callum," he pleaded. "Please help me."

I nodded inside my space suit, too deep in concentration to even reply.

A red warning light flashed and a shrill beeping echoed inside the helmet of my suit. A tiny fuel gauge popped up on the helmet glass. The jetpack was running low. Just my luck to get the jetpack space suit that was almost out of gas.

Physics was on my side though. Newton's first law, which I remembered from school, said that an object in motion stays in motion in a vacuum. That's just what space was. I was moving toward Dehqan now, and that meant I could save the last fuel to get us back to the Ark's surface.

Just a few more inches.

I was right there. The left shoulder of my suit came close enough to Dehqan's hand that he got a handful of the material. Grabbing me like a kitten by the scruff. He pulled me in until he could get his hands on my arm.

He let out a massive sigh, and now I could hear that he was on the verge of crying.

"Thank you, Callum," he said. "Thank you. I—"

"No. I'm sorry. This was my fault. I should never have pushed you and I should never have started arguing with you in the first place," I said.

"Just get us back to the Ark," he said. "We can make friends later."

I nodded. I had nearly killed one of my fellow crewmembers. Even now, at Dehqan's order, I felt compelled to argue with him, to tell him not to tell me what to do. Was there something wrong with me?

I gently moved the joysticks to turn us around and then engaged the thrusters one more time. We started back toward the Ark as the warning light flashed and the alarm blared. I gave it one last big burst and listened as the engine roared, grumbled, and then sputtered out. We were going the right direction at least, riding the last wave of energy it had in the tank.

When we touched down on the Ark's surface, the friendly feeling of magnetic boots gripping its metal surface reminded me to take a breath.

The other Arkonauts had followed us along the hull of the ship and encircled us when we landed we hit the hull of the giant ship. They grabbed us by our arms, making sure we didn't fly off again.

Dehqan locked his boots down, and nodded at me silently. He turned, breathing heavily, and then ran toward the larger group of Arkonauts still gathered by the airlock. A couple of the others embraced him.

Illarion, Gerlinde, Ogwambi and Maiara all stayed to help me up. They were chattering about the jetpack flight, and how close we had come to disappearing into the deep night of space.

"I'm just glad it wor—" I began.

Then the jetpack blew up.

20
FLOATING AWAY AGAIN

Inside my helmet was a combination of blinding lights and deafening sounds. Something about overheating or a leak. I couldn't understand it in the moment.

The jetpack didn't blow up like a grenade or anything, but one of the tanks must have ruptured, with just enough fumes still remaining, and the canister burst. Unfortunately, the blast radiated downwards, which was more than enough to blast me back out into space like a rocket.

Illarion, Gerlinde, Ogwambi and Maiara, still holding onto me, flew up and away from the Ark with me.

We all screamed.

But Gerlinde screamed loudest. She had lost her grip, and started to drift away from us. We all tried to reach for her, but we couldn't without letting go of one another.

I started to panic when my nanite memories kicked it. My heart stopped racing almost immediately, and my mind cleared until there was only a single thought: *Call One.*

"One? One! Can you hear me?" I shouted over the comm-system.

"Yes, Callum?" One replied, in a tired, exasperated voice. "The plasma is nearly secured. What do you need?"

"Five of us lost our grip on the Ark we're tumbling off into space."

"How did that happen?" he asked, his voice now resonating with seriousness and a tinge of fear.

"My jetpack blew, and the blast sent us away from the Ark."

"Who else is with you?" he asked.

"Illarion, Ogwambi, Gerlinde and Maiara."

One was silent for a moment.

"Yes. Callum, Ogwambi should be wearing a suit with a jetpack as well."

"Ogwambi, you should have jetpack capabilities too," I said.

Ogwambi looked at the sleeves of his suit. All the writing on his was in Russian.

"Ilarion, what do these control say?" he asked the Russian.

"Er, er, those buttons there start up the jetpack," Illarion explained.

After tapping a couple of buttons, two engines grew from Ogwambi's suit as well, then two mechanical arms. They looked a little different from mine, but the technology seemed to be the same.

Ogwambi clutched the two joysticks, thumbs hovering over the buttons.

"Now what?" he asked.

"Angle the thrusters so you can get to Gerlinde," I said. "Then get down to the Ark before we're unable to return."

"Don't worry, Gerlinde," Ilarion said stretching out for her. "We'll get to you."

Ogwambi hit the thrusters.

He was surprisingly smart with the controls. We nimbly turned toward Gerlinde and a burst of the jets pushed us toward her. But now we were going away from the Ark.

Gerlinde was spinning, but she was almost in Ogwambi's reach.

I looked back at the surface of the ship. The small crowd of Arkonauts was shrinking away from us.

Ogwambi released another burst of the pack and Gerlinde's hand scraped the dome of Ogwambi's helmet.

She twisted and grabbed his mask with both hands. Her momentum then mixed into ours and we tilted in space, now floating in a new direction.

"Gerlinde, you have to move around to the front so I can use the thrusters," Ogwambi said.

Gerlinde climbed around.

We continued to drift away from the Ark.

I clung to Maiara, she clung to Illarion, and Gerlinde to all of us.

"Ogwambi," One crackled over the comm. "I am in the control centre and I can see you on the sensors. I need you to angle your thruster up and give them a good blast. Do not release them until I say so."

"I understand," he said.

"Good. Ready. Set. Fire," One ordered.

The blast jolted us all. Our momentum began to slow down. Ogwambi carefully adjusted the output so we wouldn't start spinning.

Then I saw a red light flash in Ogwambi's mask.

"Ogwambi—?" I began.

"Guys, I'm running low on fuel here," he said.

"Do not panic," One said. "Keep applying thrust."

Ogwambi looked around at us. There was fear in his eyes.

I think we all felt the same thing in that moment.

If our motion didn't stop and reverse our direction before the fuel ran out there was nothing to stop us from flying right past the hull of the Ark.

He kept his thumbs on the thrusters.

Finally, we came to a stop.

Ogwambi's face was lit with red flashing lights. His forehead was covered in sweat.

"One?" he said.

"Keep applying thrust," One said. "You are nearly there."

I looked at Maiara and wanted to say something to her, but I couldn't find any words. I was simultaneously in awe of space and terrified.

Then we started going back down towards the Ark. The hull of the ship, slowly, but steadily, rose to meet us.

I breathed a sigh of relief. I could tell from Maiara and Illarion's fogged helmets that they did the same.

The Ark was getting closer and closer.

Then Ogwambi's pack vibrated and sputtered. It was out of fuel too.

"That's it for the fuel tank... One, are going to make it?" Ogwambi asked.

"I am calculating your approach vector now," he responded.

"Calculating what exactly?" I asked.

"You are drifting down towards the Ark, but very slowly and the ship is moving underneath you. If you are not moving fast enough you won't catch the ship, and you will be left behind in its wake."

"Then slow the ship down," Maiara said.

"I cannot slow the ship down, we don't have the power to fire the engines."

If the Ark was moving along underneath us, I could barely tell. There was nothing out in space to compare motion to. Still, One was surely correct. We would have to be lucky now to connect with the Ark before it went by. And I didn't want to imagine the thought of us missing our ride.

"One?" Maiara said. "We're scared."

"Hang on, please," One said. "I am calculating a minor change of momentum."

We waited for an agonising moment.

"Yes. Good. You are going to make it," One said.

We all sighed in relief.

"However—"

21
HITTING THE DECK

"However what?" I almost screamed.

"You are going to hit the hull of the Ark really hard and at the wrong angle. Since it is heading forward you might bounce off or roll along its surface."

"Is that all?" Maiara asked sarcastically.

"Actually, there is another problem," One said. "You'll be quite far from the airlock you came through and you do not have enough oxygen to walk back."

We all fell silent.

"Do not worry. We must first get you back to the ship. Two and I have repaired the plasma damage and the ship is safe. The crew can now return. And we will all be here to help you get back into the Ark."

"How long until we reach the Ark?" I asked.

"Three minutes, seventeen seconds," One said.

"Holy crap," Illarion blurted out.

"I know," Ogwambi said.

"I am so sorry, everyone," I said.

"Don't worry, Callum. It's not your fault," Maiara replied.

"Not his fault!?" Gerlinde said.

"He didn't blow up his own canister," Maiara retorted.

"We wouldn't have been outside if it wasn't for him," Gerlinde said.

"Maybe we can talk about this later." Ogwambi said.

"No, let's talk about it now," I said. "We all might die and I need to say this. I'm sorry. This all my fault, I got us into it. I started the argument with Dehqan. I pushed too hard. I'm responsible."

I felt tears well in my eyes. And I was happy my helmet obscured them from clear view. I couldn't let them know I was crying.

"That's big of you," Ogwambi said.

"Yes," Gerlinde added. "Now we'll try to survive the mess you got us in."

I nodded, still fighting tears.

"We're going to hit the Ark soon," I said. "The only way we don't go skipping off the surface is by making sure our magnetic boots hit the—"

"Back to giving orders?" Gerlinde sniped. "What new trouble should we prepare for you to cause?"

"He said sorry Gerlinde," Illarion said. "Let's just get through this."

Gerlinde went silent, but I could swear I heard her pouting.

"We need to get into a formation," I said.

"We're not a football team," Gerlinde said.

"What I mean is we all need to be in a chain, so we all need to hit the hull of the Ark feet first, together."

"Callum, I don't think we can do that," Ogwambi said. "If we start moving around we could change our momentum or start rotating and we have no way to stop it."

"He's right. We need to stay where we are, and just try to put our feet down as we go," Maiara said.

"Arkonauts are you there?" Two said through the comm.

"We are," Ogwambi responded.

"In just under a minute you will hit the hull of the ship. Hold on tight to one another and really try to plant your feet," she said.

The hull was very near, but we were coming up close on the engines, roaring bright, and that couldn't be good.

"What about the engine?" I asked.

"Based on our calculations, you'll hit the hull just above the thrusters. It is important that your boots catch because you will tumble into the engine if they do not."

"There's no way to survive that," Gerlinde said.

"Get ready. Here comes the hull," Ogwambi said.

We held each other tight as the hull approached. Even though we were drifting slowly, the huge ship seemed to come at us fast..

Maiara and Illarion crashed down first. They both cried out as our momentum coursed through their legs into the hull.

"Okay, we're locked onto the hull," Maiara said. "We got you, Ogwambi."

They pulled down on Ogwambi's legs, but the effort tilted him forward and he couldn't get his feet beneath him.

He hit the hull with his knees, and he, Gerlinde and I deflected along the surface of the ship.

It was terrifying to be so close to the hull but see it just out of reach. This could be it.

Then I felt a hand wrap around my leg. It was Illarion, Ogwambi and Maiara, she was on their shoulders like a human ladder. And for a moment Gerlinde and my momentum almost stopped.

Until Illarion's boots broke loose and we all tumbled.

We were sliding again, just above the ship, toward the roaring purple glow of the engines.

"Plant your feet," Gerlinde screamed over her shoulder.

Illarion and Maiara slowly swung their weightless legs under them and tried to kick down at the hull. The soles of their boots hit the metal surface and clicked on. Illarion took a strong stance and Maiara followed. They were able to stop Gerlinde then Ogwambi, but that just made them a kind of axel around which our remaining momentum swung.

They pulled loose of the hull again. I felt for sure this was it. The engine was too close. There was no way we could stop in time.

Mid-spin, Ogwambi kicked out his feet and caught the hull. The magnets did the last bit of work for him. He got low on to the hull, grabbing a seam between the outer hull panels and rolled his back. The momentum of all of us trailing him swung us over his head and right into the hull.

We smacked into the hull hard, but we hit it square enough this time that we could plant our feet.

There is no more wonderful feeling that that of magnetic boots securely touching the hull.

I watch as Illarion and Maiara came down.

Illarion's boots didn't hold, but Maiara's did.

And he grabbed for her, his momentum pulling her off the hull again.

Maiara shrieked.

Illarion cried out.

I thought I was going to watch my girlfriend die.

Then Maiara swung her arms and legs, putting her and Illarion into a tight spin. I don't know how she did it, but she tucked into a ball, then fanned her arms and legs out before stomping at the very edge of the main hull. As her boots locked on, she was splashed in purple light, almost like a halo. She gave Illarion a tug on his arm and the boy landed on the surface too.

The rest of us clomped over to them. The engine roared and I could feel the heat through my suit.

I wrapped my arms around Maiara. She smiled.

I let a tear or two slip out, and I hoped she'd seen them.

"I thought we were going to get roasted," Illarion said.

"Let's get back inside," Gerlinde said.

There was no argument from the group, so we marched away from the engine walking along the Ark's hull looking for any point of entry.

The radio crackled to life.

"Well done everyone. We see you on our screens," One said. "I have activated a beacon trail along the hull. Please follow it as quickly as you can."

"A trail to the airlock?" I asked.

"The airlock is miles away from where you are now, and with your low oxygen supplies you will not reach it in time," One said. "There is an access point where the top section of the ship meets the bottom. It leads to the lower sections of the Ark."

"Wait. Isn't there—" Illarion said.

"It's full of water," Maiara said.

"Water?" Gerlinde added with a tinge of fear.

"Yep. All the water the Ark managed to suck up when it got to Earth."

"Correct, Maiara. Also, the lower section is under zero gravity, As such, the water will be floating in the air," One said.

"I'm not going in there," Gerlinde said.

"One, is this really the best plan?" I asked.

"You cannot reach an airlock before running out of oxygen," One said.

"How do we open the access door?" I asked.

"I will open it from here. For now, please just follow the beacons. And no more talking, as that will increase the use of your remaining oxygen."

"Won't we need oxygen once we're inside?" Maiara asked.

"There are reserves in the lower section of the Ark. Please follow the beacons."

We trudged across the hull of the ship, not bothering to admire the view. We just kept our eyes on the trail of beacons.

22

THE INLAND SEA

It took us two hours to reach the opening into the lower half of the Ark.

I couldn't talk to the others, for fear of running out of oxygen, but I could see they were tired. Lifting these boots and dragging an ill-fitting suit along left me drenched in sweat.

We could see the giant door. Its circumference was massive like a meteor crater.

"Bear right with the beacons," One said. "I will open the hatch a small amount so I can close it quickly after you enter. You will be sealed in a very large airlock for lack of a better word. You will then have to float through to the next hatch, which I will open for you. Once past that hatch I will lose contact with you, so pay close attention to the next instructions."

"Do not speak," Two said. "It will be your instinct to ask questions, but it is imperative at this time that you do not."

Then One continued. "All the water stored in this section is suspended in zero gravity. There are the remains of the old pipe network, hulls of various naval ships sucked up by the Ark, and some rocks and sand from the sea floor.

"The inner structure is made of a criss-crossing network of support beams, like a spider web. You will have to walk across the beams upwards to the top section. Near the top you will see a shaft.

Move up the shaft, and it will lead to the bottom of the engine room. Two and I will meet you there."

It sounded like a long route, but simple enough.

"There is one more thing," One said. "It is possible that some sea life might have been sucked up into the Ark, and may still be alive."

We all stopped walking and looked at each other.

"Keep walking and we will explain," Two said.

"Be cautious. It is unlikely that anything dangerous survived, but it is important to stay alert." One said. "Now, I am opening the hatch."

All along the rim of the massive portal we saw air escaping in plumes as the hatch opened. The surface of the ship rumbled, vibrating up through our boots and then us, as giant gears turned to move the door.

We neared the lip of the giant hatch, now open just wide enough for one of us to fit at a time. In its original design, the Ark would have deployed a pipe from this opening, with the intention of sucking up huge quantities of water.

We all looked at each other.

I decided I should volunteer to be first to go inside. I stepped through the small opening and found myself in a long tunnel. It seemed to be hundreds of metres long.

Maiara was next in and she joined me, taking my hand. It was awkward in our thick space suit gloves.

"This is amazing," she whispered.

"You're not supposed to talk," I said.

"Neither are you. Don't worry, we have plenty of air left. After all that's gone wrong today at least our oxygen supply decided to behave."

Gerlinde and Illarion came next, right behind, and holding hands too. Ogwambi was last in, and once he was a few metres in, the hatch closed and sealed itself tight.

One's voice crackled over the radio, "We are about to lose contact. Remember to stay alert and watch for moving wat—"

His voice trailed off and disappeared.

We were on our own.

We walked ahead toward the second hatch, already opening.

"Can you believe this? We're going to see what the bottom section of the Ark is like," Maiara said, almost giddy with excitement.

"How much water do you think is in here?" I asked.

"I remember that sea levels dropped a little because of the Ark, so it must be a lot," Maiara said.

"Do you think anything could have survived?" I said.

"I don't see what it could have survived on. There is no sunlight down here. No food," she said.

"I hope we see something. Think of all the species that died when the Earth was destroyed. Down here we may see cod, or stingrays, or jelly fish. It'd be like home. Plus it'd be kind of nice to be taking some other animals with us," I said.

At the second hatch, where I was expecting a dark cavernous underbelly, instead we found a well-lit space.

"What's causing that?" I asked.

"Who knows? No one has ever been down here," Ogwambi said.

We all passed through the hatch, and then stood in silence marvelling at the sight.

The lower section of the Ark was impossibly massive. The crisscrossed supporting beams banded all over but the space was large enough that we could still see very clearly. The space was filled with a warm yellow glow that emanated from a network of conduits running from the ceiling all the way down to the base of the ship. Everything was floating. Water floated around in globs and blobs from the very tiny to hundreds of metres in diameter. It was like a giant had used a bubble wand to blow a whole room of bubbles but each one was made of seawater, and many had some relic of the sea floor inside.

We all gasped in awe.

Wreckages of old ships floated around, their hulls shining in the light. There was even an older ship, maybe from World War II, covered in coral and lank seaweed.

"Those look like power conduits, supplying the engines," Gerlinde said, pointing at the glowing cables.

"And they are providing the light," Ogwambi commented.

The ceiling had a shallow domed roof, and in the very middle was what looked like an opening. The passage that One had mentioned. Half of the shaft held the network of power conduits, braided together to pass through the centre of the Ark.

All the light and water threw rippling patterns of shimmer and shadow across the beams and walls.

"The other power conduits in the ship don't have lights on them like these," Gerlinde said.

"Maybe the aliens wanted to see what they were doing when they worked down here," Illarion said.

"If there is light, then maybe there's something for the fish to eat?" I said.

"You think these could replicate sunlight?" Maiara replied.

"Maybe? If there was algae down here surviving on it, there could be small fish, and then bigger fish," I said.

"That seems like a stretch."

"Watch out for sharks," I said.

"We need to start moving," Illarion said.

"Yeah. We can't stay here and admire the view forever," Ogwambi said.

"How do we get up there?" I asked, eyeing the opening.

"I say we walk up the walls," Gerlinde said.

"Wouldn't it be quicker to cut across using some of these support beams?"

"That would be dangerous," Maiara interjected. "We don't know how sturdy they are, or what would happen if one of us fell off."

"Plus it seems as though water is gathering around the larger beams," I said pointing across the space.

Little lakes had formed around the power conduits and giant support beams. I bet if life did exist down here that's where it would be.

"I say we take the walls," Gerlinde reiterated.

"Agreed," Me and Maiara said together.

"Me too," Ogwambi's said.

Illarion nodded.

"We better get going," I suggested.

Just then a melodic sound rippled through the air.

"It can't be?" Gerlinde said, seeming to recognise the sound.

Near a large support beam, a glob of anti-gravity water shuddered and something giant erupted from it, singing.

Its massive fins flung water everywhere. A humpback whale soared through the air, exiting one water blob, then diving into another.

"My goodness! That was a whale," Maiara said.

"How is that possible?" Ogwambi asked.

"It must have got sucked up years ago?" I said.

We watched the dark shape of the whale swim around its new home, popping in and out of each blob of water, drifting through zero gravity.

I could think of nothing better than to be bringing a whale with us on the Ark. Part of me didn't even want to leave the lower section now.

We watched the bubbles of ocean bob and float for a while. We saw more whales, pods of them. There were whole families from Earth, like us, who got sucked up into the Ark.

This place was magical.

The hatch behind us then closed. One might not be able to communicate with us, but he must have realised we had passed through the hatch.

It came down with a thunderous boom that echoed around the lower section of the Arc.

The noise was amazing to hear in the space, like the biggest bass you had ever heard.

Another noise seemed to respond.

It was a roar. It was deep, and crackled with power.

A primeval instinct was suddenly activated in my mind.

That was not a good sound.

"What kind of whale makes that noise?" I said.

"None," Maiara said. "Look."

When I looked where she was pointing I saw it.

Bursting from metal beam to metal beam, flinging mist and foam violently as it shredded through bubbles of water, was a something more terrifying than a whale, with yellow eyes and rows of sharp teeth.

It was as large as a jumbo jet.

And it headed straight for us.

23
THE CREATURE

"Holy sh..." I began to say.

"Callum," Maiara interrupted.

"What is that?" Gerlinde said.

I couldn't move.

None of us could.

We were transfixed on this giant creature speeding from girder to girder. In the distance we only caught the light reflecting off its eyes and teeth. As it got closer we saw it better. It was some kind of giant crocodile, but its body was thinner, and it had three pairs of legs, with is rear legs closer together nearer its tail. One of the legs ended in a heavily-scarred stump. It had a very thin, very long snout too, above which sat four, glowing yellow eyes.

It smiled as it came towards us, giddy like a dog.

"What do we do?" Gerlinde asked.

"What do you think we should do?" Illarion said.

Gerlinde turned and pounded on the hatch.

"One, let us out of here," she yelled.

"He can't hear us," Maiara said.

"We need to hide," I said. "Get behind a beam."

We ran as fast as we could to get behind the nearest one, clustering there.

"It probably saw us move," Gerlinde said.

"Maybe we got lucky? Maybe we're not its kind of snack?"

"I've never seen an animal like that before. Where do you think it came from?" Maiara asked.

I peered over the brace. "I don't know, but it might smell us."

The creature bounded to the hatch and brushed its snout along the rim of the portal, pausing and then sniffing at the empty air. Then its large yellow eyes grew wider.

"Do you think it can track us?" Gerlinde whispered.

"Crocodiles usually wait for animals to come to them," I said.

"Callum, that's not a crocodile," Maiara said.

"What else would it be?" I replied.

"If it was a crocodile, it would be smaller," Maiara said.

"Shut up both of you," Illarion hissed. "It'll hear us."

The creature repositioned its feet, its the claws gouging the metal beams and walls as it turned to scan the area. Its large forked tongue slithered out between its closed jaws and lapped the air.

"It can't smell us," Ogwambi said. "That's why it's tasting the air."

"Can it taste us?" I asked.

"We're wearing space suits. So, I doubt it," Ogwambi said.

We all held our collective breath for a few moments as the creature tasted the air again, huffed, and snorted. Then it turned away from the hatch, and peered down into the deep recesses of the Ark.

Then another whale appeared, leaping out of a nearby bubble of water. It passed right in front of the creature whose head turned slowly to watch it pass, curious. Like a whip, the beast's tongue shot out from its open mouth and wrapped around the whale, squeezing it violently as it did.

The whale cried as the tongue retracted, and it was drawn into the creature's jaws. There was a sickening crunch as its maw crushed the whale between sharp jagged teeth.

Blood and blubber flew everywhere as the creature lazily chewed and slurped the remains into its mouth.

Satisfied, the creature leapt down into the darkest place below the decks.

We all breathed out.

"It must be some kind of alien creature," Ogwambi said.

"What?" I asked.

"The Ark could have sucked it up from another planet?" he replied.

"And it's been living on whales," Illarion said.

"There *is* an entire ecosystem down here," I said.

"We have to get out of here," Maiara said. "Let's get to the roof."

"What about that thing?" Gerlinde hissed.

"Hopefully it won't be hungry for a while," Ogwambi said.

"And what about sharks? If there are whales here I bet there are sharks in those waters too," Gerlinde said.

"We stay out of the water," I said. "Up the walls, like we planned."

"What about—" she said.

"Gerlinde, are you afraid of the ocean?" I asked.

She shook her head, too much.

"She is," Illarion said.

Gerlinde punched him in the arm.

"She had a bad experience once on holiday," Illarion continued.

"Stop telling them," Gerlinde screeched.

"We'll stay out of the water."

"We might not have a chance," Ogwambi said.

He pointed toward the base of the Ark. Another blob of water was moving toward us. And given how far away it was, it going to gigantic when it got to us.

Gerlinde screamed.

Ogwambi reached out to stop her.

"It's hard to see where it's heading," he said. "It might miss us."

"Let's go. Let's go!" Gerlinde yelled.

"What if moving now puts us in its path?" Maiara pointed out.

Gerlinde froze.

"We can't stay here," I said. "We start walking now. We'll stay behind the beams and watch for the creature. We'll be fine."

After a moment, they all nodded.

We started walking amidst the mini-seas, whales, and shipwrecks all around us, listening for the sound of claws scraping on metal.

24
THE WAVE

Every odd sound we heard caused us to stop in our tracks and scan the space around us.

We had to keep an eye on the seas moving across the room threatening to engulf us, watch for the monster and any other sea life, and keep on course for the exit. It was a lot to take in.

I felt more comfortable. We had all removed our helmets, breathing in the fresh non-recycled air around us. It was like being by the seaside.

"Guys," Ogwambi said, from the head of the procession. He stopped suddenly, holding up his hand to stop us.

"What? What do you see? Is it a shark?" Gerlinde said.

"Mussels," he said, pointing at a huge bed of black-shell molluscs stretched outward like a field before us. Each one was closed tight.

"Is it safe to walk on them?" I said.

Ogwambi crouched down and his gaze followed the line to his left and right.

"It'd be too far to go around," he said.

"And if we crack the shells, that thing might hear us," Maiara said.

We could still see the beast's four eyes glistening like a cluster of stars in the dark distance of the lower Ark. It hadn't come out again, but it was still looking, at least in our direction.

"It can't hear the cracks of shells from there," I said. "I hope."

Ogwambi's gingerly stepped out onto the bed of mussels.

We all watched him as if it were a high wire act at the circus.

He took a few steps, his feet sliding a bit, but there were no loud cracks, and soon, Ogwambi turned and gave us the thumbs up.

"It's like walking on river stones. Just watch your step."

"Let's get going," I said, stepping out next.

We cautiously walked across the black field. It was harder than Ogwambi made it look. Our magnetic boots could cling to the hull as well through the layer of shells, so we had to trudge very carefully. It was like tromping through a snowbank, but with each step we had to make sure our boots had enough bond to the hull. If not, we would have gone floating off into the lower Ark, easy pickings for the creature.

Then Ogwambi stopped again, and turned. There was a look of horror on his face.

"What now?" I said.

"We've made a mistake," he replied. "A big one."

"What? We forgot the butter?" Illarion joked.

"No. Mussels only close like this when the tide goes out!"

"Oh, no," Maiara said. "Mussels can't live outside of water indefinitely. That means that this whole area must regularly be covered in water."

Behind us, that huge body of water slowly traversed the inside of the Ark.

"We're right in the line of that huge water blob," I said.

"More than likely, yes," Ogwambi said. "It must orbit the inside of the Ark at regular intervals.

"We won't survive that," Gerlinde said. "If the force of the water hitting us doesn't knock us off the wall, then we'll drown, or be eaten by something else."

Ogwambi stared at the body of water. "At the rate it's moving, we have about a half an hour."

"We can beat it. Let's keep moving," I said.

We all tried to sprint, but our boots couldn't get enough grip. We ran, as best as we could anyway, for a few minutes, but we didn't get far and we were all breathless.

And that miniature sea was edging closer and closer.

"What do we do now?" Maiara asked, panting.

As the sea moved nearer, it looked like it could be two or three hundred metres deep. We weren't going to outrun it by staying down where we were. Above us there were support beams reaching far enough up and out, and if we could get to them, then we could stay there while the sea passed underneath us.

"We have to jump," I said.

"Jump?" everyone said in response.

"Yes we need to get over to those beams. We'll be beyond the water's path," I said.

"And if we miss we'll go careering out into the lower section of the ship!" Gerlinde said.

"We don't have a choice," I said. "See that beam there? We can't miss it. We'll crouch down, deactivate our boots, and then push off."

Gerlinde rung her hands. She wasn't convinced.

"We have to do this," Maiara said.

The front edge of the bubble of water lapped at the field of mussels, jostling them.

Illarion gripped Gerlinde's hand and I grasped Maiara's.

Ogwambi huffed in annoyance at being the only single person there. I do not know why he cared. This wasn't romantic. Illarion then held his hand as we all then did, creating a long chain of Arkonauts sticking together, with me at one end.

Together we crouched, deactivated our boot magnets, and pushed off. As we lifted off the bed of shells, the glob of water splashed into the field, churning as it hit the hull beneath. Some water splashed at the edges of my feet, white caps forming atop waves as the water fell back into itself.

And I saw that one of those waves was going to hit me. I was trailing the others, having not leapt as quick and hard as they had. If

147

the water hit me while I held onto the others it would drag us all back down.

I watched as Ogwambi, Illarion, Gerlinde, and Maiara were soaring toward the safety of the support beam. I saw the wave coming closer, ready to punch me hard across the body.

There was only one thing to do.

I closed the helmet of my suit, and then I let go of Maiara's hand.

"Callum! What are you doing?" she asked. "Callum!"

"I'm sorry, Maiara, but it was the only way. If that wave hit me, it'd take you all with me."

Now they were all looking at me. Gerlinde screamed too. But Ogwambi landed safely on the beam, then Gerlinde, then Illarion, then Maiara. They each reactivated their boots. They were safe.

Water spray spattered my helmet. The light refracting through reminded me of the time Sanna and I, had scrambled with the crew to fix that leak on our first day on the Ark.

Once I had been struck by a wave.

It had come out of nowhere. I was walking on the coast with my family. I hadn't been paying attention. I was occupied with my feet in the sand.

This wave was much more sedate, in the low gravity inside it didn't have the same force. It just sort of swallowed me, gathered me up and rolled me around gently.

The glob of water was a mess of random currents, each created when the water struck beams and walls as it travelled. I imagined this was a bit like being caught in the clothes washer, but much larger. I was being tossed in circles and dizzied, and mussels were peppering me like BBs, but I started to think I could survive this.

Then I noticed the support strut that it was carrying me towards.

I tried to gain control over my momentum, I tried to swim. My muscles screamed at me with the effort of trying to fight the water.

Then I struck the beam.

And my helmet hit the beam first, knocking it loose. My precious oxygen hissed as it escaped through the gap. Water seeped into my helmet. I lost my vision for a moment, and gasped as I spit out salty water. Then I scrambled to seal the helmet again. Barely.

There was red in the water too. And a metallic taste. I had hit my head. I was bleeding.

I felt exhausted. My head was dizzy. Everything went dark.

***

I came to, no longer underwater. I had not drowned.

I was slowly spinning through the air. I checked my watch I had been blacked out for an hour.

As I rotated I saw the exit shaft at the top. I couldn't see the others, but thankfully I had not been thrown too far away.

And I still had 12% oxygen remaining.

I sighed in relief and retracted my helmet, letting the water inside escape so I could breathe without spluttering.

All I had to do was wait until I struck a beam, or the opposite wall. Then I could walk to safety.

I floated for a moment, just breathing. I reached up and touched the wound on my head. The blood flow seemed to have stopped. I hoped that the others had made it out safely. They must have, I decided, to think otherwise was too horrible to contemplate. My mind began to wander. What game could I play with my own mind, until I hit something to grab on—

I hit something. But it didn't feel like a beam because it gave away behind me, slowing me down until I came to a stop in mid-air. It didn't matter, I had hit something stable, something I could connect my magnetic boots too.

I turned to look, and my relief turned immediately to terror.

It was a big black-clawed foot.

Like giant tweezers, one claw met another with my body in the middle, and my rotation stopped. I waited for the sharp nails to puncture my suit, and then me, but they didn't.

Instead, a snout came into view. Then four yellow glowing eyes, set above a wide, wild toothy grin.

The creature's tongue slithered out from between its teeth and tasted my space suit.

Then its jaws opened wide.

25
SURPRISE

"Hello," the creature said, its voice booming like thunder.

I was ready to scream or pee myself.

My gut was tight, my body frozen.

But all of a sudden I was too confused to be scared.

This thing could talk.

26
KRAKEN

The creature gazed at me expectantly.

"Er... hello," I said

There was a deep, baritone chuckle from within the belly of the beast, like crashing waves in a storm.

"I surprised you! What fun! You were not expecting me to talk?" it said.

It cocked its head to the side and peered at me with its giant yellow eyes. The huge nostrils on its snout were positioned right above me. The creature inhaled twice with such great force that my hair was pulled upwards.

"Hmm... Definitely human," it said.

I grasped for the only available question in my mind.

"H-h-h-how can you speak?" I said.

The creature looked slightly annoyed at this statement.

"What arrogance," it said. "Whatever made you think I couldn't speak?"

"Well... Crocodiles don't usually speak," I uttered.

"The others used this same term. What is a crocodile?"

The creature brought its mighty, toothy jaws close to my face. Its eyes wore a look of expectation.

I was too shocked to speak. My mind was racing, but couldn't compute what was happening.

"Speak, I say!" the creature barked, its hot breath washing over me.

"I-i-it's a large reptile from Earth... Where I grew up," I replied.

"Well, I'm not from where you grew up," it said. "Earth? What a silly name for a planet!"

The creature bounded away, up two beams above me, then swung back around. It dangled, claws clutching the steel spars above me.

"I trust we have left orbit of your little homeworld?" it asked. "I sensed the thrust of the engines long ago."

I didn't know how to respond. I was still paralyzed with fear.

"Are you stupid, human? Should I devour you and go find another of your kind who is more intelligent and talkative?"

"No," I exclaimed, suddenly feeling emboldened. It wasn't going to matter if I was scared or not. This thing was going to keep talking to me. "No devouring, please. Yes, we have left Earth's orbit. Why do you want to know? Who are you anyway?"

It paused, maybe perplexed by my response.

"I never had a name before I met humanity," it said. "There was never any need of one. But a human called Ghost named me 'Kraken.'"

"Dr. Ghost? You knew Dr. Ghost?"

The beast nodded.

"I knew him. He did the deal with me didn't he?" the beast said, gazing off into the middle distance, as if somewhere else.

"How? How did you know him? How did you get here?" I asked.

"For eons there was peace and joy in the great sea I called home with my people. Then this monster of shiny rock struck my planet and swallowed me into its belly! For years I have lived in its stomach, surviving on the other creatures it devoured. It was a lonely existence, but I was never want for food. One day, tiny, hairless creatures ventured down into the belly from above."

The creature gestured upwards, pointing at the exit portal at the top of the room.

"They came down here and crawled all over the shining core, banging on it with shiny sticks and using crackle boxes to talk over great distances. They were very tasty."

"Y-y-you ate them?" I asked.

"Of course! Never did get full though. Such tiny morsels! They came back down to the belly again. There were many more this time. They had shiny sticks that spit little rocks at me, and birds with tails of smoke."

They must have sent soldiers down to try to kill Kraken, with machine guns and rocket launchers.

"Of course, they all died. I ate them all. Their shiny sticks gave me indigestion."

"How did you meet Dr. Ghost then?" I asked.

"I was getting to that," Kraken hissed. "After the humans stopped coming, a four-legged creature with curious splotches on its body dropped into the belly from above. Pity it could not swim. All it could do was emit a mournful moo sound.

"After I ate it something happened. My mind changed. I began to see squiggly pictures and hear sounds in my head when I saw creatures and objects. It was a language, but not that of my planet. And then I heard a voice from the hole above the belly. It told me its name and I understood. Then it explained that it wanted to bargain."

I was stunned. Somehow whoever was in charge of the Ark had managed to spike some food with nanites to teach this creature to speak English.

"Bargain?" I asked.

"The man wanted to fix this monster of shiny rock. He told me that his people controlled it now and were going to fly it away. He needed me to stop eating the little people with the shiny sticks so they could do work and make the monster live again. We agreed that I would leave the humans alone to work, and that they would no longer try to kill me. It was also promised that I would be freed from the belly of this creature when it was safe to do so."

"And you agreed to that deal?" I said.

"Of course! I long to be free of this place! To swim a larger ocean again! To feast on its many delicious forms of life! I tire of the meagre pickings here."

I nodded, hoping Kraken would keep talking while I tried to get access a nanite memories that knew what I should do. Unfortunately, Dr. Ghost had not given me knowledge as to how to deal with giant sea monsters.

"Enough about me," Kraken bellowed. "The better question is why *you* are here I was told there would be no more humans here until we arrived at our destination."

"We had a little mix up... But we haven't arrived yet," I said.

The creature swept around me and grasped me in its claw. It pointed me toward the Ark's core, and the glowing bundle of cables that led to the engine.

"'When this pillar burns bright twice, you will have arrived.' That is what Ghost said. The pillar has burned brightly twice. I have seen it! We *have* arrived. Why have I not been released?"

I was terrified. I was also angry with Dr. Ghost for everything he had kept from us. It was about to get me killed.

"But we haven't reached a new world yet," I stammered. "I promise."

Kraken roared and raked its claw down one of the beams.

"Liar!"

"No! It's true. Those two flashes... We had to fire the engine early to correct our course in space," I said.

"Deceiver!"

"I'm not lying. Please. I can help you. Why would I lie?" I asked.

"So you can leave me to rot in this belly, amongst the carcasses of these dead shiny beasts! I will not have it! If I am not freed, I will destroy this ship to gain my freedom."

Kraken rested a claw on one of the wrecked boats, and in one clench, crushed the ship like an empty soda can.

"You don't have to do that," I said. "I can help you, but I need to get back to my people. If you take me to the door, I can explain everything to them and we'll help you together."

Kraken paused as if to think.

"I don't think so," it declared. "You will be my hostage."

"Hostage?" I asked.

"Yes. If your people care as you say, then they will come for you. Until I am released, you're staying with me."

27
THE DALLAS

Kraken looked upwards then bellowed "Do you hear me, Ghost!? I have your child! Release me or I will eat it!"

Then Kraken stopped, craned its head, and looked around.

In the distance, metal was clanking loudly. Was One doing something? Had he come to rescue me?

"Turso," Kraken said, spitting the word with rage and scorn. It darted about the support beams frantically. Kraken was looking everywhere, but wasn't finding what it sought. It just paced and paced, trying to track the sound of clanking steel.

I suddenly bumped into a support pillar. I quickly activated my boots and clung to its surface. Finally, I had the means to go where I wanted.

This was my chance to escape.

I kicked my boots onto a beam and activated their magnets. I'd have to move quickl—

There was a splash of water above me. A submarine cruised out of a glob of water. It was even closer to Kraken. The ship bore an American flag and the words *U.S.S. Dallas* painted on its hull. What was weirdest of all, its propellers were spinning. The ship was running.

Kraken gasped and then whimpered.

The ship was too fast, and even as the creature tried to dodge, the submarine smashed into the beast's stomach.

Kraken cried out as the submarine drove it downwards where it pinned the monster against a pillar. Kraken pushed the submarine away in the low gravity then cradled its stomach as the sub entered another body of water and disappeared.

Even with my magnetic boots, I couldn't walk away quickly enough, but if I leapt from strut to strut I could make up distance faster.

I bounded from beam to beam, carefully planting my feet, getting a little head of steam, and leaping on the anti-gravity that would carry me to the next.

When I leapt the third time, Kraken flew up toward me, its jaws wide.

"You will not get away, morsel!"

Just as its jaws were ready to close around my legs, I heard a strange whistle, and saw a tube flying at Kraken. A torpedo.

The submarine's shot hit the beast square in the head. The explosion sent Kraken reeling, tumbling back down into the dark recesses of the Ark.

The submarine slowly approached me.

Then its hatch opened. I was ready to thank them for saving me, unless of course, they wanted to shoot me too.

I waited, feeling tense, for who would emerge from the ship.

Then Ogwambi popped his head out of the submarine.

"Callum," he shouted. "Get over here."

I leapt towards the sub, my boots clinging to its hull. I walked to the hatch where Ogwambi had been and peered inside.

Two pairs of hands were waiting to pull me inside.

28
IKU TURSO

Deep red light assaulted my face as I was pulled from the dark confines of the entry hatch tube into the sub. The emergency lighting threw crisp shadows against the decks and riveted walls, and everyone present looked like they were in a horror film.

Gerlinde, Illarion, Ogwambi and Maiara, all beamed at me. They had dumped much of their space suit's paraphernalia on the floor of the submarine, but they kept their boots to maintain their footing.

I gawked; surprised to see them. The submarine was pretty gross inside. Puddles were everywhere and the place stunk of fish.

"How did you guys get a sub?" I asked.

"It's not ours," Illarion said. "It's—"

Before Illarion could begin to explain, Maiara leapt toward me and kissed me. She hugged me so hard at the same time that it kind of hurt.

Still, I enjoyed the unexpected affection.

When Maiara finally came up for air she said, "I'm insanely happy to see you alive! Thank you for saving me."

I leaned in and kissed her again.

The other Arkonauts groaned at the display.

"What was that for?" she asked.

"Well, if we're saying thank you, I should thank you for being my anchor when we were outside."

"One thing though: Don't ever scare me like that again," she warned.

The others sniggered.

I decided to turn the topic back to our surroundings. The inside of the sub was hot and humid. Plus the fishy smell didn't help. It was like being inside a garbage bin.

"It's awful in here," I stated.

"Don't worry we'll be getting out of here soon, I hope," Maiara said.

"Yeah and never coming back," Ogwambi said in delight.

Gerlinde, still terrified of the sea nodded emphatically.

"Now, if I may continue explaining how we got this submarine," Illarion said. "This is the *U.S.S. Dallas*, an American sub—"

"So that makes Maiara the captain?" I interrupted.

"The ship already has a captain," Gerlinde said.

"Who? How?" I asked.

Had the ship been sucked up during the first battle with the Ark? Were there crewmembers on board? That thought filled me with apprehension, the last time we had military people on board the Ark it didn't go well.

"The original captain of the ship is still alive. He's been here ever since the Ark sucked up the *Dallas* back when it landed.

"Him and his cabin boy," Ogwambi said, giggling.

"Cabin boy?" I said.

"Why don't we go see him," Maiara said.

She led us through the ship, a labyrinth of small corridors, leaking pipes, and locked doors to various rooms, some bearing warnings.

"What's wrong with those rooms?" I asked as we passed the cafeteria. I was famished.

"Hull breaches in those, so we can't go in," Illarion said.

We then passed through a room of racks stacked high with twelve huge missiles.

I gasped.

"Don't worry. They aren't nuclear," Ogwambi said. "They're what's called MOABs. I guess you need a special code to detonate them."

Next we approached the bridge. The Captain was staring through a periscope when we entered. The sound of our footsteps on the deck plates alerted him and he turned towards us. He wore a faded, dirty officers' uniform complete with insignia and hat. He had a beard that had been crudely trimmed. His face was weather-beaten and pallid. Clearly he had not been eating or drinking well since ending up in the Ark. He scratched at his head absentmindedly.

"So you must be Callum. Welcome aboard! Have you met my EX-O?" the Captain said, pointing over my shoulder.

When I turned, I found myself looking into the eyes of a fish.

Well, not a fish precisely, but an alien that resembled a fish.

The alien was a little taller than me. It wore robes that glistened like wet seaweed. Its hands were webbed and its skin covered in scales. There was a pronounced hump on its back, which gave it a hunched appearance, even though it appeared to be standing up straight. The alien smiled, sharp and toothy, like a moray eel, and then raised one of its flippery hands.

"High five," it said.

I obliged. The five was slippery and slapped.

"The Captain has taught me human ways and language," the fish said. "You've handled meeting me well. The others really freaked out."

"Man, I was hoping you would jump and scream," Ogwambi said.

"Told you. You owe me your dessert if we get back to that part of the ship," Illarion said.

"I've just been talking to a giant crocodile monster. I don't think anything can shock me for the rest of the day," I said.

"That thing can talk?" Maiara said.

"Yeah. Dr. Ghost gave it nanites."

"That is Kraken," the fish said. "He does not like unwelcome guests."

161

"You're telling me," I said to the fish alien. "What's your story... umm... What do I call you?"

"My name is Iku Turso," he said, motioning to the captain of the *Dallas*. "We picked up your friends an hour ago. We found them walking up to the ceiling."

"How did you get here?" I asked. "Did the Ark suck you up too?"

"Yes, right before it destroyed my planet."

Iku Turso stepped towards the command station of the submarine, and displayed a map of the lower section of the Ark.

"Near the top of this section is a room where the original designers of this ship controlled this area. There is substantial coral growth around it and so it is safe from Kraken," Turso explained. "I discovered it shortly after I first arrived here. It has screens and controls that allowed me to see outside the ship, but I still couldn't stop what it did to my homeworld."

"Iku Turso comes from a race who lived under the seas of their world," Maiara explained, giddy at describing an alien culture.

I was a bit excited too. Meeting an alien for the first time was an awesome thing. This was someone who had seen different stars and lived in a completely different reality from ours.

"And you found the submarine after the Ark came to Earth?" I asked.

"Yup. We were sucked up several years ago during the battle to stop the Ark," the Captain interrupted, still scratching his head. "We tried to leave the ship, but that monster out there ate my crew. Turso is the only reason I'm alive. He knows this weird environment like the back of his... fin. And he can breathe underwater, which has helped us navigate when we had to, and stay away from that monster. We've survived down here ever since."

Something about what he said gave me pause, but I couldn't put my finger on it.

"How have you avoided Kraken all this time?" I asked.

"There are places to hide down here. That's where we're headed now," the Captain said.

"And can we get to the top? To the exit hatch?" I asked.

"I will take you there in a few hours," Iku Turso said. "First I need to get something from my home."

"What about Kraken?" I asked.

"He'll be knocked out for a while. And he fears this submarine. The torpedoes give him trouble," Iku Turso said. "We took off one of his legs once. He was not too happy about that."

"Whoa," Ogwambi said.

"It was really tasty too," Iku Turso said, smiling wide and toothless.

We all groaned, disgusted.

Turso shrugged.

"You eat what you can down here. Every time the Ark visits a new world we get new sea creatures. But it's been a while since it sucked anything up, and we are running low on supplies."

The fish alien strode over to another station and worked to direct the ship to wherever it was going.

I turned my attention back to my fellow Arkonauts.

"So, how did you all get here?" I asked the others.

"We made it to the support beams like we planned," Ogwambi said.

"We thought you had died," Maiara said.

"In the end we had to keep climbing."

"While we were climbing this submarine turned up. After we stopped freaking out about meeting an alien, we told them about you and they said we'd go find you," Illarion added.

"Thank you for rescuing me," I said to our unlikely comrades.

"Come here humans. This is where we are headed," Turso suddenly said.

A camera feed from the periscope displayed on the computer terminal. It was one of the corners of the Ark. Three walls met there. This was where the northern and southern hemispheres of the Ark connected in the middle. Everything was heavily encrusted in coral.

"That coral is enormous," Ogwambi said, pointing at the screen.

He was right. The coral was gigantic, and even more colourful that any I had seen on Earth. Some of it grew long, reaching out like the branches of tree. Some were rocky clusters, too, and some of it was flat, like palm fronds. The coral had grown to form a kind of tunnel.

"It's not all from your planet. Some of it is from mine. It grows bigger," Iku Turso said. "Kraken will not enter here. The coral is too sharp and strong, and he will not want to cut himself."

The mass of coral was enveloped in a blob of water, and it didn't seem to be moving like the others outside. Maybe the artificial gravity in the upper section of the Ark held it somehow.

The submarine went inside, swallowed both by the tunnel of coral and dense schools of brightly coloured fish. There were even some creatures that weren't fish at all. Maybe they were remnants of species from Iku Turso's homeworld.

After a few hundred metres, the tunnel opened out into a cavern that domed beyond the water and was completely dry. Iku guided the submarine inside until the tower on top cleared the ball of water. He brought the sub to a halt, and it drifted in the low gravity.

I could hear the metal sides scrape against the coral surrounding it.

"Won't the sub drift away?" Gerlinde said.

"No. The coral grows fast and will soon encase it, holding it in place. When we leave the new coral will break away," Turso said. "Welcome to my home. Follow me."

He took us to the base of the tower and led us up to the hatch.

"There's breathable air in this cave. A little bit of magic from the alien coral," he said. "Now, everybody out."

We exited the sub and stood on its hull, looking out around the small waterless void.

"Turso was here first, of course. He found me when Kraken had devoured my crew and led me here. We've worked together ever since," the Captain said, scratching his head.

"My house is over there," the alien said, pointing at a dwelling carved out of the base of a large coral growth. "We have to leap across."

Iku Turso steadied himself and made the leap, flying across the void, twirling in mid-air, and landing feet first.

One by one we did the same thing, save for the twirls. We weren't as good as him at that part.

Ogwambi managed it just fine.

The rest of us not so much.

We landed together, head-first, with outstretched hands keeping us from head-butting the ground, or belly flopping onto the coral floor.

Whatever weird gravity mix up was going on in this cave seemed to be just fine. It felt like the Ark or Earth here, other than the alien coral and the alien fish person, and the floating submarine.

"Follow me inside," Turso said.

His home, carved from the coral, was a generous space. A small kitchen set up on one side, and a sleeping area with a seaweed rope hammock on the other. The walls were decorated with what looked like starfish, although they hardly brought the room together.

On the far wall was a throne. It looked like it was made out of four big, black claws. They must have belonged to Kraken.

Turso sat on the throne and gestured for us to sit where we liked. The Captain sat on a stool near the kitchen.

I sat on the shell of a dead turtle, which was discomforting. The others found small coral growths to sit on.

"We will rest up, and plan our course to reach the exit shaft you mentioned," Turso said. "I know of it, of course, having explored this place extensively. I once climbed the shaft, but the hatch was sealed off."

"You climbed it? Without magnetic boots?" I said.

"There is a ladder. Gravity is low, so the climb is easy, though still long."

"When can we go?" Illarion asked.

"Before I answer that, I have a request. Let me come with you. I wish to leave this place and join you in the world above." he said.

We all looked at the Captain. He was the only adult in the room, and we instinctively felt we should be asking for permission.

"It's alright. He's trustworthy," the Captain said, smiling.

I wasn't sure what I should say, or if. I looked at the others, who were avoiding Iku Turso's pleading puppy dog stare.

"I... I guess that's not a problem," I said finally.

"Yeah, I think so," Ogwambi added. "We have limited air and water supplies, but I'm sure you would be allowed. You *did* save our lives."

"Yes, One is kind. He'll probably say 'yes'," Maiara said.

"One? Is that your captain?" Turso said, pointing at the only captain he knew.

"Kind of. He's a little different from this captain," Illarion replied.

"Different how?" Turso asked.

"He's probably stronger, and more intelligent. He's the most powerful person on this ship."

"Really?" Turso said.

"Indeed."

"Now I feel insulted," the Captain said.

"Sorry," Illarion replied. "We can't all be specially engineered superheroes."

"No, I understand," the Captain replied. "Helming a space ship of this size must be difficult. Please tell me what has happened. Why is the ship in space? Are you the children of the crew? Is this a colony ship now?"

"Captain, this isn't a colony ship," I said. "We're the last survivors from Earth."

"What!?" he asked despondently. "How? This ship was defeated! It couldn't have destroyed Earth!"

"While you were in here another alien ship dropped onto Earth. It was a much larger one. One we couldn't stop. It stole most of our water, and when it left its engine blast destroyed Earth. This ship was made to be our life raft," I said. "Us and two hundred others are the only crew. We're traveling to a new planet to try and start over."

The Captain stared into space. Then he stood up and paced Turso's living quarters.

"I had a family on Earth. Could any of them have survived?" he pleaded.

"We are the only survivors. Us and the rest of the kids in the upper section of the Ark." Maiara said, staring at her feet.

The Captain picked up the stool he had sat on and threw it, denting the seat, and knocking coral off the wall.

"I'm sorry, Captain," Turso said. "Please try to calm down. You're alive and your family would be glad for that. Plus you're about to be free of this life."

I guess after several years down here, Turso and the captain had become good friends. The Captain did indeed compose himself.

"Yes. You will be free. One will definitely welcome you aboard," I reassured.

"I'm glad to hear that," Turso said, speaking for the Captain. "Down here it's a daily struggle to find food and stay out of the reach of Kraken."

"Yeah. How will we avoid Kraken on our way to the exit?" I asked.

"I will create a distraction far away from the shaft. When the beast goes to investigate, we will run for the exit. Kraken won't have time to stop us from getting to safety. And the shaft to the exit narrows near the top, so he won't be able to follow us."

"What kind of distraction?" Ogwambi asked.

Turso crossed the room from his throne to a veil of seaweed covering a wall. He lifted it like a curtain, and revealed a hidden console. He brought the console into the middle of the room, and we crowded around it.

It looked like he had ripped it from the wall. The metal was damaged, and a long thick wire led from the base across Turso's hut, and disappeared into the opposite wall.

"This was on a workstation. It allows me to see all that is happening outside," Turso said.

The screen showed a 3-D image of the Ark's lower section, slowly rotating.

"It tracks where the water is going and even shows me Kraken," Turso said. "Look! There he is."

A red dot on the screen moved around the display of the lower section of the Ark.

"He's awake," The Captain said.

"So, how are we going to distract him?" I asked.

"As you can see, two seas are rotating around the outer walls of the... Ark. The sub can travel through one of these towards the lowest point. Kraken will want to follow it. He loves the shiny objects and by the time he realises it's unmanned we will have escaped."

"Unmanned?" Gerlinde asked.

"It can be programmed to run on autopilot," the Captain said.

A green dot suddenly appeared on the console screen. It was moving very fast. Faster even than Kraken.

"What is that?" Maiara said.

"I don't know. It looks like it came from the exit shaft," Turso said.

"How can it move that fast?" I asked.

"It must be swimming. There is a big mass of water passing between us and the exit," Turso said. "Whatever it is, it's heading right here!"

29
HELP FROM ABOVE

Outside, we saw whatever it was, a dark shape heading through the water darting around the coral surrounding Turso's home.

The thing burst out of the water fell through the void of air and somersaulted landing on its feet.

It was Two.

She whipped her water-logged hair back and stood up straight. She wore a wet suit and webbed gloves. Strangely, she had no breathing gear or goggles. Could One and Two breathe underwater, or anywhere?

She scanned our faces, then burst into a big smile.

"You are all alive," she said, overjoyed.

"You found us," I said.

"How did you know we were here?" Gerlinde asked.

"One and I were trying to activate consoles down here so we could relay communications through them. When a console switched on a few moments ago, One sent me to find you."

She pulled us together and gave us a hug.

She was less excited to see Turso and the Captain. Two pushed us behind her, and quickly drew a long blade, seemingly from nowhere.

"Whoa, whoa, whoa," I said, grabbing her arm.

"They are friendly," Gerlinde said.

Two accepted this without question and sheathed her blade.

"I am sorry," she said to our hosts. "I am required to protect these children."

Turso placed his palms together.

"I understand.

Two examined his alien appearance

"Who are you?" she asked.

"My name is Iku Turso," Turso replied.

Two examined his alien appearance, again.

"What are you?" she asked.

"He's an alien," Ogwambi said. "Can you believe it? An alien was sucked into the Ark years ago. Before it came to Earth."

"I am the last survivor of my people," Turso added.

"Welcome to our family of Lasts," Two replied.

She focused on the Captain next, inspecting his shabby uniform.

"The *Dallas*?" she asked. "And you've been down here since the Ark landed on Earth?"

The Captain nodded.

"I am so sorry sailor. Do not worry. You are safe now," Two said. "The *Dallas* was fondly remembered. I understand after you were taken into the Ark, there was a ceremony for your ship. A model of the ship was part of the Ark memorial, etched with the names of the crew. Your country mourned your loss and celebrated your sacrifice,"

The Captain teared up a little.

"Thank you."

I smiled.

This is what Two had over One: the ability to make friends quickly and easily. Two seemed to know the right thing to say.

"Now, we need to get you all to the exit and back to the top of the ship," Two said.

"But the water blocks our path," Illarion said.

"Of course we will wait and use the walkways once it is clear."

"Walkways?" I asked.

"The top of the Ark is crisscrossed with handy walkways, we can use them to get to the exit shaft."

"Walkways are great, but did you know there's a giant monster here?" Maiara asked.

"Kraken is still alive?" Two said.

"You did know," Gerlinde said.

Two sighed.

"We thought Kraken had died. The Ark was in human possession for several years, and no one thought a creature like it could survive on the meagre food supply inside this section of the ship. Clearly, we were wrong. I am sorry that we endangered you here."

"Humans, let's go back inside and rest while the water clears," Turso said as he wandered back inside his home.

Two watched Turso go, and then turned to us.

"Are any of you hurt?"

"No, we're okay," we all said, practically in unison.

She hugged us all again, in a big bunch.

"It will all be fine now."

We all wriggled out of her embrace and followed Turso back inside his coral house.

"Time to rest. It's a long walk from here to the exit!"

I lingered outside, hanging on to Maiara's hands, and keeping her with me.

"What is it, Callum?" she asked.

Alone outside the house, I looked her in the eye and gestured the scene around us.

"Here we are in this amazing place, and I want a moment to share it with you, and only you."

We watched the blob of water swell here and there, watching the submarine hover metres away, amongst the massive, beautiful coral.

"This is date number... Umm... I've lost count, but I think, so far, it's one that we'll remember most," I said.

"Yeah," she said. "Age fourtee—"

"What? Here? Now? You want me to tell an embarrassing story now?" I asked.

"I do," she said, taking my hands. "It will make this moment perfect."

She smiled.

I smiled too, though I was exasperated by the timing.

I pulled her closer and thought back. At fourteen, I was mostly in the grip of the government then, being trained for the moment I would join the Ark. There was one story I would rather not tell, but a deal was a deal.

"Let's see... umm... When I was fourteen, before I was taken to the army base, my school had a final celebration. Without water in the school's pipes it had to close down, so the head tried to organise a sort of talent show for everyone before the whole school said goodbye.

"My form teacher decided that her class were all going to do juggling tricks. I don't know why? Maybe she was just super into juggling or something? But when the day came, my class was lined up and we would each do a certain juggling trick. I had to juggle three balls, toss them in the air at the end, and catch them in a top hat."

"A top hat?" Maiara asked.

"Not my idea," I said. "Anyway, I fumbled the whole thing several times. The whole school laughed at me. Eventually I had to leave, and I cried off stage."

"Jeez. Keep it light, Callum," Maiara said.

I mustered a smile.

"I was dealing with a lot at that point. I had only just received this scar," I said, running my finger down the ragged flesh over my eye.

There were actually two scars now: thanks to the Minister whose knife caught me during the battle between the Chinese and American spaceships not long ago. "The bad times are chances to grow stronger."

Maiara reached out and touched the scar.

"I understand," she said.

We nuzzled closer, and sat, our hands linked as we watched the dancing water. We could see fish swimming beyond the bubble of water. A sea turtle broke the surface of the water and came flying out of the blob and across the void, flapping its fins in desperation.

Maiara jumped up and caught it. We looked at it for a moment. Wondering where it thought it was, what it must have felt in this place where nothing is like the world it ever knew?

Maiara set it down on the coral and the turtle dragged itself back to the water where it disappeared again.

"I didn't think I would ever see any life again that wasn't human," she said.

"Me too," I said. "Weird isn't it? When I think about it, I never really saw many animals other than squirrels and foxes. I saw some zoo animals, but that's not the same."

"I've seen wolves in their natural habitat, and sharks off the coast of Texas when we were on holiday," Maiara said.

"Do you think our new home will have animals?"

"Maybe. Unless that world is in its dinosaur phase."

"That would be cool," I replied.

"Are you kidding? You must have seen *Jurassic Park*. It doesn't end well..." Maiara said.

I laughed and then she laughed.

I had another question for her but I hesitated to say it, opening my mouth again and again, but not saying the words.

Maiara seemed to read my mind.

"You're worried about what happens when we get back up top?"

"I have to face the music. Everything that happened was my fault."

She didn't say a word.

"Wow. I was expecting you to comfort me," I said.

"It's not your fault," she conceded. "Not all of it."

I stared off into space, thinking.

"Thanks. I don't think I'll ever make up for it, though," I said.

"What do you mean? You already saved Dehqan. And you saved me," she added.

"If I hadn't then you and Dehqan dying would be on my hands," I said, my voice quavering. "I had a youth leader at my church who told me that no good deed pays for the bad. The good was what you always should have done no matter what."

"Sure, but wallowing in self-pity doesn't help either. You can only learn not to repeat the mistakes of the past. That's what the eighteenth memory was always doing, I think," she said. "I'm worried that without it we won't learn, and that the squabbles that brought us here will just get worse."

"I'm not worried," I said. "This is how we learn. We make mistakes. We fix them. We learn from them."

"Humanity doesn't work like that. We make the same mistakes over and over again."

"That was the *old* humanity. We get to be the *new* one. We don't need the eighteenth. We can get there on our own."

I let my head rest against her braided hair.

"I like our conversations," I said.

"Yeah. Me too," she replied.

We sat there in silence, watching the light dance on the water.

30

THE CAPTAIN'S PLAN

An hour before we were due to leave, the Captain sat us down in Turso's home.

"Here's the plan. We will program the *Dallas* to sail down the sea that's due to wash over this area soon. Kraken will spot it and follow it. If Kraken believes the sub doesn't notice it, then it probably will attack. And the ship is still sturdy enough to keep that beast busy for a while."

"But won't Kraken destroy the *Dallas*?" Illarion asked.

"It doesn't matter if it gets us up top... It doesn't matter," the Captain said

"Won't Kraken come after us once the sub is wrecked?" I said.

"Unfortunately yes. Once the beast knows the sub is empty it will most likely search for us. Hopefully we'll be long gone before then," the Captain explained.

"We better get aboard and start reprogramming," Turso said.

"Yes," the Captain agreed. "Can one of you join us?"

I looked around at the others. None of us seemed eager to go back into the sub. It stank. Plus it was hot and uncomfortable. I realised that I should probably volunteer since it was largely my fault we needed to escape the lower section of the Ark.

"I'll go," I said.

"Perhaps I should go instead," Two said.

"No Two," I rebutted. "I'll volunteer. It should be me."

I regretted my decision immediately. When I stepped back onto the sub, the smell overpowered me. It was a rank and rancid mix of seawater, mildew, and rotting. But I had to show the others that I was remorseful, so I held my nose and worked through it.

The Captain led Turso and me to the bridge, and once there he brought up a computer map of the *Dallas*.

"Okay, Callum, Turso, while you seal off areas of the ship to maintain hull integrity, I will plot the course," the Captain said. "Turso, start with the communications room, seal it and power it down. Callum, you start in the cafeteria."

"The cafeteria? I thought that was already sealed?" I asked.

The Captain twitched.

"Yes," Turso added. "It filled with water long ago."

"Of course," the Captain said. "Instead, go to the crew quarters on deck B and seal them."

"Yes, sir."

The crew Quarters were very depressing. There were knick-knacks, photos, and personal belongings of the former crew. I imagined what it must have been like for them to be pulled into the Ark. The fear they must have felt as they tried to escape, and a beast they had never imagined came to devour them... They didn't even know what they had signed up for when the first battle began.

I whispered a prayer, and then I sealed the crew quarters.

I returned to the bridge just as Turso was exiting.

"I'm off to the officer's mess," Turso said cheerfully.

"Where to next, skipper?" I asked.

"Skipper... The Chief of the Watch used to call me that," the Captain said, a warm smile on his face. "The torpedo bay. Check the torpedoes are all secure and then seal it off."

I was fascinated by the torpedoes. There were dozens of them, all stacked on racks from floor to ceiling like a grocer. I wondered if we could activate them and use them as a mine to kill Kraken. Though, maybe a big explosion shouldn't happen next to the ship's engines?

After sealing the torpedo bay, I returned to the bridge.

"Okay, Callum. It's time to seal off the cafeteria," the Captain said.

I paused. Suddenly I was wondering if the Captain had a terrible memory, or he was losing his mind. He *had* been here for years. He had lost his crew gruesomely. It made sense that he might not be completely with it. I would have to ask Turso, since the alien had known the Captain the longest of all of us.

"The cafeteria is already locked up, Captain," I said.

The Captain looked dismayed, and then stared off into space.

Turso entered the room as the Captain gave my next orders.

"Weapons locker, Callum," he said. "And whatever you do don't touch the guns."

I nodded and left the room, but I stopped just outside the doorway to the bridge and waited.

Turso came sidling out, heading to his next assignment.

"Turso, is the Captain alright?" I asked.

Turso looked confused.

"As alright as anyone in his position could be," Turso replied.

"Does he have problems, you know, forgetting things?"

"For years he's only dreamt of getting out of here," Turso said. "He's probably just thinking about seeing humans again and isn't very focused. I would feel the same way. I wish there were other members of my own race out there."

I nodded. Maybe I would direct the Captain to see One when we got back to the upper section. I left Turso and found the weapons room. There were austere metal lockers filled with rifles and other guns, but I wasn't interested in them. Especially not after the violence I'd seen. I simply sealed the door and left.

I referenced the map of the sub on the wall, so I could find my way back. Here, the map showed a close-up of this section of the *Dallas*, set over the smaller map. The torpedo bay, crew quarters and weapons room were all really close to the cafeteria. Only a few doors away. The communications room and officer's mess, both places the

Captain had Turso check were on the other end of the ship, far from me.

Why had the Captain told me to seal the cafeteria when it already was? Had he sent me to all the adjacent rooms on purpose, hoping that I'd check the cafeteria anyway?

I checked the map again and found the cafeteria door. Now I was curious. I wondered what I would find inside. Would it be dangerous?.

When I yanked open the door, there was no spray of water. There was a new smell. One more powerful than any other on the ship. It was horrible. It made me want to puke. Then I heard a sound I had not heard in a long time.

The buzzing of flies.

I peered into the cafeteria. The room was still intact. There were no holes in the hull at all.

Then I saw. The flies hovered in swarms over several bodies in naval uniforms. The floor was strewn with them. There were more than I cared to count, lined up carefully, rotting, and covered in flies.

It had to be the crew of the ship.

I wanted to throw up as I backed out of the cafeteria. I was overcome with sadness. The crew had died and the Captain had laid his comrades to rest in this room, unable to bury them. No wonder he had locked off this section.

I wondered why he wanted me to see this?

Then I remembered what the Captain had said before. He had told us his crew had been eaten by Kraken. The bodies shouldn't even be here. They should be gone.

Then it hit me. Kraken had never mentioned the crew of the sub. The beast gloated about eating other humans, but only those who came to fix the power conduits, and the soldiers that came to protect the technicians.

Why hadn't the captain contacted Dr. Ghost or his crews when they were working? The radio on the submarine would have worked.

Maybe he didn't want to be rescued? Maybe he wanted to stay on the Ark, realising Dr. Ghost's plan? Was he another stowaway?

178

No. That didn't make sense. Why send me to the cafeteria, to the bodies? The Captain must have wanted me to figure out he was lying. And why would he lie unless he was forced? No one would stay down here unless someone was making them...

Turso.

I had to get back to the bridge and tell Two.

Then a familiar, alien voice spoke behind me, "If you hadn't seen that we could have continued to be friends."

31
TURSO'S PLAN

Turso shoved me into one of the chairs on the *U.S.S. Dallas*'s bridge.

The Captain held a gun at his side. He looked troubled and nervous.

I begged him, with my eyes, to shoot Turso, but he didn't and Turso tied me up with lengths of seaweed.

"You killed the crew of this ship," I said. "The Captain's crew."

Turso nodded, but didn't say anything.

I struggled against the seaweed binding me.

"He killed your crew," I yelled at the Captain. "Why are you helping him?"

Turso sauntered up behind the Captain, and brushed the hat off his head. Underneath, right where the Captain kept itching, was a starfish just like the ones hanging up on Turso's wall. It had dug the ends of its arms into the captain's head.

"This is something from my planet. We tamed the sea creatures of my world to maintain order. This bio technology allows me to tame any creature, and makes them obey me. Thankfully, it works as well on human minds.

"This means the Captain obeys me. He has done so ever since his ship arrived. The crew obeyed too, at first, but over time they proved to have strong minds and they resisted, so they were no longer of use to me. The Captain, though, is weak and always obeys," the alien said.

"Why would you do this to them?" I demanded.

"They came into my domain. They told me of the Ark, their world, and their mission. They showed me that this prison was actually my ticket to a new world all my own."

"We *are* going to a new world," I said. "You can come with us."

"You're going to the wrong world," Turso exclaimed. "I will find a world for my people, and my people alone."

He indicated to his pouch. "In here are a set of eggs that I can use to restart my race. I won't live on a new world with you vile, wretched *things* who might hurt my people."

"But... We can co-exist."

"I've learned your history. Humans can't even cooperate amongst themselves," Turso snarled as he stalked around the bridge. "I will take control of your Two, and then your One. And with their help I'll turn this spaceship toward the planet I have in mind."

"You can't," I said. "Our course is already set. There's not enough power to—"

"Of course I can," Turso replied.

My pulsed raced. I had to convince Turso of the truth.

"The others will tell you the same thi—" I began.

"The others won't know my plan until it's too late. If you think you'll have any chance to rat on me think again," he said. "You'll be going on a suicide mission with your friend, the Captain."

"Suicide mission?"

"This submarine is a diversion, but I was never going to *program* it. The Captain, and now you too, will distract Kraken until it eats you and this ship alive."

"They will find you out! You don't have enough of those starfish to control them all. I saw the two you have in your house."

Turso grabbed the glove of my spacesuit, the material stained with my blood from when I hit my head.

"This place is some of the richest life anywhere in the universe. These are good feeding grounds. If Kraken didn't get you, perhaps a shark did?" Turso snarled. "Your friends will believe me when I give them evidence."

Turso tore off the glove and held it over me. "Especially when I tell them how horrible it was that Callum, the boy hero, tried to save me and died in the process," he mocked.

I lunged at the alien, but the seaweed restraints were too strong.

Turso laughed and then turned to the Captain.

"Take off as soon as I'm clear of this ship. Complete your mission as written."

The Captain nodded, but there was a subtle pain in his eyes

"Turso! Please!" I yelled.

The alien didn't listen. Turso disappeared up the exit hatch of the *Dallas*.

I heard a hatch slam closed, loud and reverberant.

The Captain started up the sub. Its engine roared.

On the monitors, I could see that we were reversing out of the ball of water surrounding Turso's home.

"Captain, don't do this," I yelled. "You have to fight it. You have to help us."

It didn't matter. The Captain just piloted us out, using a giant body of water to cruise far away from the Turso's hovel.

I struggled against the seaweed again. I just wasn't strong enough. Even as I pictured Turso lying to the others, I couldn't muster the force to break them. Then I thought of Maiara. She'd be angry thinking I was dead. She'd demand Turso show her my body. Or was Turso just convincing enough, able to calm her anger and convince me with some story of me being a hero?

I hoped that Two would show up and save me. I waited, counting minutes in my head, but nothing. Two didn't turn up. Two must have believed Turso. This was it. I had run out of luck.

I spent what felt like hours shouting at the Captain, but he ignored me.

He had his back to me most of the time, at least, so I had time to think about how I could get loose from my bonds. I tried to bite at it, but my spacesuit was awkward and inflexible. I thought of anything else. My legs were free. But I couldn't get the leverage to stand, and while occasionally the Captain would come into reach, there was no point kicking him.

With no other options, I dipped into a set of nanite memories I had kept repressed since the day they were injected. I didn't like the person the military memories turned me into, but they were all I had left. My head flooded with strategy, precision, and violence. As I peered around the submarine I saw how everything could aid me in my mission to survive, and what stood in my way.

Kill the Captain, Captain Amis and my military memories ordered.

That thought might solve one problem, but it wouldn't win the day, so I ignored it.

Remove the starfish.

That could work, but the question was how. There was no way to reach the Captain's head from my chair, unless...

I waited for the right moment. The Captain had to be facing the right way. I considered the trajectories, did a little mental geometry. And then he stepped to the left at just the right time.

I kicked with both legs, as hard as I could. My feet struck the Captain square in his back, sending him head-first into a steel support pillar.

The starfish atop his head absorbed most of the impact. It screeched and recoiled, loosing its hold on the Captain's head.

For a second the Captain was dazed. Then he grabbed at the starfish and yanked. The starfish shot out a spine that pierced his hand, but the Captain didn't let go. He pulled the creature free and then smashed it against the pillar until it fell limp.

He fell to his knees, cradling his face in his hands. After a moment, he looked around, confused, as if he had woken from a nightmare. Then he saw me and stood up.

"I'm sorry. I'm okay now. Let me get you free," he said.

As he reached toward me, he noticed his hand. It was turning green, with the deepest colour surrounding the wound the starfish spine gave him.

"Poison," he uttered, shaking his head.

He tore at the seaweed holding me, but it was even hard for him. The Captain was starting to look weak, pale.

"I couldn't fight back I wasn't strong enough," he said through tears, barely forming the words beyond gasping them. "He made me kill my crew... made me serve him... You have to get back to your crew, and save them before it's too late."

As the Captain ripped the last piece of seaweed holding me, he fell to the floor. His head listed to one side, and he slumped over against the control panel.

I had just watched the Captain die. And I didn't have time to mourn him.

I had to get back to the upper section of the Ark, and to do that I to pilot the *Dallas*. I stepped up to a console, but it was all gibberish to me.

Captain Amis, can you help me here? I asked the nanite memory.

I was a soldier, not a midshipman, the memory replied.

Fat lot of good you are.

I reached out and pressed a button at random.

The submarine suddenly jolted to the right.

"That can't be good," I said.

I tried other buttons, and even spun a steering wheel of sorts. The submarine rocked and shook. It was probably flitting all over the place. I mashed at another button. The ship twisted violently, much more violently than it had before.

Metal groaned. Glass smashed. Sparks flew from damaged power conduits. I fell back into the captain's chair, and that's when I saw them.

Claws, huge ones, had speared the sub, digging into the hull from both sides. Water drizzled in around their edges as they rent the submarine in two.

I gripped the arms of the chair and watched helplessly as the *Dallas* broke apart.

The dancing light from outside entered the submarine, as well as the spray of seawater, and as the other half fell away in the darkness,

I came face to face with Kraken.

32

THE NEW BARGAIN

"You again?" Kraken said. "Where is Turso?"

I opened my mouth to tell the beast, but then I realised Turso's location was my only bargaining chip.

I tried to make by best angry face as I braced myself against one of the submarine's consoles, sparks flying all around me.

"Turso betrayed me," I snarled. "He forced me onto this sub to be a distraction while he leads my friends to their doom. We're on the same side. I hate him too."

"What are you talking about?" Kraken said.

"I will tell you where Turso is, but you have to take me with you."

"I will eat you right now if you don't tell me."

"Then you will never catch Turso without me."

"Oh, little human, you've already told me enough. If Turso sent you down here to get my attention, Turso and your friends must trying to get to the exit hatch."

I was caught. I had to think of something.

"You can stay here. I will go devour Turso and your friends and then I'll deal with you," the beast said as he jetted out of sight.

I heard the groaning of support beams as he ascended toward the top of the Ark. I had to warn the Arkonauts. The submarine was wrecked. I needed another way to chase Kraken. There was nothing of use on the bridge. Maybe the ship had diving suits, or life rafts, but how could those get me anywhere?

Hang on. I was still wearing a jet pack. In the low gravity, it could get me up top fast, but no. It was broken, no good.

But Ogwambi was wearing a jet pack too. Hadn't he and the others left their suits in the *Dallas*?

I ran through the ship, dodging cutlery, books and pens that floated through the corridors. When I arrived at the sub's entry hatch, I found Ogwambi's suit with attached jet pack and hurriedly changed out of mine and into his.

Then I looked at the fuel gauge. Empty. I had to think.

There must be a fuel source somewhere, or even a tank of pressurized air. Then it hit me, diving gear. They had to have it on board this submarine.

I checked the map on the submarine's wall. The diving gear storage was in the other half of the sub, the half that was floating away from me after Kraken sheared the ship in two.

I ran to the open end and saw the other half listing a hundred metres below. All I had to do was jump. The problem was, if I didn't get it right, I might be speared by the jagged metal surrounding the opening. But I had to risk it.

I set my feet, took a deep breath, and jumped. I soared through the air, covering the hundred metres, aided by the low gravity, and landed on the severed side of the bridge. I managed to just scrape by jagged edging, but smashed into another console, knocking the wind out of me.

I panted, recovered, and carefully walked to the diving gear room. There were only three tanks, but it was what I needed. I struggled to hook the air tank to the jet pack, my fingers fumbling from the stress. I had to force some connections that weren't designed to be hooked up.

When it was done the jet pack fuel gauge showed fifty percent capacity, but very low pressure. All the thrust I would get would be brief and pretty weak, but it would have to do.

I returned to the jagged hole I had arrived through, and waited as this part of the ship rotated around to face the roof of this section of the Ark.

Once it was pointing in the right direction I leapt towards a support beam.

I needed to conserve the jet pack, so I tried to leap with all my might. And I rose fast, but it wasn't enough to get me to the nearest support beam, so I reluctantly used the thrusters. I used small bursts to save fuel, and soon I was soaring, dodging among the struts and globs of water.

I was on my way.

33
THE ATTACK

As I nearly missed beam after beam, and dodged through other ship wrecks, I had managed to save about twenty percent of the jet pack's fuel.

I was near the exit hatch. Kraken would be close. I needed to be stealthy. But, strangely, there was no sign of the beast.

The base of the exit shaft was lined with a network of walkways and power lines that ran up the interior. The power lines intertwined to form the main strand that led down to the engines. From one walkway an enclosed ladder rose up to the hatch at the base of the engine room. It was going to be a long, tight climb. I really wished Dr. Ghost hadn't destroyed the lifts.

I made my way to the exit, watching for the giant monster, but he was nowhere to be seen. I worried that he had intercepted the others before they could get here.

Then I heard a familiar voice, distant, quiet, but familiar.

"One... One can you hear me?"

It was Two.

There was movement on the walkway just below the ladder.

I climbed toward them, and I heard One's voice.

"I am ready at the exit hatch," One said.

There was a chorus of sighs. The others were okay.

"Is everyone accounted for?" One said.

"All but Callum. He did not make it," Two said quietly.

Everyone was silent for a moment.

"I see. We will discuss it further once you all are safe," One finally replied.

"Be advised, we are also bringing an alien. It has been living here for years. It saved the children, and needs our help escaping the beast. It is still alive."

"Very well," One said.

My blood boiled at the thought of Turso getting into the Ark, and as a hero.

"Okay, Arkonauts. It is time," Two said.

One by one my friends filed up to the ladder and started the long ascension.

I moved closer, still watching for Kraken. I wanted to shout that I was alive, but I couldn't risk Turso retaliating, or letting Kraken know where I was. Then I noticed that one of the walkways opposite me was torn apart.

I crawled to the support pillar directly beneath the shaft.

The others had not noticed me yet, but I could still faintly hear them.

Two said, "One, can you open the hatch up top? Seeing the light of the engine will calm the children."

I looked up expecting to see a blaze of light to guide my way.

"I do not understand," One said. "The hatch is already open."

"I cannot see any light. Are you certain?" Two said.

One was quiet for a moment.

"Something must be blocking the shaft. I cannot see down either."

"Maybe there's a ship stuck up there?" Illarion offered.

I squinted and tried to see what was in the way.

It wasn't a ship.

Four yellow eyes opened, shining like torch beams.

Kraken. The beast opened its mouth, roared, and tore down the shaft towards Two and the Arkonauts on the ladder.

The beast had been hiding there the whole time.

34
SALVATION

"You thought you could trick me, Turso?" Kraken roared. "I will devour you for taking my leg."

"Everyone stop. We must climb down now," Two yelled.

I watched the group halt and begin descending the ladder, then I hid myself, as best as I could, from Kraken's view.

"We will retreat back to Turso's home. Stay together. We will be safe there," Two said as the group stepped down, onto the walkway.

"But it's miles away," Gerlinde protested.

"It is the only choice we have," Two said.

Two was right. Kraken was almost upon them. Two barely shepherded the group away from the shaft entrance when Kraken pounced.

The beast's huge claws swiped at the ladder, throwing sparks into the air. Kraken's momentum was too great. It couldn't stop itself. But it still nearly slashed the others on its way down. Kraken fell into a large glob of water passing beneath the exit shaft and disappeared. There was a thrashing of water, and then the monster came flying back out, its powerful tail driving it up through the water. It was headed, once again, at my friends.

I wanted to scream and shout, but that would only draw Kraken to me.

I watched helplessly as Two gathered the group and tried to protect them.

Kraken crashed into the walkway just ahead of them, completely destroying it. There was now no route back to Turso's hovel and the safety of the coral reef there.

Two put herself upfront to shield the group.

Kraken turned his head and stared down at them, laughing viciously.

"I have you now, Turso," it said. "I will eat you at last and then you humans will set me free or be eaten too."

"We have not arrived at a new planet, Kraken," Two said. "There is nowhere to escape to."

"Liar! If you will not cooperate, I will destroy your only exit from this place," it said, raising a claw to strike the ladder, permanently cutting the others off from the shaft.

Then something came shooting out of the shaft from above. It struck Kraken on his snout and exploded.

The beast tumbled back.

My mind raced. What could have hit him?

The answer arrived quickly. One blasted down from the shaft, stopping in mid-air. He held two guns in his hand, one a grenade launcher and the other a machine gun. The jet pack on his back rumbled as One levitated, holding his aim on the beast as he zipped to the walkway, and tossed the machine gun to Two.

"Get them up the shaft now," One ordered. Then One flew across Kraken's path and fired another grenade at the creature.

Kraken recovered and snapped at One. But One was too fast and the beast's jaws clapped at nothing. It twisted in the air trying to lash at One, but the jet pack was too great an advantage.

All the while, Two hurried the others up the ladder.

One didn't even use the jet pack half the time. His strong legs combined with the low gravity allowed him to dart from support beam to support beam, dodging Kraken's bites. Each shot from the grenade launcher knocked the monster for a loop, dizzying it. And One's aim was precise as a sniper's.

Kraken roared with rage, and it echoed all around us. It flailed wildly, never hitting One, and it was clear that the beast was tiring.

There were sparks and smoke everywhere and it was clear the monster lost sight of One.

And so did I. One had disappeared. Or at least seemed to.

The beast looked everywhere for him. "Show yourself!" he bellowed.

One did. He came hurtling out of a smoky cloud and landed right next to Kraken's face, his gun pointed right at the monster's eye.

"If I fire you will die," One said. "The explosion will go through your eye and into your brain."

Kraken didn't reply. It's eyes dilated trying to focus on One, who was so close. Kraken raised a paw above One, out of sight of my captain.

"Do not attempt it," Two yelled, from the base of the shaft.

Kraken grumbled. It knew it couldn't hit One before One fired.

"Did Dr. Ghost tell you about me?" One said to Kraken.

"He did. I did not believe any human could be so strong."

"Understand this," One said. "On this ship, I am the only predator."

One knelt down and secured a beeping device next to Kraken's eye.

"This is a bomb. I am going to join my friends and we are leaving. If you try to stop me, I detonate it, and you will lose a significant portion of your face. If you try to scratch it off, it will detonate. Once my friends and I are a safe distance away I will disarm it and you can be on your way."

"How do I know you won't detonate it anyway?" Kraken said.

"You will have to trust me. My father made a deal with you, and so far you have not eaten or hurt another member of my crew, despite yourself. That deal still stands. When the bomb stops chirping it will be safe for you to remove."

Kraken growled weakly.

One leapt away from the lizard and sped toward the exit.

After a few moments, the beeping bomb on Kraken's snout fell silent.

The beast scratched it free, and howled in rage, thrashing about like a temperamental child. Then Kraken seemed to remember something. The beast moved quickly, deliberately...

...in my direction, or what he thought was my direction, back into the depths toward the submarine.

This was my moment. I couldn't wait any longer. If I made it to the hatch and the others had already moved on, there was no chance I could get back to safety. I would be stuck here.

I heard Kraken clattering in the distance. It must be miles below already. I moved as quickly as I could, with every bit of my strength, up the beams toward the ladder. If I keep moving it will never catch me. The end of the shaft was closer than I thought and I had to brace myself to stop myself from crashing into it. Unfortunately, while I didn't hit the metal, my jet pack did, and a loud clang echoed.

The thunderous roar that rumbled up to me was deafening. I looked down and there was Kraken. The beast was charging towards me with speed and a manic look in all four eyes.

"At least I get you as a consolation," it growled.

I grabbed the thruster controls on my pack and gave them all they were worth. I shot up the shaft. There was a pin prick of light where the hatch was still open. Then it disappeared. The others must have just closed it.

"Come on," I muttered.

I had to get there before they exited the base of the engine room and wouldn't be able to hear me knock.

Kraken's claws scraped along the walls of the exit shaft as he chased me. The beast was catching up.

I pressed the jet pack control buttons harder, hoping it would mean more thrust. Warning lights flashed on the pack. It was almost out of fuel again. I reluctantly released the button, knowing that I needed some fuel left over to slow me down so I wouldn't splatter on the closed doors.

Kraken was closing the gap.

I swear I could feel the wind of its breath.

The shaft began to taper down. Maybe it would be too thin for Kraken. If I made it up far enough in time.

The beast's jaws snapped beneath me. Its legs crowded against its body as the tube grew narrower.

Finally the monster growled, and stopped.

And I kept going.

Kraken was stuck beneath me

I laughed to myself, but my heart was racing too fast to really enjoy the moment.

As I saw the roof fast approaching, I toggled the jet pack and slowed myself down. Then I reached out with a hand and grasped the cage around the ladder. I forced my body through a gap in the lattice, quickly dropped the jet pack, and then hauled myself onto the ladder. In the low gravity the climb was surprisingly easy.

After climbing a bit, I peered down at Kraken. It was still shimmying its way back out of the narrow tube.

"Bye, Kraken," I said.

It roared its hatred at me.

I continued up the ladder to the hatch, and knocked on its underside, hoping someone was still there to answer.

35
THE CONTROL

I wasn't sure how thick the hatch was, or if anyone could even hear me.

"Did anyone else hear that?" Gerlinde's muffled voice said.

"I think it came from the hatch," Ogwambi said.

"It must be Kraken. Ignore it," Turso interjected.

"The shaft becomes too narrow at the top for the creature," One said.

"It's me! It's Callum!" I yelled.

"Callum!?" Maiara shouted, surprised and joyous.

Suddenly the hatch clunked and opened. The multi-coloured light of the engine showered down on me from above. Then as my eyes adjusted, I saw One there, his arm extended toward me.

I grabbed on, and One lifted me into the engine room as if I was weightless.

Before I even got my bearings, Maiara grabbed me and hugged me.

I hugged her back. For a moment, everyone was crowded around me, happy, and then they turned to Turso.

"You said Callum was dead," Two said.

Turso took a step back. He was reaching for something in his pack.

Then I remembered the mind control devices. Turso still had some. My mouth went to frame the words, *take him down*, but I was too late.

Turso had already retrieved the starfish and had thrown them at One and Two.

Luckily, One and Two were smarter and quicker. Their hands shot up, and they caught the armed creatures out of mid-air.

"You have to smash them," I said. "But watch out for the spines they are poisonous."

The starfish slithered through their fingers, crawled up their arms, and made way for their heads. One and Two snatched at the starfish on the other, but the starfish had time to defend themselves.

Spines shot into One's hand and he winced and dropped the creature. The same happened to Two. They should be poisoned just like the Captain, but maybe the nanites in their systems isolated the poison because neither of them looked ill.

Unfortunately, the creatures continued toward the tops of One's and Two's heads. The starfish on One's head clamped down, and suddenly his eyes turned cloudy and white.

But when the starfish on Two's head clamped down she screamed. Smoke or steam or something rose from the starfish's arms, until it suddenly shuddered, withered, and fell off.

Turso yelped in surprise at Two's reaction.

Then I heard Captain Amis yell a battle cry, my mind went blank, and I lunged at the alien.

"Protect me," Turso commanded.

One slithered over and kicked me in the side.

I collapsed onto the floor, totally winded.

Two staggered back, holding her face. The spot on her head where the starfish had tried to attach was scorched.

"How did yo—" Turso sneered.

"I am not built like One," Two said, composing herself.

"Then you're of no use to me. One, kill her," Turso said.

One lunged for Two's machine gun. They struggled, but One took it and aimed it at Two. Two threw a kick at the gun barrel just as One pulled the trigger, and the shot went high. Then One turned to fire again, and Two flung herself between us and One. She knocked the other Arkonauts to the side and out of the way, leaving a clear path between One and me.

I don't why, but I went for One. I wanted to grab the gun from him.

Turso turned his focus on me. And as if telepathically ordered, One turned at me and fired.

I saw the gun on me. I heard the boom of the gunpowder. My legs had turned to jelly at the thought of being shot. It was over. One was a crack shot. I waited for the pain.

Instead, someone knocked me to the floor.

The only pain I felt was my hip smashing on the engine room floor. In my confusion I saw the other Arkonauts were everywhere, running to hide behind pieces of the engine to avoid the gunfire.

Who had saved me?

Then I looked up. Maiara was standing where I had been.

I cried out. I didn't even form words. I was overwhelmed. I just knew. I knew what had happened. I was paralyzed and devastated.

There was smoke everywhere. The air had a horrid stink of cordite. We all looked at Maiara. Strangely, she seemed fine. She didn't look hurt. I didn't see any blood. I just saw her beautiful face.

She was looking down at me in shock and horror.

One had stopped. He dropped the gun, and it clattered as it hit the floor. His hands were shaking. Maybe he had momentarily overcome the starfish's power.

"Maiara, are you oka—" I said

I tried to get up, to stand, so I could get to her. I had to make sure she was alright.

A pain shot through my chest. I couldn't bear the thought of her dying.

"No, Callum. Please do not move," Two said.

Maiara was looking at me in total shock. So was Two. And the others. But they weren't looking at me, so much as my chest.

The pain I felt hadn't subsided. It was strange. I looked down. Blood was seeping into my clothes from a bullet hole next to my heart.

36
THE LOSS

"It's alright Callum. You'll be okay."

Maiara practically threw herself down to the floor to cradle me. Two knelt down beside her and tore at my spacesuit trying to get to the injury.

I curled into Maiara's arms. She was so warm and soft. I don't know if I'd ever felt so comfortable before. Out of the corner of my eye I saw the bullet wound fountain blood.

I could taste it in my mouth, too. Metallic. Coppery.

I started thinking about odd things.

I could see Turso and One disappearing from view, taking a lift upwards, but all I could think about was Jack, my little brother. For a moment I thought I saw him. He wanted to tag along. He was waving for me. Why wouldn't he come closer?

Two was pressing on my chest. Her hands felt cold. Everything felt cold.

I saw Earth, my parents, the base. I saw the soldiers, Dr. Ghost, the Destroyer. I saw...

Maiara held me closer. Was I going numb?

Captain Amis boomed in my mind. "I'm sorry, soldier. You're not going to mak—"

My eyelids were heavy. I'd never felt so tired.

"Twelve," Maiara stammered.

"What?" I said.

"Tell me about you, age twelve," she said. "Don't close your eyes. Keep talking, Callum. Please keep talking."

I looked up at her. She was almost a blur.

"I can't Maiara. I don't remember. I don't know," I said.

"We made a deal!" she said. "Tell me a story about you, age twelve!"

Two ran over to the lift and tried to call it back down, but it was committed to its ascent with Turso and One on board.

"I... I don't know. I was bullied a lot. Once they stole my PE Kit and the teacher forced me to do it in vest and pants," I said. "I was so sweaty and uncomfortable the whole time, but I did it."

There were tears in her eyes, but Maiara chuckled at that.

I chuckled too. The laughing hurt.

"I'm sorry you had to go through that," she said.

"Don't worry. It made me stronger," I replied. "I was so frustrated that I never took any bullying from them again. Bad times... Maiara. The bad times are chances to grow stronger."

I heard Captain Amis whisper to me again.

I was out of time. I could feel it, too. I silently recited a prayer.. Everything was all going to be fine. Everything started to feel warm. And I felt almost completely relaxed.

I looked up once more at Maiara.

She was crying, her face screwed up in sadness. I never wanted to make her feel this way. And there was no way I could fix it. I just needed to tell her something. Something that would let her know it would all be okay. Something to remind her that she's stronger than this... than me.

I reached up, and gently pulled her face down toward mine.

I kissed her once on the cheek, and I stroked her hair.

"Don't let them drift apart," I said. "Get these kids to a new home. Make it the best one anyone could dream up. Tell them all, tell Dequan, I'm sorry."

Maiara shook her head. She just kept saying "no" as tears streamed down.

"Stay strong," I said. "They need you."

She squeezed me close to her, kissing me on the forehead.

I looked up at her again. "I love you. I do. I really do."

I heard her say, "I love you" but her voice was muffled.

Everything seemed to wash away in an instant. Then there we were, Maiara and me in the engine room, the great machine giving off its shower of luminous colourful sparks. We were holding hands. She was smiling. I was nervous and wondering if now was the time to kiss her.

"It's the most beautiful view on the ship," I whispered.

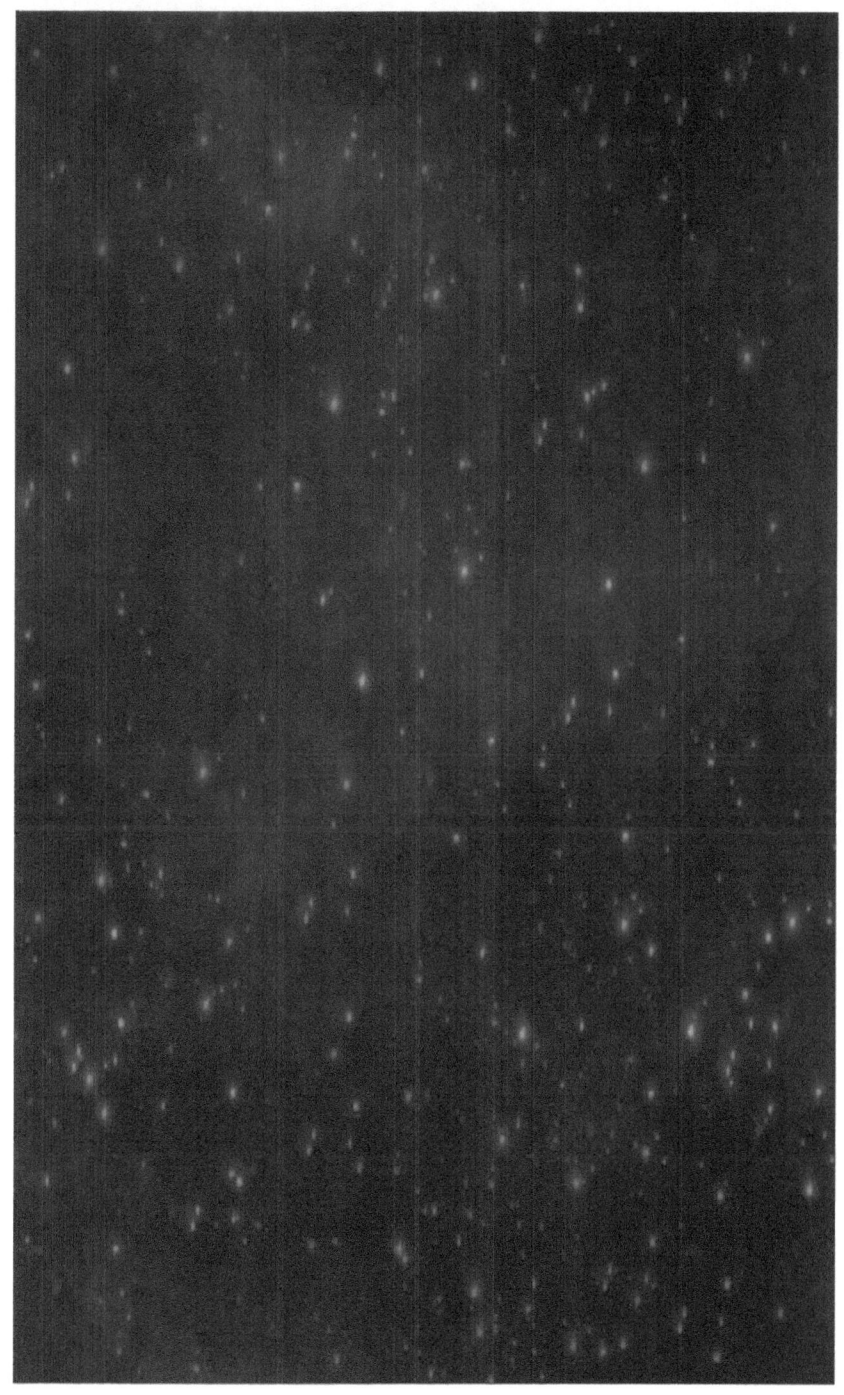

203

1

PAIN BEYOND PAIN

I went blank for a moment, like someone had slung me in and out of a coma.

Two put her hand on my shoulder and squeezed.

"I am sorry, Maiara," she whispered.

For a moment I forgot that I was holding Callum. My mind drifted to Nuan. This was how she had died too—a bullet in the chest, gasping for one final breath, and gone with thoughts of the crew on her lips.

The ringing silence in my ears turned to crying and moaning behind me, as the other Arkonauts broke down. We had lost another of us, senselessly, and right after we thought we were finally back to safety. And this... after the rush of hope, seeing Callum alive again, after thinking he was dead. I was shattered. I lost him when Turso said he was killed by Kraken in the submarine. I had listlessly marched to the exit, overwhelmed with sadness. It had been the second time in one day I thought he had died and was gone for good.

And then we heard a knock. And suddenly, the boy who had filled the hole in my heart left by lost family, was back. Returned from the dead. I actually thought we were going to live happily ever after. I though that everything was going to be okay, no matter what.

But I was wrong.

There were no happy endings.

Mine lay dead in my arms.

Gone, with so much potential left.

Callum had been amazing. He had revived One. He was always the first to stand up... to volunteer. He could be a man and see the error of his ways, even though he was still a boy. He had even crossed time to save us.

And he was now dead.

All because I wasn't quick enough.

Guilt wasn't going to get me anywhere. It wouldn't bring Callum back. I knew exactly who was really responsible. And I knew that I needed to make them pay.

As if he could read my thoughts, the one thing I hated most in the universe started speaking over the Ark's intercom.

"Humans on board the Ark, if you don't know of me I am Iku Turso. Your captain... Your One... is at my command and so your ship is at my command. You will all gather in the... theatre immediately. This will give me the opportunity to convey what is happening. Don't worry, you will all be allowed to live. We will just be changing course to a system you call Alpha Centauri. I will explain further. Oh, yes, and the gathering is mandatory. Anyone who does not go to the theatre will be killed. Thank you."

The speaker system clicked off.

"We cannot allow Turso to change our course. We will not have enough power to change back and continue to the wormhole," Two stated.

"Why does it want to go to Alpha Centauri?" Illarion asked.

"Turso's motives do not matter," Two said. "We just need to stop it before it's too late," Two said.

"But won't he kill us?" Ogwambi asked.

"We could not reach Alpha Centauri without lowering the Ark's power requirements. The easiest way to do so would be to limit life support services. I believe Turso intends to kill us all regardless of our cooperation," Two said.

"So he murders Callum and now he's going to murder us. I'm going after him!" I said.

"Maiara, he still has One under his control," Two said. "You cannot fight him alone."

I didn't listen to her. I didn't want to. There was rage drowning out everything and I wanted it. I wanted that alien scumbag dead. I sprinted up the path, my hard, angry stomps clanging on the gangplanks surrounding the engine. I pushed by the other Arkonauts in my path, rushing to the long stairwell leading past engine control and up into the passenger section of the ship. My legs burned, but I didn't slow down. Each footstep was me crushing Turso's skull, and each one brought me closer to the hateful thing that took Callum from me.

I had no sense of time. It was dozens of flights of stairs, but they went by in no time. Suddenly I was at the door to the cargo bay.

The door hissed and groaned as it opened. I trudged inside, and found what I came for on a shelf near the entrance.

Beside a motorbike, now worthless without its battery, guns and radios, were several military issue bionic backpacks. The Colonel and his crew had worn them when they invaded the Ark. The packs had given them speed and strength, as well as preventing muscle atrophy from the months in zero gravity. The bionic mechanisms would give me the strength and speed to have a chance against One and Turso, and since I hadn't been in zero gravity for months, it would be even more effective.

And all I wanted right now was to cause Turso pain.

Two clambered into the cargo bay, looking surprised at my speed.

"Maiara," Two said. "Please stay here. Do not endanger yourself. Even with this suit you will not be strong enough. I will go after Turso."

"No, Two. I'm doing this," I said.

"It is my duty to protect you. I cannot allow it."

Two reached out toward me and I slapped her hand away.

"This is all my fault! I should have been quick enough to save him!"

Tears welled in my eyes.

"Maiara—"

"No! He was sorry! He was in pain! He was going to face his mistakes and grow up and now he will never get the chance. Turso has to pay, and I'm going to make that slimy fish wish it'd never existed. Even if I die in the process, I will get revenge on Turso for taking it all away from me."

"Taking what away from you?" Two said.

"I meant to say 'taking it all away from him'," I said. "For not giving Callum the chance to say—"

"Maiara, you are not in the proper mind set to—"

As I slipped into the backpack and locked its braces around my arms and legs I threw up one finger and placed it before my lips, cutting Two off as she spoke.

"We're doing this my way, Two," I said.

I powered up the bionic pack and strolled out of the cargo bay, feeling stronger than I ever had before.

2
THE SHOW

The theatre was packed when Two and I arrived.

Turso and One were already on the stage. One looked glassy-eyed and vacant. He held in his hands two knives made of sharpened coral. Turso didn't know about the weapons in the cargo bay, so he had furnished One with the ones he had.

Not one Arkonaut would sit down. All of us stood at the back of the theatre, keeping our distance. Lots of kids were shaking, terrified. Others were glaring at Turso, muttering insults under their breaths.

"Thank you for joining me," Turso began. "Now that we're all assembled, I'd like to explain what is going to happen. But first, a little background.

"I was brought on board this ship against my will many years ago. For a very long time I have been stuck down below, in the lower recesses of this amazing machine. I stayed there, helpless when my own home was destroyed. And then had to watch as this ship attacked planet after planet, capturing more and more creatures before eradicating their worlds.

"I tried, in vain, to gain access to this top section of the ship countless times, so that I could take control, and take this ship to a new planet. Every time I was foiled, but then, I happened to meet a group of your friends who made my egress possible once and for all.

"Now I have control of this ship, and it will take me to where I need to go. We're heading for a planet not far from here. The Ark passed it on its way to Earth, and it's perfectly suitable to start my race anew. You see, I only want to take you on a brief detour, nothing more. Once I have disembarked on my new planet, you can all be on your way."

Turso smiled. "I think it's a rather fair proposition."

All around the theatre, Arkonauts started to chatter. They seemed at ease, and not at all bothered by making a stop for Turso, especially given that he might kill us if we didn't.

Turso's smarmy speechmaking made my skin crawl.

"We don't have enough fuel for that," I yelled.

"Maiara is correct," Two added. "This ship will never have the power to do that. We will be stranded on this new world of yours."

Turso's smile faltered.

"I am not lying," he said.

"Why would Maiara lie? Why would Two?" someone yelled from the crowd.

Suddenly, the Arkonauts were all yelling at Turso, questioning him, demanding answers.

"Enough," the alien commanded.

And One took an aggressive stance with his daggers.

"Arkonauts, please exit the theatre immediately," Two said.

The other Arkonauts rushed into the corridor, as Two stepped up to the stage.

"I will not let you harm this crew," she said, drawing a blade of her own.

"You forget I have your captain."

Turso glanced at One.

One stepped up to Two.

While I snaked through the crowd, trying to stay low and out of view, I wondered how long Two would be able to hold One off. They were pretty evenly matched, but One probably was stronger. After all, he was built for fighting.

One lunged at Two, spearing at her with his coral daggers, then swiping them in a powerful X-shape across her body.

Two was quick. She dodged the stab with a sideward turn, then hopped back and slipped away from the slices. Even though One was wide open, Two had a clean shot at his back, she didn't attack. That was her weakness. She would not kill One.

One, under the influence of Turso, would kill anyone.

I dialled the bionic backpack up to full power and charged. I felt like I had simultaneously drank coffee, energy drink and had a shot of adrenaline at the same time. I was unstoppable, and a little out of control. I sprinted down the side aisle, leapt over rows of seats, and bounded toward Turso.

The alien saw me coming. Turso glanced at One and Two, and must have realised that One couldn't protect him from me without giving Two an opportunity to attack. Turso took a defensive stance, ready to fight me.

As Turso's face grew closer I could only imagine beating it to a bloody pulp, assuming aliens like it had blood. I wanted nothing more than to end its existence. And I could feel my bionic arms and legs surge with strength at the prospect.

Turso ducked my first punch and tried to respond with another of his coral knives.

I parried the blade, deflecting it with the carbon-cased metal bar powering my right arm.

Off balance, Turso was overextended.

I had a clean look at his face, and I punched it. But my strike was off. I hit Turso in the neck.

The alien winced, and made a lazy swipe of the knife across my belly.

I hopped back, dodging the blade, and then threw a roundhouse that caught Turso's arm and cracked it against the alien's chest.

"You're quite skilled, girl," the alien sneered.

"You're trash," I said.

The alien launched at my face, but I all I had to do was step back. Then a second slice caught the wiring on my bionic suit's left arm, cutting its power. Luckily, though, the blade was jammed in the elbow joint.

As Turso struggled to pull the weapon back, I spun around, smashing my right elbow into the alien's face.

Turso cried out, and fell back. The knife fell to the floor, bounced and skittered away under a seat.

The alien cowered on the floor.

That's when I heard voices behind me. There were other Arkonauts behind me, ready to join in. They swarmed Turso.

"Help me," the alien screamed.

Immediately, One turned away from Two and ran at all of us to help his master.

Illarion, Dehqan, Pilar and Ogwambi, all pinning Turso, looked up at the approaching, powerful One and started to back away.

It was going to be me and One, one-on-one. I steeled myself for the attack, trying to watch his every hand movement to be sure I'd see each strike coming.

"One," I said. "We don't have to fight. Fight the mind control!"

Two then leapt on his back, and grabbed the starfish on his head.

The starfish shot a spine through her hand. Two cried out.

Callum had said it was poison. I just hoped that Two could resist a second dose.

One flung Two off of him. She slid against the back of the stage and grunted.

There was nothing between One and me, now.

The other Arkonauts started to scatter, but One was too fast.

"Kill your crew," Turso said. "Kill them all."

One lunged toward us wildly. He snaked toward Ogwambi and raised his blades to attack.

Ogwambi raised his arms in front of his face, just trying to defend himself.

As One's strike came down, I burst forward, jumping with bionic power, and shoulder barged One, knocking him aside.

Then I knocked into One again.

And again.

And then I was on top of him, trying to hold him down with all my strength, and hoping Two would sort him out.

One started to get up.

I wasn't going to be able to hold him for long.

"Everyone! Quickly," Ogwambi called.

He and other Arkonauts piled on One, pinning his arms and legs, tangling him.

"Get up," Turso screamed.

But Two had made her way to One's side. She grasped the starfish once more, and another spine pierced her flesh again. Now she had a triple dose of the poison, but it did not seem to bother her.

Two tore the starfish from One's head, taking some of his skin with it and leaving a bloodied raw wound behind.

One slumped. His eyes cleared. He looked at us with recognition. He was free. Then he seemed to remember what he had done. One looked at his hands, shaking, seeing the blood on them that left no physical stain. He breathed fast, and then stared down at the floor, rocking, and repeating Callum's name.

I wanted to stick by One's side, to console him, but there wasn't time. Turso needed to be dealt with. I turned back to Turso, but the alien was running away.

Turso had picked up his knife, and as he ran around the interior of the theatre he swiped it at any Arkonaut who came near. Then the alien ran for the exit.

I tried to push through the mass of Arkonauts still crowded at the back of the theatre.

"Maiara," Two called, over the din.

I ignored her and pushed on. I had to catch Turso. The alien wasn't going to get away again.

"Maiara," Two shouted again.

3
THE PIT

I caught up to Iku Turso at the bottom of the engine room. The crystalline remnants of engine problems from earlier were still coating parts of the room, refracting brilliant colours.

My eyes were fixed on the alien, trying to operate the hatch leading back to the base of the Ark. If it made it there, then Turso would be free. There was no way I could pursue the alien, and if I did, he would have the advantage.

Turso didn't have a chance, though. The alien always used others to accomplish its goals. On its own, Turso was worthless. A snivelling rat.

It must have been the whining of the gears on my suit that gave me away, because Turso rounded on me when I stepped off the last step to the ground floor.

The alien snarled and came at me with the knife. But the blow was slow and laboured. Turso was too tired from running.

I kicked the blade from its hand, and the alien backed away.

"Maiara," Turso said, spreading his arms as if greeting an old friend. "I'm sorry. I'm so sorry for what I've done. It was all for my people. I'm the last, but I can rebuild my race. Can't you understand how important that would be?"

"I understand," I said.

I walked over to the hatch, and operated the controls, opening it. The large circular door clicked loose, revealing the long descent into the base of the Ark.

I stood at the edge, holding the hatch open, and looked down. The tube was illuminated by the warm yellow glow of the engine, and its shining master cables. I could even see the blobs of water floating and flowing around, and the shadows of the sea life within them.

Iku Turso's eyes were darting between me and the open hatch.

I then let the hatch open all the way, and it dropped to the floor with a clang that reverberated down the shaft below.

"Get out of here," I said, pointing to the exit.

The alien flashed a smile, and then stepped forward carefully.

"Thank you! Oh, thank you, Maiara!" it said. "I am sorry for what I did. This ship is yours and I was wrong to try to take it. Oh, being alone down there can make even the wisest creatures a bit batty, you know. Thank you, Maiara. You are very smart and very kind."

I gritted my teeth as the alien approached the open door. It was loud enough to hear.

"We'll forget all about my foolishness," Turso said. "I'll just wait down here to die. That's for the best, isn't it?"

I had had enough. This slimy monster wasn't going to guilt trip me, not after he had taken Callum from me, not after he had hurt One and Two.

I punched Turso in the face with my bionic right arm.

The alien rocked back.

Then I punched at Turso's stomach. Then I threw another blow to the head. Before the alien could fall to the floor I grabbed it around the throat and dangled it over the open hatch.

Turso chuckled, confidently, through broken teeth.

"I see. Good. You just wanted to punish me a little before letting me go. It makes sense, of course. I understand," he said. "And I forgive you."

"You forgive me?"

Rage overtook me. My vision went white. I could only see flashes of Callum dying in my arms, of Callum waiting in my doorway for our date, of Callum flying off to save Dehqan, of Callum leaning in to kiss me under the sparkling light of the engines.

"I won't be forgiven by the likes of you," I said. "You're a disgusting, heartless weasel and you deserve far worse than you'll ever get."

A part of my mind, my better part, was crying out for me to stop what I was doing. It knew my secret intentions, the desires I tried to hide even from myself.

Turso nodded and smiled.

"You're right. And I am grateful for your pity."

"It is pity. But that's not all. You deserve punishment. The only kind a murderer like you will understand."

Turso looked suddenly confused.

"What are you do—"

Beneath us there was a cacophonous roar.

We both looked down.

A giant mass had taken up position at the base of the exit shaft and four yellow eyes were peering hungrily up at us.

"Kraken?" Turso said.

"Yeah, you'll be better as a snack than you ever were as a scheming murderer," I said.

"Wait! You can't do this. You'll be killing a whole race of people. All of our history and achievements will be wiped out. It will be like we never existed."

The alien tried to struggle, but he was too weak compared to my bionic arm.

All I had to do was let go. That's all it would take. Turso would fall down into the open mouth of Kraken.

My revenge would be complete.

But it wouldn't be justice, would it? Would Callum do this? Would revenge be enough? Did I want to be a killer, even a killer of an evil creature?

I couldn't do it. I hoped that Turso would say something nasty or something that would prove to me that he didn't deserve to live. That's all the excuse I would need. Maybe he would pull another knife from his belt, just like in the movies, forcing me to drop him.

I could always just say that happened anyway, couldn't I?

I cringed at that thought. I was justifying what I felt was an evil act, planning to lie.

He killed Callum. He orchestrated our deaths. If not for me there would be hundreds of dead kids on his hands...

On mine.

No one would ever know. How could they?

But I would always know it was a lie.

I wanted One to swoop in and take Turso away.

Where was Two? Shouldn't she be here convincing me not to do it?

Wasn't someone supposed to show up, talk me down, and find a better punishment for Turso?

Why was all of this happening to me?

Callum would know what to do, wouldn't he?

I just wanted Callum back.

Callum...

4
THE CHOICE

I started to cry.

It was all always about Callum.

A stab of pain ran through me. A realisation I hadn't thought of before. Or maybe I had thought of it, but just supressed it, I didn't know any more, there was just so much pain behind my eyes.

All this time I had been thinking about how Turso had hurt him. I wanted revenge because he had drawn his blood, made him cry out in pain. But now I realised and accepted a worse pain.

He was really dead and not coming back. Everything about him was gone forever.

I looked Iku Turso in the eyes.

As I held the alien by its neck above its potential demise, I realised that this wouldn't bring Callum back. Nothing would. He was really gone... dead. Everything about him was gone forever.

My stomach twisted and churned. My hands shook. Tears streamed down my face, clouding my vision.

Through the watery veil, I looked at Iku Turso.

The alien quivered and cowered.

"Girl, you are reconsidering," Turso said. "Good. Yes. Don't become a bad girl. Good girls don't kill, do they?"

If I let Turso live, the alien would hatch a new scheme. We'd never be safe. Who would be the next to die? Would it be me? Did it matter? Did any more lives need to be risked?

I could end it.

"You'll do it all again," I said. "I can't let you…"

My grip loosened.

"Now, now," Turso pleaded. "Let's not be hast—"

I released my grip.

Turso screamed during the fall. Perhaps it was a curse in his native tongue, but it no longer mattered. They were all just meaningless concerns.

I enjoyed watching the alien fall. And realizing that I did momentarily turned my stomach.

Kraken smiled and sort of barked in joy and moved up the shaft his arms pounding against the walls as he propelled himself upwards.

I heard Iku Turso gasp in panic, heard his cries of fear. He tumbled over and over, and as he fell every few seconds he saw the thing coming to kill him get closer and closer, knowing that at any moment those jaws would close over him.

Kraken roared in triumph as his jaws slammed shut and in one gulp he swallowed his prey whole. Kraken licked its lips and looked up at me, as if we were kindred spirits. Then he turned and headed back down into his domain.

I felt satisfied, for a moment. Then a horror overtook me, thoughts of the alien being swallowed, of screaming all the way down the gullet of Kraken. The pain it must have felt. Not unlike the pain Callum felt. I had extinguished a whole people.

I collapsed to the floor and wept. I wept for what seemed like hours, but it was nowhere near that long. It felt good to cry. It gave me more relief than I expected.

I snapped back to reality when the hatch groaned shut.

Beside me, Two had resealed the portal to the lower Ark. Her wounds had already healed some, but there was a kind of smoke rising from the scar on her head, and the punctures to her hands. It must be a side effect of her healing nanites. She knelt down and sighed.

"I'm sorry Maiara," she said.

I stared at my feet.

"What do you have to be sorry about?" I asked.

"That One and I let you all down today. And that you suffered incredibly for it."

"It's not your fault," I said, choking on my words. "I'm the one who became a killer today."

Two reached for my shoulder, and I smacked her hand away.

"It's over, Two. It's all over now, so drop it!" I yelled.

"There is no need to be angry," she replied in a calm voice.

"What do you know about it?" I said. "You didn't just kill the last survivor of a whole race! You didn't lose your boyfriend!

"I'm just like the men who killed Mathieu, the minister who shot Nuan, like Turso who killed Callum! I didn't have to, but I wanted to... I'm sorry."

"You're not like them," she said calmly.

"How would you know?"

"Did they feel shame or guilt after they killed?" she said.

I paused and thought.

"No. I guess not," I whispered.

"Did they ask for forgiveness?" she asked.

I shook my head.

"Did they cry over what they had done?"

"No."

"Then you are not like them," Two said. "Yes. You killed Turso, but you have been through things you should never have had to experience. Not at sixteen years old. And when the deed was done you didn't feel satisfied by it. You didn't boast about it or hide it. You cried and you confessed."

I buried my head in my hands and sniffed again.

"You're a good person, Maiara. Someone you love was taken from you and you were angry and you reacted, but you'll learn from this."

"Will I?" I said.

"Yes. And now you have to get up and move on. You'll never get forgiveness from Turso or his people. And this won't bring Callum back. But you will survive this. You will continue to live, but you must forgive yourself."

"I don't know how," I said.

"You will know how with time. Right now, you aren't ready to let go of your pain. It's natural to self-blame, but it cannot define you. I know you don't want to let it go. You don't want to give it up because you want to own it, even though you can't handle it. Give up the pain, Maiara. Listen to me closely: You are not a monster. Nor are you perfect. You are simply human," Two said.

I stared off into space, through tear-filled eyes. The engine room was a blur. Two was right. There was a small part of me that wanted to give up my shame and guilt. But Turso falling, the clamping down of those jaws, the alien's screams all echoed in my memory. Maybe that was for the best. Maybe by never forgetting what I'd done I would always remember the person I'd never want to become again. Even that realization was too much. I would need time to forgive myself, time to process.

When I looked up, Two was smiling at me. At least she believed in me, even if I didn't.

"Now, I need to get to the medical bay and manage my wounds," she said. "Will you accompany me?"

In my daze, I hadn't noticed, but the smoke coming from Two's wounds was pluming and overwhelming.

"Oh jeez. I'm sorry! We need to get you some bandages," I said.

"I need more than that," she said. "But I'll be fine."

She stood first, and then helped me up.

"Come along, Maiara. The rest of the crew are all waiting and they are all worried about you."

"They are?" I asked in disbelief.

"They know what you've been through. And they saw you fight Turso and free One."

We ascended the engine room. At the top, I felt overwhelmed. I didn't want to see the others like this. I needed to do something to finish Callum's business first.

"Two, I need a few moments," I said. "After you get to the med bay, can you please call everyone, into the theatre? There's something I need to do."

"What's that?"

"Please. It'll make sense. I promise," I said.

"Okay. I will," she said. "We'll gather everyone in a couple hours."

"Oh! Can you also do one more thing?" I asked.

5
THE EIGHTEENTH

The Arkonauts gathered in the theatre were talking when I arrived. Their conversations ranged from joking about not wanting another meeting like Turso's to wondering what was going on with me.

I waited in the corridor, terrified to face the crowd even though I had called the meeting.

I was afraid that I would breakdown. That I would be embarrassed, ashamed, and probably led out of the room by One or Two to be comforted.

Still, I tried to fight it, to be strong. For Callum. At the thought of him I was near sobbing. For so long it felt like we were in a movie, a fairy tale, and we were the princess and the prince. But instead of living happily ever after, my prince was dead. And somehow the fairy tale hadn't ended right there. I had to go on.

I didn't need a prince either. I don't need a boy to define or sustain me. But Callum brought love back into my life, and now there was a huge hole in my soul that hungered and starved at his absence.

Growing up was hard. Growing up as the last American girl in the universe was harder.

I waited outside the entrance and bawled my eyes out. I tried to do it quietly, but it came out. I felt ashamed even though I knew I didn't have to be.

Callum was gone. But his passing had taught me something, and I needed the others to hear it.

I wiped my face and strode through the door and up onto the stage.

I felt every Arkonauts eyes on me. My eyes teared up again, but wiped them quickly, trying to make it look like I was picking out a stray eyelash or two. I pretended to flick something to pad the lie.

Two was there on the stage with her arm in a sling. She smiled at me warmly. Beside her, One stood tall and straight with his arms behind his back. They both moved away from the dais as I approached.

One leaned in toward me and said, "I am sorry for what I did. Your heroism and strength saved me, Two and these Arkonauts. I am in your debt. Please, the floor is yours."

That One treated me as a leader, not a kid, gave me renewed bravery to speak. I wasn't going to be alone on the stage at all. They had my back.

"Thank you," I said to One. "I forgive you and I will not let you down."

I stood and faced the crowd, ready at last to say my piece. Two and One rested strong hands on my shoulders.

"I'll start by quoting our friend Two. 'What does it mean to be human?'"

The crowd fell silent.

"Being human means we're free to make our own decisions about our lives. We're free to make mistakes. Free to be good. Free to be bad. We asked One to take away the nanites that guided everyone here to the strength and wisdom to stay together and cooperate for a peace unlike the whole of humanity has shared before. We decided that it took away our freedoms... that we were being controlled.

"If Callum was with us right now I know he would admit that he was wrong to push that idea. He had realised that staying united made us more powerful, and more extraordinary. He was sorry for how he had treated Dehqan. He was sorry for the fractures that grew among us when we fixated on our differences, instead of celebrating our similarities.

"Callum died telling me he was sorry. He wanted to tell all of us. He owned his mistakes. He was so sorry for the trouble he caused, and he wanted to make it right.

"For humanity to survive, we must all exercise the greatest act of free choice we have. We can choose to give up a shred of our freedom, to create a future humanity has never had in its grasp before. We have the choice to be better than the humans who came before us. And I truly believe we can make an amazing new world together.

"Before the Earth was destroyed, the richest countries hoarded their wealth and resources to live out their lives comfortably. My country was one such nation. And I had spent the last few days defending my country the way Callum did. Not because I believed it was right, but because I felt I should. And just as Callum realised he was wrong. I was wrong too.

"We have an opportunity to be our best selves. To be the best last Earthlings. To make all the loved ones we lost proud. That's why I'm going to ask One to reactivate my eighteenth memory.

"I have a right to be free, but I'm going to give up a small piece of that right so that tomorrow, like Callum, I'm able to trust, and to lay down my life for my friends.

"That's all I had to say. Thank you."

The theatre was silent. I couldn't tell if they liked what I said or not, but I was proud of myself for saying what I believed.

One gave my speech some time to sink in, before stepping forward to address the group.

"Thank you, Maiara. I think your words might take some time for all of us to process. If anyone wishes to have their eighteenth memory reactivated, as Maiara will, please speak to me. If not, you need only not ask me. I will keep the names of those who do and do not private."

"What if half of us do and half of us don't?" Koyla shouted from the crowd.

"It will be a mess! We'll be at each others throats!" Illarion yelled.

224

"If that's the case, so be it," I said. "I remember something Callum told me he had learned from Dr. Ghost. 'Freedom cannot be forcibly sacrificed.' So, we must choose. Each of us. And if anyone chooses not to reactivate, I hope they will still try to work with us to survive, and start a new, peaceful colony without war or division. But it must be a choice for each human, and each Arkonaut."

There was silence at my words.

Two beamed at me and mouthed the word, "Wow."

"One, I'm ready," I said.

He pulled out the nanite activator and positioned it.

I nodded.

And One aimed the device and turned it on.

I felt the nanites reactivate almost immediately. Suddenly, I felt familiar to myself, like I had been wearing ill-fitting clothes and just finally got back into the ones that fit. My feelings of bitterness and jealousy smoothed out and washed away. As I looked around the room, it was as if each Arkonaut had a clean slate in my mind and heart. There was no one who meanly tagged my graffiti art. There was no history of disagreement. I was, for lack of a better description, over it. And while feeling those things are parts of being human, I didn't really want to feel them. It was an acceptable loss, and it was my choice.

I smiled to my fellow Arkonauts, and walked up through the theatre. Many of them looked lost in thought. They were probably trying to decide what they wanted to choose.

I wondered what they would choose, too.

6
GOODBYE

Callum's funeral happened that evening.

We gathered on the observation deck, as we had with Mathieu and Nuan. Callum's body rested on a table in the centre, wrapped in a blanket from his room. We draped his Arkonaut hoodie over him, too.

I kept my misty eyes down, avoiding everyone as best I could. I was lost thinking about his wit, his humour, and the funny stories he had shared with me. He would never share another story with me. I'd never know anything more about him. And he'd never be part of another story of his own again.

At that I started to fully cry.

Two stepped forward, a solemn expression on her face.

"'For in that sleep of death what dreams may come, when we have shuffled off this mortal coil,'" she began, quoting from Shakespeare, from Callum's home of England.

She paused for a moment, and then continued.

"When death comes for a loved one we all must pause. We all must consider our own mortality, and think of the eternity beyond this life. Callum lives on now like all his ancestors who came before. He is back with his mother and father, his brother, Jack. They are forever at peace. Callum, now, can rest. We will miss you. And we will do our best to be our best selves in your memory."

Two lowered her head and stepped back, and then One stepped forward, holding a sword.

"First, I must say something personal. I know that this is not normal for me, but it must be done. Callum, I am sorry. I was your killer. I pulled the trigger and shot you. I will never forgive myself for letting Turso get the best of me, and I will never slack in my duties again. I failed you. In your memory, I will never, ever let this happen again."

One stood over Callum for a few moments.

I couldn't tell if he was crying or not. I don't know if One can cry at all.

"When we reach our new home those we've lost who we honour will be buried with the artefacts of their home nations," One continued. "This sword belonged to the Royal Family of England. It's called Curtana, the Sword of Mercy. As Maiara reminded us, Callum was troubled by his recent actions. He sought absolution, forgiveness... and mercy. It is fitting, then, that he will have this sword."

One then drew it from its scabbard. The blade shined in the artificial light filling the room.

"Callum," One said, standing over Callum's body. "Even though you will own this sword for an eternity, you will never need to use it, for now you are at peace."

One laid the sword next to his body.

I hoped that Callum would suddenly wake up and take it. Of course, that didn't happen.

One stepped back and then it was my turn. I took a deep breath, wiped my eyes, and then stepped up to say something.

"I was thinking of some important words from Geronimo, a great leader of the Apache, from the land now called the United States," I began. "'I cannot think that we are useless or God would not have created us. There is one God looking down on us all. We are all the children of one God. The sun, the darkness, the winds are all listening to what we have to say.'

"We will no longer hear what Callum has to say, but he has left us enduring memories.

"Today another nation has passed entirely into the history of humanity. They will make no more marks. What they have etched in our minds and in our hearts will remain forever, and be their legacy. You may not have known him as well as I did, but I believe that Callum loved us all and wanted so much for us. I think he wanted us all to stay together for the rest of time because we are all one family in the end. The last days have seen bitterness among us, but that no longer matters. What matters now is that we stay together for ourselves, and for Callum."

I stood over his body for a few moments, solemnly. Silence ruled the room. Then I stepped back and returned to my seat.

After a pause, Two opened the floor for the others to speak. And they did. Some shared stories. Others prayed or sang hymns.

Then when no one else had something to say, One carried his body from the room. It would go into storage to await burial on our new planet.

***

The next morning, One and Two summoned me to a room I didn't even know existed. It was a clean room lined with individual pods. It turned out that it was where Two had been stored prior to joining our crew.

"So, you'll be in this pod until we arrive on New Earth?" I asked.

Two nodded. She smiled broadly. But it was a fake smile.

I could tell by the way she was looking at the pod that she didn't really want to go back inside it.

"You don't like the pod?" I asked.

"To be honest, it stinks," she said.

I laughed.

"It smells alright to me," I joked.

Two chuckled.

"You won't be in it for as long as you were before," One said.

"But why can't you stay with us?" I asked.

"Unfortunately, the starfish Turso used to try and control me did cause some lasting damage to my brain. It will need time to heal, and the best place to heal is in this pod."

I nodded. But I was sad to see her go.

"We'll miss you. Take care of yourself in there," I said.

"I will. Please look after the uniforms," Two said, fondling the seam of my hoodie. "I spent ages on these."

She gave another smile, turned, and stepped into the pod. The door closed, and then her eyes closed, and she drifted off to sleep.

THE NEW FUTURE

"That's what happened," Two, also known as Ada, said.

I struggled to process the story she had just told. I felt an incredible guilt for not being there, even though technically I was, for not doing more. Then I felt pride, proud of my other self, who had somehow pulled through. But that was quickly washed away by an awful sadness for Maiara. I didn't really know her. But I felt like I was supposed to, and I wished I did.

I began to wonder what my younger self had missed. What would Maiara and I have had, had my younger self survived? I wondered about her, and our conversations, the way she had made me feel. Plus there was the disturbing realization that I was dead.

My younger self was nothing but bones now.

Should I be afraid? At any moment, would time correct itself and erase me from existence? I technically had no past, or at least a sizeable gap, that should mean I should have had no future, including the me that existed in the actual future. Of course, it didn't really matter. And thinking about it wasn't going to solve anything. I needed to put those thoughts out of my mind.

"So you were put in the pod. Then what happened?" I asked.

"I woke up opposite Antumbra," Ada said.

"And what happened to the crew in your timeline?" I asked.

"I think we can conclude that something must have wiped them out. Something that led to the Ark being destroyed, leaving me floating in space to be picked up by the Thieves."

"What could have destroyed the Ark? There were no more threats."

"We'll have to go back in time, find out, and repair the damage," Ada said.

"No," Antumbra said. "This Rod needs to recharge. Plus I am not sure we should change time again."

"Why?" I asked.

"Don't you remember? I said before that there were two possibilities when we went back in time. Either we would create a new universe where we were certain that our people had survived or we would change time in the past, which would eventually lead to the collapse of the universe. A third option has apparently emerged. We successfully created a new universe, but for some reason the original and the new have combined.

"If we change the timeline again, what will happen? Will we just create a sub-universe that eventually will merge with this one again? Will we destroy all timelines at once? Until I can understand more about what happened, we cannot use the Rod," Antumbra said.

"So, uh, what *do* we do?" the Mouth said.

"I doubt the thieves will let us get away with stealing one of their ships," Antumbra said.

"Even with a new ship like this they'd catch up to us," the Mouth said. "We need somewhere to hide."

The other aliens looked at each other.

Hippo shrugged at Antumbra.

"There are a few planets I know of that the Thieves won't steal from," Hippo said.

"If they're looking for water, they'll be looking everywhere," Ada asked. "Where could we even hide?"

"They do not want all the water they steal for themselves. They simply want to choke off and destroy life that may grow to threaten them. Our best bet for safety would be to find an uninhabitable planet, or one that's not at all advanced," Antumbra said.

"That doesn't seem like a solution," I said.

Antumbra nodded. "There are few satisfactory solutions."

"Then maybe we can stop them?" I asked.

"No other species has the power to match them. Their fleet is huge. Only space faring species have survived because they could just retreat to another world," the Mouth explained.

"So we've already lost."

"The Thieves basically control the galaxy," Antumbra said. "Once they detect a species that has reached a significant technological milestone they send in a ship to steal its water and destroy the planet. Bye, bye future competitor."

"Yeah, I'm familiar with that part," I said. "So how did we all end up in that museum?"

"The Thieves always steal a member of the races they destroy, to preserve, kind of like a trophy," the Mouth added.

"And we've all been added to the collection over time?"

"You and Ada were there long ago," Antumbra said. "Pebbles and the Mouth were the most recent additions."

"And when was that?"

"Ten years ago," Hippo interjected. "It's odd."

"Why's that?" Ada asked.

"New races would appear every two years or so. Like clockwork. For the last ten years no one new has arrived."

"So the Thieves haven't attacked a world in the last ten years?"

"Or none of the exhibits survived."

"It doesn't matter if the Thieves have stopped or not or why," the Mouth said. "We need a plan!"

"Then we're back to getting to a new planet. How long will it take us?" I asked.

"This ship will take us anywhere in a reasonable amount of time. There is a planet I know that hosts an early space-faring civilisation hub. The Thieves didn't get to them before they had a way to defend themselves and now they keep their heads down. So far the Thieves haven't attacked them," Antumbra said.

"I thought you said your people never went into space," I asked. "How would you know this other planet?"

"We did talk to new civilisations, we just weren't interested in visiting them. There's an intergalactic community of races who share knowledge about the Thieves in hopes of staying out of their way."

"So it's decided," I said. "We'll go to this planet Antumbra knows of and then we can figure out what to do about the timelines."

"Look, when we get to this planet, that's where I'm going my own way," the Mouth said. "Look thanks for freeing me from that museum, but I think the debt is paid. When I get off this ship it's time for me to get on my own ship, and get as far away from the Thieves as possible."

Mantis clicked his bladed hands together and nodded.

The bug must have the same plan.

"I shall also be leaving your company," Hippo added. "I will need to take revenge on the Thieves, to restore my people's honour."

I looked at Pebbles. "What about you?"

The rock alien didn't say anything.

"Don't worry about him," the Mouth said, "He'll probably be content to just stay right there forever. On his planet he started off as a mountain. Over eons, he eroded down to the form you see now. He's literally millions of years old at this point. He has no desires or goals, he lets the elements form and shape his actions."

I turned to Lyger.

"I don't know what to do," Lyger said. "But there is hope for my race."

"It's a big universe," Ada said. "Perhaps you could join another feline culture?"

"Maybe," the cat replied. "But it won't be the same as my planet."

"This is fine. You have all been helpful companions. I will find a safe spot to use this Rod properly. After that, I will be free of my obligations to my people," Antumbra said. "And I assume you and Ada will begin a new race of humans."

"What?" I exclaimed.

"Yeah you're lucky thanks to our time shifting that you can restart your race again."

Ada and I said "What?" together.

Mantis held up two of his pincers then crossed the energy between them together, which then changed colour.

He then nodded.

Pebble brought his two fists together.

I suddenly realised what Antumbra was talking about. My face was flush with embarrassment. I looked at Ada, and her face was flush too.

"Look, if there was another of my kind out there, I know I'd do it," Hippo said.

"Y-yeah," I stuttered, and desperately pleaded that someone would change the subject.

"For now, let's just get to that planet I mentioned," Antumbra said. "Then we can all be free to do as we wish."

"We still have to outrun the Thieves, right?" I asked.

"We did just steal one of their largest ships," Antumbra said.

A NEW HOME

We had a ship, massive in size, its function mostly redundant as none of us had any need for a ship that could drink up an entire planet's water supply.

It would be weeks before we could go our separate ways. We agreed to work together to survive until then. And to do that we had to search the ship. It was too big to search completely, so we focused on the areas surrounding the control centre.

We found laboratories and sleeping quarters. Even though the Destroyer was automated, some Thieves would stay on board to prepare it between missions.

Luckily, we found a stockpile of food and water in a room next to the sleeping quarters. We wouldn't starve or die of thirst. It was a small victory.

There wasn't much else to do during the journey other than spend time together. We were a motley crew, but we managed to get along.

Hippo was from a culture that prized families above all else. Each family was ruled by a matriarch who did all the farming and hunting. Apparently a huge population boom had spurred them to explore space, and find new worlds on which family groups could settle.

"We had colonised several moons orbiting my planet," Hippo told me. "My family presided over one of them. My great grandmother was the matriarch, a fierce woman over two centuries in age and still quite capable."

"Without a unifying culture, did the families ever go to war?" I asked.

"No," Hippo said. "Each matriarch was ultimately related to the Supreme Matriarch. With everyone related to everyone else, we would never fight, other than a small scuffle over a feeding ground."

"And you said a probe brought you to the museum?"

"Yes. I was tasked to travel between two moons with supplies. My ship was intercepted by a probe sent from the Destroyer."

"And you had to watch your world be destroyed?" I asked.

"Yes. I was locked in a cell, surrounded by monitors that showed me the devastation of my world."

"I'm sorry," I said. "I know your pain."

Hippo's wasn't the only sad tale I heard on our journey.

Antumbra had been married to another young female of her species before the fall of her planet. They decided to send Antumbra away in a spaceship in order to use the Rod. She didn't have a choice in the matter. In fact, Antumbra had been chosen because it was deemed that she would live to be the oldest of her kind. In her species' minds the longer Antumbra survived, the more time she had to use the Rod and change history. They were a very methodical race.

"My species is made of energy, but that energy fades over time. When it was decided to send a member of my species off world each one of us was tested. By an energetic fluke, I was the one who would live the longest. I was altered to live even longer and trained to survive in space."

"And no one else wanted to go?" I asked.

"I was chosen to change time and make things better. We didn't know everything about the Rod's full capabilities, but we hoped that it could change time completely to resurrect everyone."

"And you had to leave your family?" Ada asked.

"Yes. I kissed my wife goodbye, and I said farewell to our children and left them to die."

I knew what it was like. The teleport that had delivered me onto the Ark had stolen me away from my parents. And I had been taken from my friends on the Ark, too, even if it wasn't the me that I am now. It seemed we all had hard lives.

***

Mantis was the hardest to talk to, but the most fun. A conversation was like a game of charades.

"How did you get caught?" I asked him.

He sort of jogged on the spot.

"You were running?" I said.

He nodded.

"From the Destroyer probe sent to collect you?" I asked.

He shook his head. He then pointed at himself, then sort of levelled a pincer in line with his head then moved it up.

"A bigger mantis?" I asked.

He pointed at Antumbra. Then he pointed at himself then me. Then he did the bigger mantis thing again and pointed at Antumbra.

"I think he means a female mantis," she concluded.

Mantis nodded.

"You were running from a female mantis? Why?" I asked.

He made a hand gesture, which on Earth meant only one thing.

"You had just... mated?" I said.

Mantis nodded.

"And she was trying to eat you?" I asked. "They did that on Earth."

Mantis nodded.

"So the Destroyer scooped you up while you were running from your girlfriend?" I said.

Mantis nodded.

"And now, would you have rather been eaten or caught by the Thieves?" Antumbra asked.

Mantis shrugged.

Through another long conversation I learned that Mantis was over fifty years old, and had a long career as an administrator for a school on his home planet.

Just like Hippo's race Mantis's was entering space for the first time, which had attracted a Destroyer to their world.

***

Pebbles wasn't a talker.

But The Mouth knew a lot about him. For a brief time their races had been at war. The Mouth's race were already refugees, and quite advanced. They had built a ship to escape their world. Its size matched the Ark in scale, and they ended up on Pebble's homeworld.

Pebbles' culture started when life erupted from the lava of their planet's core. The rock people spent thousands of years as mountains until erosion made them able to move, and they possessed no technology, save for infinite patience and self-reflection.

They had even worked out the meaning of life, simply because they had the time to think it over.

The Mouth's species chose the rock people's world as their new home, and landed on that planet. They began mining into it for raw materials, sparking a war.

Eventually the two species learned to communicate and found a path to peace.

When the Thieves came for their world, they scooped up the Mouth and Pebbles. And their shared world was destroyed.

***

Lyger didn't want to talk about her past, but she seemed hopeful that other members of her race might be alive. Her world had been peaceful, mostly because her race slept for twenty hours a day. Her planet, by a quirk of physics and nature, was a wormhole nexus, so portals to other planets opened on her world and allowed her race to travel to other places in the universe. When the Destroyer arrived, it's impact separated her planet from the wormholes permanently. No one could escape, but some had been on other worlds, and should still be there. Lyger believed that her people persisted, somewhere.

We had all been through a lot. It was a pity we weren't staying together. But I understood that each of us must make our own paths.

***

As our journey continued, Antumbra showed me information from the Destroyer's database. It told the history of the Thieves.

"The Thieves are one of the oldest species in the galaxy. They are more advanced than any other," Antumbra explained. "This is their leader."

It looked like an octopus, rounder than the squids I had seen, and it was suspended in a hovering cradle. Unlike the other thieves, this one's face lacked mechanical masking. And it was seated, plump and in repose.

"It is called the Overlord," Antumbra said. "The Thieves exist within a loose hive mind, with the Overlord at the top. Underneath it are Greatlords, and below them, many others. Each lord controls a domain and answers to the lord above. The entire race is cybernetic, and each Greatlord commands a Destroyer-class vessel,"

"But why do they do what they do?" I asked.

"The Thieves became the most advanced race in the galaxy. Why would they share when they had the power to take? They believe in taking. Nothing else guides them except for their shared race."

"And the water?" I asked.

"They don't even use all of it. They dump it on another barren planet, hoping that it will eventually create an ecosystem, and one day, a planet they can steal from. All they want to do is sit at the top forever."

The Thieves had impacted all of our lives, ruining all of our worlds. It was more important than ever that we find a way to change the timeline and save those who had been lost, including Maiara, and the Arkonauts, and myself.

***

There was one other person I had to get to know.

The last other human in the universe.

Ada.

We were the last two humans left alive. I was male and she was female. There was an obvious course of action for us to take, but I was never going to broach this subject with her.

No. The human race was gone.

But maybe she was different? Maybe she was like One, bound by a duty that drove her to serve the crew of the Ark. Maybe she was programmed to continue humanity? I wasn't going to talk to her until I knew.

One day, I went to the gallery. It was a cavernous space filled with the air the Destroyer had drained from other planets. It had its own atmosphere and you could see all types of weather. Clouds formed, rain fell, and there was even snow.

I found Ada looking out over the edge gazing at the view. A tornado was spinning around in the distance.

I could have walked away, but I wanted to chat.

"How is the weather?" I asked.

"Thousands of light years from home, on an alien ship, and yet somehow the Englishman still starts a conversation with the weather," she said.

I smiled, remembering that I was, indeed, English. The thought stung though, it was all gone.

"What did you want to chat about, Callum?"

"Who says I want to chat?" I lied.

"My purpose on the Ark was to chat to Arkonauts. I always know when someone wants to chat with me."

"I'm here," I said. "Yeah, chat to me."

"You want to chat to me."

She was right.

"What do we do, Ada?"

"I don't know, Callum," she sighed.

"Right now, I feel purposeless. All I want to do is keep living," I said.

"That's the programming you received in the pod. It only wanted to create a human capable of surviving anything, and it instilled in you a desire to live moment by moment."

"And you're still a sounding board for the Arkonauts?" I asked.

"Yes, but they are all gone. My training feels redundant."

We were silent for a moment.

"Why did they call you Two?" I asked. "Why weren't you known by your real name?"

She looked at me with her golden eyes, and then looked away.

I wasn't completely honest with you. Ada is not my original name. It's one I choose for myself, a better name. I was named Two from... birth."

"Why did you parents call you Two?" I asked.

She lapsed into silence.

"Ada?"

"One day, I'll tell you," she said.

Maybe it was too hard to talk about.

One had been called Joshua, and had told me that he was once a disabled boy who was turned into a paragon of human vitality and strength. Had the same happened to Two?

Before I could ask Ada anything more, we heard Antumbra over the intercom.

"Please join me in the control centre."

When we arrived, Antumbra told us something terrifying.

"I have detected a remote access of our vessel."

"Someone been hacking our ship?" I asked.

"Yes. And only the Thieves could do so," Antumbra said. "They are trying to get their ship back. I can block them, but I don't know for how long."

Suddenly alarms sounded all over the ship. Something had exited a vortex in front of our stolen ship.

"What's that?" I asked.

INVASION

"That is a small Thief cruiser," Hippo said.

"They're coming to take back their ship," the Mouth said.

"Can we fight back?" I asked.

Antumbra and Hippo went to nearby control consoles.

"They've already hacked us. All we can do is prevent them from opening the docking bay," Hippo said.

Suddenly there was a Thief, a Greatlord, standing beside us all.

We all leapt away.

I drew my gun.

Hippo drew too.

The walking octopus had two normal eyes and a third mechanical one.

"Don't shoot," Ada said. "It's not really here. It's a hologram."

Ada passed her arm through the alien projection.

"Exhibits located on board our ship," a voice boomed through the ship's intercom.

"They've already accessed the internal communications system," Antumbra said. Her hands flew across the controls trying to block them out.

The image didn't appear to see us. It never moved or reacted.

"You have stolen a ship belonging to one of the Greatlords of the Larceny. It is a symbol of our power, our birthright, and our heritage. We will now reclaim it. Surrender, and we guarantee your return to the museum, alive. You will each receive punishment, but your lives will be spared," the voice said, then the image disappeared.

"If they want us to surrender, that means they've come prepared for a fight in case we don't," I said, lowering my weapon.

"Can we go faster? Try to outrun them?" Ada asked.

"We are already traveling at our max speed," Antumbra said.

"Then we get ready for company," I said.

"They will dispatch a shuttle to the docking bay," Antumbra said. She enlarged the feed of the ship that cruised next to our stolen vessel. The Thief cruiser took position near the upper section of our ship. The ship had a long pyramid base, like the Destroyer, but also had a ridged, skeletal structure around that hull, giving the appearance of fins. It also had long, mechanical tendrils that pulsated as the ship moved forward.

Antumbra continued, "And considering how we were able to defeat some of their forces on the planet, they will likely send heavily-armed soldiers."

As Antumbra predicted, the ship ejected a shuttle.

Then it ejected two more.

"Course tracked. They are heading for the docking bay," Hippo said.

"They will board us. We must plan accordingly," Antumbra said.

"And these will be the more elite troops?" I asked.

"I see no other outcome," Antumbra said.

"Why don't we escape?" Lyger said.

"Escape?" Ada asked.

"This Destroyer has to have escape pods or support craft!"

"There are escape pods, but they won't get us far quickly enough," Antumbra said.

"So we're trapped," the Mouth said.

"We need a plan to fight back," I said. "I know we're at top speed, but maybe it's not more power we need to go faster."

"We could lose some weight to gain momentum," Antumbra said.

She tapped some buttons on the nearby controls. The dome above us showed the interior of the Destroyer. The lower section was coloured completely blue.

"They have not unloaded the contents of the ship," she said. "We are currently carrying a planet's worth of water. Ejecting it should provide a boost to our speed."

"They've reached the docking bay," Hippo said, panicked. "They are overriding the commands trying to unlock it," he said.

"Try to block them," I said. "We need a little more time."

"I might be able to buy us fifteen minutes," Hippo said.

Suddenly Mantis tapped its front pincers together. It was like it was clapping in joy.

"What is it Mantis?" I asked.

Mantis's front mandible reached down and tapped at the image of the platform ship that was parked in the docking bay. It kept miming with its pincers. It looked like it meant to be shooing a fly away.

"I think he's making an explosion," Ada said.

"Blow up the platform ship?" I asked.

Mantis pointed at me, empathically.

"That makes sense," Antumbra said. "If we blow up the platform ship it will bombard their shuttles with shrapnel."

"Won't blowing up a ship inside this ship tear this ship to pieces?" I asked.

"Not necessarily," Hippo said. "If we blow up the platform ship and open the docking bay at the same time the escaping pressure should direct the explosion outwards."

"And it destroys any way off this ship," Antumbra pointed out.

"We'll still have the escape pods," I said. "Hopefully we'll have time to find a suitable planet. Any objections?"

No one spoke up.

"Once we blow the docking bay, and clear their ships we'll eject the water and then our engines can propel us away even faster," I said. "So how do we blow up the platform ship?"

"I can handle that," the Mouth said.

THE PLAN

Me, the Mouth and Ada volunteered to go to the docking bay to try and destroy the ship we had left there.

I kept stealing glances at Ada. Her presence felt alien to me. I should have been happy to see an old friend. Besides, there was another human still alive.

But I was clouded with questions and uncertainties. Were we supposed to try to get revenge? Should we try to restart the human race? The responsibility of shouldering millennia of human history was no longer mine alone and that only seemed to make it more complicated.

I wanted to talk to her about it, but we had bigger concerns.

"How do we destroy this ship?" Ada asked the Mouth.

"I was a miner on my planet. My species preferred flat land so we reduced every mountain, hill and mound we could. For a time I worked crafting explosives for that purpose," the Mouth said. "Plus, I'm pretty eager to blow them up. They held me in that museum for ten years."

"Ten years?" Ada said.

"Yes," he replied.

"I'm so so—" I began.

"Don't worry about it, human. After all that time, I'm just happy to be alive, and be free of expectations and pressure. It's just me and the universe from now on."

"Sounds lonely," Ada said.

"Sure, but it beats the judgment I used to deal with among my people. And, hey, even when I'm alone, there are an infinite number of life forms nearby."

The Mouth's philosophy was interesting. I wondered if it could ever work for me.

In the docking bay, we found the platform ship, just as we had left it, in a broken heap. We followed the Mouth as he led us around to the back of the ship.

"We need to get to the reactor core. We can ignite the fuel," the Mouth said. "Ada, scour the ship for any energy weapons. The bigger the better. Then meet us in the engine room."

"Callum, you're coming with me to assess the core."

"I don't know anything about engine cores. Should I look for weapons, instead?" I said.

"Nope. You're my bodyguard."

We climbed up the hull of the platform ship toward the entrance. The ship was tilted, making the climb intense, and once we were inside, we had to walk on the floors and the walls at the same time.

Ada went for the cargo cache to find weapons.

The Mouth and I descended into the back of the ship. There were dead ends all over, each created by collapsed corridors or piles of dead Thieves.

The platform ship's engine core was like a miniature version of the Ark's with a small piece of multi-coloured crystal attached by cables to the core casing.

"This mechanism holds incredible energy."

"And it'll explode?" I asked.

"Definitely," the Mouth said, checking a nearby control console. "One problem: it's currently over half full so the explosion will probably do too much damage to the Destroyer."

"How do we use some energy?" I asked.

The Mouth tapped on some more controls.

"I'm activating all the ships systems that are still active: heating, lighting, and environmental controls."

The Mouth flicked another switch and then spoke into thin air, "Ada, I am going to activate some of the platform ship's systems, including the engines. Please don't be alarmed."

The ship shook as the engines came on. The lights glowed brighter, and it was definitely getting warmer inside. Then the ship's internal communications activated.

"Fellow escapees, the Thieves outside have gained access to the computer. They can open the docking bay door. I will be able to regain control and shut it, but the docking bay will lose some pressure. Brace yourselves," Hippo said

The giant bay doors groaned and inched open. The air in the docking bay flowed immediately out into space. The air even leeched from inside the platform ship.

We braced ourselves against the consoles. I hoped that Ada was okay. I was starting to get light-headed, it was so hard to breath against the escaping pressure.

Then the docking bay doors stopped and began to close.

I took a deep breath. The air was still thin, but at least I could catch some.

"They will be able to do that again in a few moments. Ideally you will be ready to blow up the platform ship when they do," Antumbra said over the intercom.

Ada scrambled into the room, holding a large gun, panting.

"Will this one do?" she asked.

The Mouth took the gun and inspected it.

"This is good," he replied. "But we need more firepower. Can you get another?"

Ada nodded, but her expression was weary. She ran out to find another gun.

The Mouth pried the gun's casing open, and then dug around inside. After a moment, he retrieved a small piece of metal. And the weapon flashed.

For a second the room's lights flickered, and the consoles restarted.

"What was that?" I asked.

"I accidently triggered a small electromagnetic pulse when I rigged the gun. It'll only last for a second," the Mouth said, and he went back to fiddling.

Soon, Ada returned with another of the same gun.

"Can you show us how to do that?" I asked.

"Sure, but keep up."

The Mouth opened the second gun and showed us what he'd done.

"Don't let those two green bits separate, or you'll trigger a small electromagnetic pulse and all electronics in the area will power down for a moment."

The Mouth finished tinkering and closed up the second gun.

"Once I pull the trigger on the first gun, it'll try to fire, but the energy flow is blocked. The unreleased energy will build up until it explodes. It should be enough to damage the core. And the second gun will be our fail safe."

Ada and I nodded. We were ready.

The Mouth set both guns beside the engine core and pulled their triggers. The weapons hummed, but no blast came out, as planned. Instead they shook and the humming seemed to get louder with each second.

"Time to run," the Mouth said.

We scamperd back through the tilted corridors of the platform ship until we got to the entrance, and climbed out into the docking bay.

"Antumbra," I called out. "The bomb is set."

"We can see the device on the sensors. We are tracking the energy build up. Get as far away as you can. We will open the bay doors right before the bomb goes off."

"Confirmed. We'll see you as soon as we can," I called back.

The depressurisation of the docking bay had shifted some of the debris, so we had to move more carefully than we did on the way in.

We passed by the body of a thief, no longer covered with some metal panelling.

I looked at it as we passed. Then I saw it was moving. It was breathing.

I wasn't fast enough to react.

A tentacle rose up and shot toward me. It wrapped around my neck, and lifted me into the air. I wanted to yell, but I couldn't. Then the tentacle threw me against the wall, and pinned me to it.

The injured Thief's mechanical and electrical parts sparked and fizzed and it tried to stand on its remaining tentacles.

The Mouth leapt to my rescue and clamped his jaws on the tentacle holding me. With one swift bite the tentacle split in two.

The Thief's blood sprayed everywhere. The alien raised a metallic, clawed, tentacle and try to thrash the Mouth.

Ada grabbed that arm before it could do any damage. She wrenched the arm downward and twisted it, snapping wires and sending rivets flying. Then she pulled hard at the tentacle until it ripped from its socket.

With the Thief defenceless, it scrambled around trying to throw its body at us, but it was clumsy and slow.

"Get out of there," Antumbra's voice boomed.

We ran toward the door to the docking bay. I could hear the gears of the door whine and shudder as they reacted to conflicting commands to open and close. We climbed over refuse and debris, and made our way through the door, back into the corridor and back to the command centre.

Antumbra nodded at us as we entered.

"I've closed all the doors from here to the docking bay," she said. "We should be safe from the explosion here."

"The Thieves are going to open the door again," Hippo said.

"And the platform ship is about to explode. Let them open it," Antumbra said.

Hippo let go of the controls.

We all looked up at the dome to see.

The docking bay opened. Three ships hung back from the entrance. When the door was wide open, the ships opened fire on the platform ship.

"Wait. What are they doing?" I asked.

"They are trying to dislodge the wreckage so they can land," Hippo said.

"Ten seconds until detonation," Antumbra said.

"This is going to be amazing," Hippo said, smiling wide.

The Thieves stopped firing, and maneuvered into the bay.

What remained of the platform ship exploded. Energy and light filled the inside of the docking bay. A bubble of colourful fire expanded from the inside of the ship and enveloped the whole area in an instant.

The Thief shuttles vaporized. All of them were destroyed. There was nothing left but smears of black ash.

I waited for the ship to tremble and shake, but there was only a tiny ripple through the floor.

"We got them," Antumbra said. "Unfortunately, the docking bay remains usable. They may come again."

Another Thief hologram appeared before us.

"Exhibits," it said. "We will take your actions as a message of non-compliance. Now, no mercy will be given."

Five new shuttles came streaming from the larger Thief ship. They were flying, full-speed, toward us.

"We need a new plan," Lyger said. "We don't have any more ships to blow up now."

"Wait," I said. "That's not entirely accurate."

THE NEW PLAN

"You want to blow up this ship?" Lyger screamed at me. "The one we're on."

"Yes I do," I said.

"Explain?" Ada said.

"We set up the Destroyer to self-destruct, then get in the escape pods. The explosion will be more than enough to destroy these invaders," I explained.

"Escape pods can't take us anywhere," the Mouth said. "They are short-range craft meant to be temporary lifeboats."

"They don't have to take us far," I said.

"Then where do you want to go?" Hippo asked.

"There," I said, pointing at the screen where the smaller Thief ship hovered.

"You want to invade them?" Antumbra asked.

"Why not? It's the last thing they will be expecting," I said.

The aliens all looked to each other, waiting for someone to protest. But none came.

"Are we really doing this?" The Mouth asked.

"I want to take the fight to them," Hippo said. "Let's try taking their ship."

"There is nowhere safe on this ship. Why not?" Lyger said.

Pebbles shrugged and Mantis nodded its head.

"How do we blow up this ship?" Ada asked.

"Let's do what we did last time," I said looking at the Mouth.

"A normal gun won't do it. We need something bigger," he said.

"Do we just have to breach the engine's containment core?" Ada asked.

The Mouth licked his giant lips and teeth.

"Yes. That's all the explosions from the guns did. It created a chain reaction."

"So we don't need an explosion, just something of sufficient strength to crack the core of this ship," Ada summarised.

"What are you thinking, human?"

"The Destroyer has giant pipes inside it that are heavy and thick. What if we used one of them to strike the core?" she suggested.

"That sounds promising," I said.

"We can control the pipes from here. The problem is that the top section of the ship is separated from the lower section. And the pipes are all down below," Antumbra said.

"If this ship is anything like the Ark then there is a hatch at the bottom of the engine room with a shaft that leads to the lower section," I said. "We could bring the pipe up through that hatch."

Antumbra paused for a moment to think, her eyes disappearing into her energy like skin.

"Yes. This will work. I need you to get that hatch open, and direct the pipe I will control up the shaft," she said.

"Ada, Lyger, come with me. I might need a hand," I said. "The rest of you, stay here, and do what you can to fend off any attackers. And keep a path clear to the escape pods."

Ada, Lyger, and I headed for the engine room hatch. The layout of this Destroyer was much like the Ark. There was a flight of stairs not far from the control centre that led to the engine room.

The engine of the ship was monstrously huge. It was four times larger than the Ark's, which was about as tall as the Gherkin in London. This engine was more like the Empire State Building in New York.

We found an elevator and took it down to the base, where we found the hatch.

"Thank goodness these Thieves don't change their designs much," Lyger remarked.

The hatch was so heavy that all three of us had to lift to move it. When we got it open, we looked down into the lower section of the Destroyer.

Unlike how Ada had described the Ark's lower section, this one was almost completely filled with water.

"Antumbra," I reported. "We're here."

"Give me a moment," she replied. "I have taken control of one of the pipes now. I think I'm moving it up toward you."

We watched down the shaft and saw a pipe rise, slowly out of the water like a sea monster. It had metal tusks mounted around its open end.

"We can see it," I said.

"Which way does it go when I do this?" Antumbra asked.

The pipe suddenly moved up and right scraping the side of the shaft and tearing into the metal.

"The head of the pipe is moving upwards," Ada said.

"Let me know when to stop," Antumbra said.

The pipe then started heading straight towards us.

"Not yet," Lyger said.

After a few seconds Antumbra said, "Now?"

"Not yet," I said.

The pipe was only a couple of hundred yards from us.

"Stop," Ada yelled out.

The pipe continued to ascend.

"Stop," Lyger and I yelled. "We said stop!"

It did not stop.

The pipe was going to smash right into us. I grabbed Lyger and Ada, held them under my arms using my new super strength, and jumped away from the hatch just as the pipe ploughed its way through the floor.

THE ESCAPE PODS

Metal tore and screeched as the pipe punched through the floor. The hatch went shooting over our heads, flung upon impact, and embedded in the opposite wall. The pipe powered forth, stuck into the underside of the engine, and finally came to rest.

We all held our breaths, waiting for the engine to blow, but thankfully the impact did not trigger a reaction.

"We told you to stop," I said to Antumbra.

"Apologies. These pipes are not designed for this," she replied.

"Now what do we do?" I asked.

"Leave it where it is, and come back up here," Antumbra said.

Once we were back in the control centre, the screens showed the Thieves landing their five new ships in the remains of the docking bay.

"We have to get to those escape pods now," I said.

"There are two sets we can use," Antumbra said. "I suggest we split into two teams, double our chances, and split their forces into more manageable chunks."

"What about destroying this ship?" Lyger said.

"I've inputted a set of commands into the computer, set on a delay. Once out of here, the instructions will make the pipe we chose swing wildly in the engine room. It should break the containment around the engine, leading to an explosion," Antumbra said.

"In the meantime, we'll be trying to take the Thief ship for ourselves. I imagine that much of their fighting force is arriving right now in those shuttles, so their main ship will be undermanned," Hippo commented.

"Is everyone ready?" I asked.

The motley crew of aliens then nodded.

"Lyger, Antumbra, Hippo and Pepples: you're one team," I said. "Ada, Mantis, the Mouth, and I will be the other. See you on the other ship."

"And be careful," I added.

We were, at the moment, each other's only friends.

We parted ways, running for the escape pod bays.

I knew that somewhere Thieves were disembarking from their ships and heading deeper into this Destroyer to find us. Suddenly my ears pricked up. I heard something behind us. My super-hearing was like One's had been. I heard footsteps. Lots of them, but it was impossible to know how many Thieves were coming since they walked on multiple tentacles like upright squid.

"They are coming up behind us," I said.

"Maybe they're tracking us," Ada said.

"We need cover. If we're going into battle," I said.

I checked my weapon out of habit.

"I memorised the layout of this level before we left the control centre," Ada said. "There is a room up ahead at the end of this corridor."

"Let's go."

We hustled inside the room. It was a laboratory of some sort. Medical benches and equipment dotted the room. In its centre was a large circular cell. And inside the cell was dark.

"Up end the tables and push them to the door. We'll hide behind them," I said.

Mantis put two of its pincers on a table, knocked it over, and then pushed it towards the door.

Ada and I grabbed another table, scattered the equipment from it, and lined it up next to Mantis'.

We then knelt down behind the barricade, watching down the corridor for the Thieves to arrive.

"They're close," I said, turning my right ear to the sounds of scuttling tentacles moving nearer.

"Guys, what is this?" the Mouth said, standing by the cell.

"Who cares? Pay attention! We have Thieves closing in," I said.

The Mouth walked around the circumference of the cell, once he had done a loop, he said, "Hey, there's a switch."

The cell lit up when he flipped the switch.

Staring at us from inside was a creature from my worst nightmares. It was like an insect and reptile smashed together, with a hundred eyes, and thousands of teeth. Its body was horrible. It seemed to be made of mouths and limbs contorted and tangled into the vague shape of a four-legged beast.

We recoiled in fright. Even Mantis, intimidating as it was to behold, backed away from the creature in the cell.

The thing sent shivers down my spine, but it didn't seem to be moving. It didn't even blink or look our way. It was frozen in its pose.

"What is that?" I asked.

"Never seen one before," the Mouth said.

"I think I can guess," Ada said. "Antumbra said this ship was still full of water, which means this Destroyer had only recently returned from another planet. I think that it is one of the inhabitants of that world. We are all samples of the worlds the Thieves destroyed, so maybe this creature is too."

"Should we let it out?" the Mouth asked.

"No!" Ada and I exclaimed.

Mantis frantically shook its head and waived its front scythes in the air.

"Why not?" the Mouth said. "It's like us. Trapped by the Thieves."

"It's a nightmare," I said. "Why on Earth would we set it free?"

"That's a bit prejudiced isn't it? It could be a sweet heart," the Mouth replied.

We didn't have time to settle the discussion because the Thieves arrived. Twenty of them rounded the corner and were coming straight for our room.

"Blast them," I said.

Ada and I raised our weapons and fired. Both of us were genetically engineered to be faster and stronger than we had been before, so our aims were excellent.

I shot off three blasts and three Thieves went down.

Ada got off four shots and four Thieves went down.

Then came the retaliatory fire.

We ducked down as laser blasts flew into the room, blasting apart the equipment we'd scattered around when we moved the tables. Some of the laser blasts struck the cell holding the creature, damaging its outer casing.

The Mouth and Mantis ducked into the corners, away from the crossfire.

"Try this," the Mouth said.

He threw another gun towards me, and I could see that he had removed its cover and modified it to explode like before.

"You've got ten seconds," he said.

I chucked the overloading gun into the hallway, and took a quick looked.

It bounced under the nearest Thief and slid down the corridor. The attacker recognised it for what it was and retreated, but some of the other Thieves didn't notice, and the exploding gun threw them through the air, up over our barricade, and into the room.

One Thief struck the cell, cracking its casing further. This Thief was different from the others we had seen before. It was larger, with tentacles coming out of its head and lower torso.

Three tentacles, armed with mechanical pincers, shot at me and speared the floor and table.

It was about to launch more tentacles at me, but Mantis swiped them with its claws, cutting them like spaghetti.

The Thief tried to lunge forward again, but the Mouth bit down on some of its other limbs and started chewing, drawing the thief into his maw.

Mantis cut the thief again. This time, the strike split the Thief in half. One part dropped uselessly to the floor, as the other half disappeared into the Mouth's mouth with a slurp.

"They are regrouping," Ada said gazing down the corridor.

I reloaded my gun, took a breath, and waited for the next attack.

"Uh... Guys," the Mouth said.

"What is it?" I asked.

"The cell," he said, pointing at the damage.

The alien's cell flickered, and then its lights went out completely, filling the inside with darkness.

There was a low rumble and then the whole cell burst apart in a shower of metal and ultra-thick glass.

The creature inside stepped out. Its skin seemed to writhe all over the rest of the body. Its mouth opened several times, with each set of jaws opening to reveal another set inside, and another and another. Its eyes jockeyed for position on what I would charitably call its face, with some of them moving to, and peering from its wriggling limbs.

So far in my life I had seen a skeleton of a Mantis, a walking shadow, and a walking stone. This thing was more alien, and more terrifying, to me than any of those.

The creature studied us for a moment. Then it looked around the room, and as it did, another group of mouths opened up on its legs.

I pointed my gun out of instinct.

The creature didn't react. It didn't seem to care about the gun.

I wasn't sure what to do, but the sound of the Thieves charging again stole my attention. They were almost here. I took cover and waved for the others to do the same.

"What do we do, Ada?" I asked.

"Don't shoot it," she said.

"Are you sure?" I asked. "It could be dangerous."

"It was a prisoner of the Thieves. We are not it's enemy," she said.

The Thieves fired into the room again. The blasts that missed our tables, struck the creature.

The creature started to bleed from where it was shot, but its flesh quickly covered those wounds, and it seemed to be healed.

It seemed to see the Thieves, and then crouched on its rear legs and leapt over the tables.

I didn't see what it did next, but I heard the screams from the Thieves.

When it was quiet, I stood up and looked. The carnage I saw made me nauseous, and I threw up.

Ada stood up and looked as well. She looked shocked, but wasn't sick.

Mantis and the Mouth looked too.

The Mouth threw up his recently eaten Thief meal.

After I was done vomiting, I looked at the creature. It was covered in wounds, and it stood, panting, over a pile of dead Thieves.

Then it slumped to the ground.

I gasped.

We all walked out to inspect the bodies of the dead Thieves. They were everywhere, literally, even on the ceiling.

The Mouth approached the creature, picked up a tentacle and offered it to the creature.

"Eat. You'll feel better," he said.

The creature looked at him but seemed too tired to do anything except bleed on the floor.

"I don't know if it will survive," I said.

"If it does not, its sacrifice was noble," Ada said. "It seemed to know that the Thieves imprisoned it and had its own revenge."

"Human," Hippo said over the communicator.

"What is it?" Ada said.

"We didn't make it to the escape pods."

"Come to ours. We've taken care of our Thieves," I said.

"I don't think we need to," Lyger said. "The Thieves are leaving."

"We must've fought them off," I said.

I high-fived Ada and the Mouth. Mantis held up a pincer, but not wanting to lose my hand, I regrettably declined.

"No. The Thieves got Antumbra," Hippo said.

"What?" Ada said.

"They didn't want all of us. Just her."

THE FLOOD

We regrouped in the engine room.

The Mouth decided to stay behind with the wounded creature. I hoped he would catch up with us soon.

"We got separated from Antumbra, then they grabbed her in containment field and disappeared."

"There she is," Hippo said pointing at a screen.

We watched as Antumbra was forced onto a Thief ship.

"We need to stop them," I said. "They're already taking off. As soon as they are aboard they will take her back to their planet.

"Does it matter now? We're free," Lyger said.

"Antumbra is one of us," I said.

"One of what?" Lyger replied. "We all escaped together out of convenience. We don't owe her."

"The Thieves must have taken her for a reason," Ada said.

"She knew the risks. We don't need to go after her," Lyger said.

Did I owe her anything? She wasn't human. And the odds were against us to rescue her. I pondered the situation until Ada yelled.

"Oh no!"

"What is it?" Hippo asked. "More Thieves?"

"No," Ada said. "There is only one reason to take Antumbra, and no one else. It's the Rod. Antumbra has the key to time travel."

"So what?" the Mouth said. "We proved it doesn't change anything. Your race is still dead. You changed nothing."

I raised my hand. "I'm a change. I'm not nothing."

"That's right," Ada said. "Plus remember what Antumbra said. She needed to study why Callum and I are still here. She didn't know as much about time travel as we think. And the Thieves might be able to figure it out and use it to their advantage."

"Why else would they want it?" I added.

Hippo nodded.

"If they figure out how to time travel, they would be unstoppable. They could undo battles, rebellions. They could modify time so that they always win."

"We have to get her, and the Rod, back," I said.

"Fine, but we don't have a capable ship," Lyger said.

"I can use the escape pods," I said.

"You won't get there in time," Hippo said.

"Maybe we can slow them down," Ada said.

I searched the control panel, hoping for some tractor beam controls or something similar. No luck, but there were controls for the pipes and hatches on the lower half of the Destroyer, where all the water was stored. I had an idea.

"Hippo, can you position the Destroyer to line up the underside hatches near that Thief ship?" I asked.

"I can."

"Do it now," I ordered.

Hippo worked the controls.

"The Thieves are moving their vessel clear of us," he reported.

"You won't be able to hit their ship now," Lyger said.

"I'm not trying to," I replied.

"We're in position," Hippo said.

I activated the controls to open one of the Destroyer's side hatches. Then I watched on the screen as millions of gallons of seawater floated out of the lower section of the Destroyer. It crashed over the smaller Thief ship, first as water, then as vapour when the vacuum of space boiled it, and finally freezing to ice crystals like snow.

Back at the controls, I activated a pipe from inside the Destroyer and maneuvered it towards the smaller Thief ship. With flicks of my wrist, I started wrapping the pipe around the vessel. Once the ship was sufficiently wrapped, I tried retracting the pipe, which pulled it tighter and squeezed the other ship like a boa constrictor.

"It can't go anywhere now," I said. "I'm taking an escape pod, and I going over there to get Antumbra."

"Wait," Ada said. "I'm going too."

"I will go as well," a new voice said in my head.

It was odd. My brain seemed to hear the words even though there was no sound.

The Mouth entered, and behind him was the creature that had been locked in the cell.

The creature seemed healed, at least partially, its wounds were slowly disappearing.

We all backed up.

"W-what is that?" Hippo asked.

"A creature we found when we were holed up fighting Thieves."

"It's not a creature," the Mouth said. "It's like us. The last of its kind. And this one is special."

"I was created to take revenge on the Thieves," the creature spoke telepathically. "Every enhancement my people could find was imbued in my body. I wish to go with you and kill as many Thieves as I can."

"And you're telepathic?" I asked.

"It provides advantages on the battlefield when one's enemy cannot hear one's communications," it said. "I will not take no for an answer. I will fight beside you. I will do my duty."

I was never going to say no. Not to a creature with so many mouths and teeth, and especially not after what I saw it do to the Thieves.

"Great. You're in," I said. "Everyone else, hold down the ship. We'll be back soon.

"Oh and before I go... I need any guns you can spare."

THE INVASION

The escape pods were not actually pods, but simple shuttles. Without Lyger to pilot them, it was difficult, but I managed. I wasn't going to perform any death-defying stunts, but I kept us on course.

The Thief ship was firing its thrusters at full power, trying to pull away from the pipe that had ensnared it. The pipe was stretching, and it wasn't going to hold forever.

"Callum, I have a bad feeling about this," Ada said.

"You didn't have to come."

"I couldn't help it. A part of me needs to protect you."

"I think I'm capable of protecting myself, but I appreciate it," I said. "We talked earlier about how neither of us really knows what to do. I have this pure instinct to survive. And that feels so hollow. Is my only role now to exist? Just stay alive until I'm not? My life has to have more meaning than that, even if I have to ignore my instincts. Antumbra is a friend, and she has no one else. I can't leave her. I need to get her back. That's my purpose right now."

Ada beamed at me, like she was proud.

"Don't look at me like that!"

"Like what?"

"Like... My mother," I said.

She barked a laugh.

"Well, I'm not your mother, but I can still be proud. And I sincerely hope you have a plan for defeating the Thieves on that ship."

Ada looked at the stockpile of guns."

"And I hope it's more than just shooting them all," she said.

"It is. Trust me."

"I hope that we will rip them all limb-from-limb," the creature said telepathically.

It was clear that this creature's sole purpose was revenge.

For a moment, I contemplated the ways some species prepared to meet their ends. Mine had resolved to save enough people and resources to start again. Antumbra's had sent her away to change time. And this creature was purely a blunt instrument, to pummel the Thieves until it took its last breath.

As we neared the ship, it launched a few shuttles. They didn't fly toward the Destroyer, instead they turned and fired on the pipe that held the ship.

"We need to get aboard fast," I said.

Then one of the ships broke formation and made a beeline at us.

"They must know we are coming," Ada said.

I piloted the escape shuttle as wildly as I could, hoping to dodge the incoming ship's fire and buy us some time.

"I will meet you on board," the creature said suddenly.

"What do you mean, meet us?" I said.

But the creature was already in the airlock, sealing and depressurizing it.

"Get closer," it said telepathically.

The creature opened the outer door and clambered out across the side of the hull. It must have been clinging there, waiting for me to guide our escape pod in.

I steered the ship toward the Thief shuttle, barely avoiding its weapons fire.

As we lined up, we heard a loud noise as the creature leapt from our pod over to the Thief shuttle. It floated through space, seemingly unaffected by the vacuum or cold. Then, as it passed in front of us, we saw its writhing form change shape. Large wings, like a butterflies, erupted out of it. Somehow it used them to propel it toward the Thief shuttle.

The creature smacked into the hull, folding up its wings and gripping the metal with its claws. Those claws tore into the ship, instantly depressurizing it. The shuttle stopped firing and went adrift.

The creature leapt off, unfolded its wings again, and streaked at the other ships.

"This is our chance, Callum. It's distracting them."

I nodded and steered us at the docking bay of the main Thief ship.

"I just hope he stays on our side," I said.

As we approached we saw that the docking bay had no protection or weapons. Not even a metal door. It seemed to be sealed by an shield that allowed ships to enter, but kept atmosphere in. We could also see that the Thieves were ready for us. A welcome reception was already there, armed, but not firing. Just waiting.

We landed, and still they didn't fire or advance.

"Maybe they think we're here to surrender?" Ada said.

"They're going to be disappointed," I said.

I grabbed a gun, loaded it, and walked to the airlock, depressurizing the first seal.

"What about these other guns?" Ada asked.

"We'll come back for them. I need only the one right now."

"If they see you're armed, won't they shoot?" Ada said. "We won't have time to get out of the way, even with our speed."

"Don't worry," I said. "I have a plan."

I took one of the guns I carried and made the same modifications that the Mouth had before, carefully avoiding a possible EMP.

"Don't set off the EMP," Ada warned.

"I know, I know," I replied.

Then I closed up the gun, and opened the pod's door, holding the weapon out as if I were surrendering.

Four thieves levelled their guns at me as soon as the hatch opened. One Thief, with three rotating mechanical eyes seemed to be the leader.

"Surrender is wise," it said. Its voice was wet and slimy.

"Yep. That's why we're here," I said.

Then I tossed the gun forward. It skidded across the floor and stopped right next to the four Thieves.

The Lead Thief slurped saliva before speaking again. "Good. We would have killed you. But now we can torture you like we have the other."

"You are torturing her?" Ada said, horrified.

"She is our property, and she has information we need," the Lead Thief said.

I stared at the gun I had tossed, waiting for it to overcharge and start glowing.

"What kind of advanced race are you?" Ada said. "Kidnapping? Torturing? Murdering?"

"We're much like you," the Lead Thief said.

It cackled as the gun started to glow.

"Can you excuse us, please?" I said.

I reached forward, grabbed the hatch to the pod, and pulled it closed.

"What are you..?" the lead thief began but I cut him off after closing the door.

The explosion of the gun outside vibrated the hatch door, and the escape pod rocked in the docking bay.

I grabbed all the other guns we had, and gave some to Ada.

Ada opened the hatch, and we saw that three of the Thieves had been killed by the blast, and the Lead Thief was embedded in the cargo bay ceiling.

"Let's go get Antumbra," I said.

Before we could set off, the creature soared on its wings into the docking bay. It was severely injured, but its body kept writhing and healing itself. What was strangest was that the creature seemed to be shrinking.

"Coming with us?" I asked.

"Yes," the creature telepathically intoned. "In a moment I will be healed. Once I complete the sacrifice."

"Sacrifice?" Ada asked.

"I must give of my body to heal," the creature said. "Until I can give no more. I am here to kill Thieves. When that is done, I will take their ship back to their world and kill more."

"Well, we're not going to stop you. And we'll be grateful for your help."

"Good," it said.

We set off to rescue Antumbra.

THE RESCUE

Ada and I were like lightning and thunder.

The explosion in the docking bay had told the Thieves that something was wrong. Now the corridors were filling with them, and they were heavily armed.

Too bad they were no match for Ada and me.

Our aim was perfect every time.

The thieves were good shots too, but we were just too fast.

One Thief, though, managed to surprise me. It popped out of a side corridor that I hadn't noticed. I didn't have time to aim at the body, but my shot still sheered off the tentacle, and disarmed the Thief of one weapon.

Another tentacle, this one of machine parts with three metal spikes at the end, thrusted at me. I dodged, and then blocked it with my palm, my fingers splayed between the spikes. I parried the arm, jumped back and fired twice, severing the tentacle and then killing the Thief with a shot to its head.

In its death throes, another tentacle waggled, and slapped my gun from my hand just as another Thief came at me.

The charging Thief fired, and I dodged, barely avoiding the laser.

I lunged in, amongst the Thief's tentacles, and grabbed onto a piece of machinery embedded in its torso. I wrenched it from the alien's flesh.

The Thief howled in pain. It swung a tentacle at me to shoot.

I grabbed the arm, twisted it, reversing the gun in its grip, and fired. The shot blasted the alien to pieces.

Meanwhile, Ada was kicking a Thief, hurtling it away.

As it flew, it wrapped a tentacle around Ada's leg.

She stomped her foot with all her might, causing the Thief to snap back towards her, like a ball on a string. Ada grabbed it by its mechanical eyes and smashed it with a head-butt.

"Nice work," I said, picking up my gun.

"Let's keep moving," she said.

Since the Thief ship was a lot like the Ark or a Destroyer, I assumed the control centre was located near the top of the vessel.

We made our way up and up, dispatching more Thieves with ease. And when we reached the control centre, ready to open the door, gunfire assaulted the door frame.

"I've been watching you wreak havoc through this ship," a slimy, deep voice said. "Did you really think you could surprise us? Step through that door, and you will die no matter how fast you are."

"That must be the Greatlord," Ada whispered.

I nodded.

"Toss your guns where we can see them," the slimy voice continued. "Then step out."

I grimaced. There was no other way into the command centre.

"Perhaps this will motivate you?" the slimy voice said.

Suddenly I heard Antumbra scream in pain.

We couldn't let them torture her.

Antumbra screamed again.

I took a superhumanly-quick glance around the door frame. My enhanced mind was able to memorize the view. And I was clear before the gunfire came again.

The Greatlord was an octopus-shaped creature with its face enclosed in a skull and two yellow eyes like rotten fruit. It stood next to Antumbra who was bound in some sort of harness. Surrounding the Greatlord were several other Thieves, all large, and all heavily armed. In one tentacle the Greatlord clutched the Rod.

"He's got Antumbra in some sort of torture device and we're definitely outgunned," I told Ada.

"The creature?" she said. "Maybe it could help us."

"We don't have time for it to get it here," I said.

She bit her lower lip, and stared off, trying to think.

Antumbra cried out again.

"Surrender now humans," the Greatlord said. "Or else."

"Distract it," Ada said.

"What?"

"Keep it talking. I just need a second."

I nodded, though I wasn't sure what I would say to a homicidal squid alien monster.

"Erm... I know you're not going to kill her," I yelled through the doorway.

"Why exactly is that, exhibit?" the Greatlord asked.

"You want to know how the Rod works," I said. "She can't tell you if she's dead."

Beside me, Ada knelt over her gun, making adjustments to it.

I made loops with my index finger, hoping she'd know the signal for "hurry up."

"I'm sure we can figure it out, but torturing her for the information is quicker. And more fun," the Greatlord growled. "And it's a nice preview for the pain that you, too, will suffer. There are penalties for stealing my family's ship, an heirloom of my kingdom."

"The Destroyer? You should know that we've damaged it," I said.

"I am well aware," the Greatlord said.

"Okay," Ada said finally. "Follow my lead, please. You'll have to do all the shooting."

She stood next to me, holding her gun out with open palms like she planned to surrender. She had loosened something inside the weapon, and it seemed she wanted to use it as a bomb.

"We'll blow up Antumbra..." I said.

"It won't explode," Ada said. "It's an EMP. Like the one that shut down the computers on the platform."

"And they have a lot of cybernetic parts..." I said.

I held my hands out, following her lead.

We walked to the doorway, arms out, palms up.

"We're surrendering," Ada called out.

We held our guns out.

The Thieves were aiming their weapons right at us, but they didn't fire, seeing that our weapons were safety dangling from our fingers.

"Drop them," the Greatlord said. "And don't try that grenade idea. If a bomb goes off in here, your friend will die too."

"We wouldn't dream of it, " Ada said. "Here."

She let her gun drop.

I plotted my next move, my superhuman senses watching Ada's gun drop in slow motion. I identified the Thieves I would need to kill first, and looked for the right moment to help Antumbra. My eyes flashed toward the falling gun.

When the gun hit the floor the piece Ada had loosened, popped off.

The electromagnetic pulse erupted in an instant. I saw the lights on the Thieves' bodies dim. Their mechanical parts, suddenly gave away underneath them and they fell. The Greatlord tumbled to the floor. Ada also dropped to the floor, but she didn't appear to be diving for her gun. It was more like her legs just gave away..

I focused on my targets. This was my chance.

I spun the gun in my hand, and whipped it around. My first shot took out a Thief, the second, another.

The lights came back on as the EMP died.

My third shot struck the harness holding Antumbra, and shattered its lock.

The other Thieves were back in the game as their electric parts came back to life.

Luckily, Antumbra was free. She quickly turned her arms into magnesium flares and swung them at the alien robo-squids, cleaving off tentacles left and right.

The Greatlord slinked back in shock.

One last Thief pointed its gun at Antumbra. It had a clear shot.

But Ada shot it first, from where she had fallen, having repaired her gun.

It was only the Greatlord and us now.

Ada and I fired, the blasts deflected off some kind of personal shield.

The Greatlord laughed and then swung its mighty metal arms, throwing us to the side.

I fired again after the rough landing, but that shot bounced off the shield too.

Then another tentacle came at me. For a second, I saw that the shield fizzled around it. The shield was allowing the Greatlord to penetrate it to attack us.

I quickly grappled the tentacle and got out of its way.

Then the arm yanked me off my feet, slamming me into a console on the other side of the room.

Ada tried to shoot at the tentacles, but the Greatlord was too quick to hit.

Antumbra tried to sheer off the limbs with her red hot hands, the tentacles had such dexterity that they avoided her, and still managed to strike us.

We were getting our butts kicked.

I jolted around to the Greatlord's back. But one of its arms picked up a fallen gun, and fired at me.

I tried to dodge, but the blast went right through my stomach.

I had been shot.

I suddenly remembered when One got shot, back in the cargo bay when we first met those workmen stowaways. One had survived that wound by playing possum until he could strike the biggest guy.

My wound wasn't fatal. The nanites in my body had already stopped the bleeding. I could even feel them mending me.

I didn't want to risk getting hit again, so I stayed on my back cradling the wound.

The Greatlord spun around, twirling and lashing its limbs like whips.

All of us were thrown and slammed into the walls.

"Pitiful creatures," the Greatlord snapped. "I have crushed dozens of worlds. My family have feasted on many peoples, and you think you can defeat me?"

"Human? Where are you?" I suddenly heard in my head.

The creature from the cell.

"I will turn you back into museum exhibits," the Greatlord said. "Not live ones. No. You will be flayed, and dissected, and mounted."

We're in the command centre, I thought, hoping the creature would hear it. *At the top of the ship.*

"I will also take back what you stole from us," the Greatlord said.

"Ironic statement to make," I said, coughing up some blood. "Considering you steal from everyone. Didn't think someone would repay you in kind?"

The Greatlord laughed.

"I will kill you now. Then I will kill that creature you brought with you. A trophy of my last conquest. Even he can't defeat me."

"Are you sure about that?" I asked.

"Anything that comes through that door dies," The Greatlord declared.

With a mighty crash, the floor erupted directly beneath the Greatlord in a tangle of metal and sparks.

The creature burst through, flying into the room.

The Greatlord shrieked and tried to back away, but its shield was useless because the creature was already inside it. The alien's tentacles tried to spear the creature, but it ignored all the wounds it took, and its limbs turned into mighty biting maw that chomped on the tentacles before they could try to strike again.

"You destroyed my world," the creature bellowed.

It opened its mouth and the mouths within those. One took a bite, then another, and another until the Greatlord was consumed entirely.

It was horrendous, disgusting, and amazing. There was nothing left but an empty skull.

The creature then roared, victorious.

It was so loud I had to cover my ears.

"Thank you, friends," Antumbra said to us, then nodded to the creature.

She picked up the Rod from where the Greatlord had been, and held it close.

"I see you've made another friend in my short absence."

"It's more of an acquaintance," Ada replied.

"A temporary ally," the creature communicated. "Now leave this ship. It is mine. I'm going back to the Thief home world to destroy them all."

"Thank you. It was nice to know you," I said.

The creature grumbled. "Go. Take one of their ships and release this one from that pipe."

"Definitely just an acquaintance," Ada said, limping to the door.

I expected to limp too, or at least feel pain from my laser wound, but it was already gone. It had completely healed.

We left the creature to its prize, and found a smaller ship in the docking bay that could take us back to our Destroyer.

In the shuttle, Antumbra sank into her chair, exhausted from the torture and the battle.

Ada took the controls.

"I hoped you would come for me," Antumbra said.

I looked at her.

"I didn't expect you to. We barely know each other."

"You're the last of your kind," I said. "You had a wife and child. You're made of energy and you have a time altering device. I'm sure those are the important things. Although, what's your favourite flavour of ice cream?"

"I don't know what that is," Antumbra said.

"You look like a strawberry person," Ada said.

"Strawberry is nice," I said. "I can't speak for Ada, but I came to get you because you're one of only seven people who know what it's like to be alone in the universe. Plus, there's an old Earth expression

276

that I think perfectly defines our relationship, 'the enemy of my enemy is my friend.'"

Antumbra pondered those words.

"I like it," she said.

"Me too," Ada said.

Then she piloted the ship out of the docking bay, and guided us back to the Destroyer.

"Do you think that creature will survive?" I asked.

"Who knows? Rage takes you down uncertain paths of self destruction," Ada said.

"Let's just hope it causes so much chaos that the Thieves don't come after us again," I said.

After a few minutes we touched down in the Destroyer's docking bay. The doors even closed, behind us. It was lucky that our platform ship bomb hadn't done too much damage.

"Home at last," Ada said.

"Don't say that. I never want this to be home," Antumbra said.

"It is for now," I replied. "We might have to get used to it."

7
THE APOLOGY

Once the pod had slowed down all of Two's functions, I said, "I'm going to miss her. I wish she were still around."

One stepped away from the pod to stand next to me. "Yes. She really brought us together."

Two was someone to talk to, in a way I didn't feel comfortable talking to anyone else. Not right now. Not One. Not any other Arkonaut.

"We will see her in a year, Maiara," One said. "Let us be patient."

He looked down at me and smiled. "I have a gift for you."

"You do?"

He pulled out a vial of swirling grey liquid.

"Nanites?" I asked.

"All nanites that humans receive have a default program that enacts when a human dies. They are instructed to latch onto the memory centres of the brain that light up when a person is dying. And record their final moments, their final thoughts."

"Are those—?"

"Yes. Callum's Nanites. I have Nuan's and Mathieu's too. Recorded for posterity. I thought that you should have Callum's. Who knows what he was thinking when he died, but maybe it was you. In fact I am sure of it."

I took the vial and stared at the liquid.

"Thank you One," I said and held the vial to my chest pondering Callum's final thoughts.

"Hey One. I have to know. How many more Arkonauts asked for their eighteenth memory to be reactivated? "

"All of them," One said.

Before I could respond, he backed away with his hands in the air waving his fingers.

"Or maybe it was none of them," he said in a spooky voice.

"No! Come on! I need to know."

One led me out of the room and sealed it behind us. He smiled as he walked away.

"We had a deal, Maiara. You said it doesn't matter. And, you know, it doesn't. We're all just human. Nothing can change that."

"Aren't you, like, super-human?" I asked.

"Close enough," One replied.

***

Over the next few days I avoided the others if I could. I made polite and quick remarks to people's condolences, but I couldn't escape everyone.

When I saw a chance to duck out of dinner early one night, Dehqan stopped me outside the cafeteria as I was heading back to my room.

"Maiara," he said. "Wait!"

"Look, Dehqan, I'm sorry. I just want to go to sleep," I practically begged.

"No. Please follow me," he said. "I have to show you something."

Dehqan took me to my painting, the one Two had encouraged me to make. Next to it was Callum's, with a bright red cross through it.

"I did that," he admitted. "I defaced Callum's painting."

I should have been angry. I had liked that painting and Callum had worked hard on it. But there was no anger. Instead I just thought about why Dehqan had done it. Callum had made himself a target, and

279

had failed to see Dehqan's point of view. Dehqan was speaking to his own suffering, but Callum couldn't see it, and at the time, wouldn't look.

"This way," Dehqan said. "There's one more thing."

He led me to his own drawing. It was a picture of him and his family. He had drawn a mountain backdrop behind them all, along with some Arabic words I didn't understand.

Then he handed me a can of spray paint.

"Put a cross on it," he said.

I took the can and looked at his painting.

"I don't want to," I said. "You didn't do anything to me. And I don't want to do this for Callum. I don't think Callum would even want that."

"This isn't about you getting revenge for Callum," Dehqan said.

"It isn't?" I asked.

"No," Dehqan said. "Do you remember why Two made us do this? It was so that future generations would come back to this ship and see what we, their ancestors, thought about the most, and what was special to us. One day they are going to come here and they're going to ask a tour guide why Callum's painting was covered over, and they'll tell the truth: I defaced his painting. And then they'll ask why you did the same to my painting. And they'll tell the truth."

"What truth?" I asked.

"Please just paint the cross and I'll show you," he said.

I wondered what he could be going on about, but I shook the can and made a cross, ruining his artwork.

Then, he stepped up and wrote, *I, Dehqan asked Maiara to do this, to show that I was sorry for defacing Callum's picture. I thought my picture deserved to be defaced to pay for the damage I did.* Then he signed it.

"Now you sign it," he said.

And I did, right beneath his signature.

"The truth is both Callum and I were right and wrong," he said.

"I think he was more wrong than you," I admitted. "He wouldn't want me to lie for him. He was upset with himself the entire time we were in the lower part of the Ark."

"But we were still both wrong," Dehqan said. "Now, at least, future generations will come here and see that two people joined together to make that point, to reset things back to zero, and they moved on."

I had to hand it to him; it was a nice sentiment. And Callum would have appreciated it. For the rest of human history, it would be proof that two people who disagreed could move on. In the future, our descendants would understand that Dequan and I held no bitterness.

I felt very peaceful, even as my heart tinged at the thought of Callum being gone. I forced a smile for Dehqan, to assure him that all was well between he and I.

"Go have a good sleep, Maiara," Dehqan said. "You deserve it."

I nodded and offered my hand to shake his.

After he was clear, my smile disappeared, and my heart ached. I collapsed onto my bed in my new room. On my bedside table, a single cactus flowered, and next to it, a vial of liquid. Random thoughts of Callum, life, growing up, death, space... kept me awake until I was too exhausted and drifted off wondering if I'd ever feel the same again.

SYSTEM ONLINE

CHECKING RESOURCE DEPLETION

     WITHIN DESIGNATED PARAMETERS

SOLAR SYSTEM SCAN REPORT

     SHIP NO LONGER WITHIN THE BOUNDARY OF THE SOLAR SYSTEM

CREW STATUS

1. ENGLISH REPRESENTATIVE DECEASED
2. USA REPRESENTATIVE MEDICAL FILE UPDATED

COURSE UPDATE

SHIP WILL REACH THE WORMHOLE IN FOUR WEEKS.

THE NEW FUTURE

"Human, come take a look at this," the Mouth said.

"Good to see you too," I replied.

Antumbra sank into a chair in the control centre.

Hippo had already released the Thief ship.

The creature was already flying it away.

On the floor in the centre of the room was the body of a Thief, lying face down. The back of its head was covered in implants. It looked weird, like a torso with a mass of tentacles for arms and legs.

"I found this as I was looking for a snack," the Mouth said.

The Thief was shot full of holes.

"What about it?" I said.

Ada came and stood next to me.

The Mouth crouched down next to the body.

"Don't you find this at all weird?" he asked.

"What do you mean?" we both asked.

"It's the same shape as you," the Mouth said.

He was sort of right, I guess. The Thief was at least as tall as me and had arms and legs in roughly the same proportion, but the arms and legs were mechanical tentacles, not real limbs.

"Antumbra did say that the Thieves come in various shapes and sizes," I said.

The Mouth shrugged. He grabbed Thief and turned it over, revealing its face.

"That's impossible," Ada said.

"How can this be?" I said.

Nothing about the Thief's face made sense to me. It couldn't be a Thief. There was no way.

The face was human.

Ada and I gasped.

We knelt to inspect the man's face. He was, undeniably, from Earth. His head was nestled in a crown of implants.

But, the only way that this could be a human was if he were a descendant of an Arkonaut. They were the only humans left in the galaxy. This man, turned Thief, must be related to my long dead friends.

"What kind of future did I create?" I whispered.

The man gasped, coughed, and exhaled.

He was still alive.

"We'll have to ask him," Ada said.

Acknowledgements

A big thank you to Nate for rounding out this book's rough edges, and to everyone at Spaceboy books who helped made this sequel possible.

Thanks to my fellow Spaceboy authors, for the support and encouragement you give me and one another.

About the Author

M. Drewery has been writing for 20 years and is a life long Sci-Fi fan. He lives in a little village in Surrey, England. The only people who know it exists are the people who live there. One day he'll write a book where a time traveller visits the village, having crossed time and space to eat at our lovely restaurants and get their hair cut in one of our many, many hairdressers. You can find him at http://www.mdrewery.co.uk/

About the Publishing Team

Nate Ragolia was labeled as "weird" early in elementary school, and it stuck. He's a lifelong lover of science fiction, and a nerd/geek. In 2015 his first book, *There You Feel Free,* was published by 1888's Black Hill Press. He's also the author of *The Retroactivist*, published by Spaceboy Books. He founded and edits BONED, an online literary magazine, has created webcomics, and writes whenever he's not playing video games or petting dogs.

Shaunn Grulkowski has been compared to Warren Ellis and Phillip K. Dick and was once described as what a baby conceived by Kurt Vonnegut and Margaret Atwood would turn out to be. He's at least the fifth best Slavic-Latino-American sci-fi writer in the Baltimore metro area. He's the author of Retcontinuum, and the editor of A Stalled Ox and The Goldfish, among others.

www.ingramcontent.com/pod-product-compliance
Lightning Source LLC
Chambersburg PA
CBHW020301200626
46814CB00006BA/2033